I'll Be Leaving You Always

I'll Be Leaving You Always

Sandra Scoppettone

LITTLE, BROWN AND COMPANY

BOSTON   TORONTO   LONDON

Library of Congress Cataloging-in-Publication Data

Scoppettone, Sandra.
    I'll be leaving you always / Sandra Scoppettone.—1st ed.
        p.   cm.
    ISBN 0-316-77647-5
    I. Title.
PS3569.C586I44   1993
813'.54—dc20   92-5096

10   9   8   7   6   5   4   3   2   1

MV-NY

*Published simultaneously in Canada
by Little, Brown & Company (Canada) Limited*

Printed in the United States of America

This one is for all my Thursday friends
who share six o'clock to seven-thirty with me . . .
then, now, and in the future.

My lifetime listens to yours.
—*Muriel Rukeyser*

We want the facts to fit the preconceptions.
When they don't, it is easier to ignore the facts
than to change the preconceptions.
—*Jessamyn West*

I'll Be Leaving You Always

Chapter
One

═══════════════════

POUNDING. Someone is pounding on our door. And there's a man's voice calling my name. Kip and I wake, startled. I sit up while Kip says something unintelligible. I look at the digital clock on the night table. It's nine-fifteen and it's dark. We'd fallen asleep. I throw on my robe, still satiated, and groggy, tuck my feet into slippers.

As I make my way downstairs I think I recognize the voice. It's William, our upstairs tenant and very good friend. Still, I live in Greenwich Village, New York City, and know better than to open a door before checking.

"Who is it?" I ask.

"It's Mildred Pierce, who do you think it is?" says William.

I undo the locks.

William, who's six feet five inches tall, is hunched over, his brown, gold-streaked hair falling forward, hiding his face. He breathes heavily as if he's been running.

"What is it? William, what's happened?"

"Oh, God, Lauren, I can't believe it," he says in a short burst.

Now I'm frightened. "Has something happened to Rick?" Rick is William's lover.

Slowly, he raises his head, his blue eyes wide with the unmistakable look of terror. "Rick, shmick, something's happened to me, now will you let me in please, or do I have to be prostrate before I gain admittance?"

"I'm sorry." I open the door wider, and still puffing, he

heads for the living room as I snap on lights. He collapses on the couch, his large body spread out like a huge fan. Even in this condition one can see that William is a very handsome man. He sports a mustache and beard, neatly trimmed.

Before I can ask him anything, Kip comes in wearing her white terry cloth robe, nothing underneath. Although she's been rudely awakened she looks as if she's ready for a modeling session, her brown eyes alert, brown gray-tinged hair looking as if it's been coiffured by Sassoon moments before. She's neat and trim and five six to my five two. I wouldn't be so conscious of everyone's height but, for a private eye, mine's a liability.

"What's going on?" Kip asks, alarmed.

We both stare at William. I see now that his usually rubicund complexion looks like unsullied snow.

"Hold up," he says.

Kip and I look at one another. After twelve years together we know what the other is thinking. I speak for both of us.

"Hold up what?"

"Hold up *me.*"

"Are you drunk?" I ask.

He shuts his eyes with impatience and speaks through clenched teeth. "I — was — in — a — holdup."

"Oh, William," Kip says, goes to him on the couch. "Shall I call Rick?"

"Not home. For a change," he says, with a touch of uncharacteristic bitterness. "And it's all his fault."

Kip says, "Do you want a drink?"

"Water."

She goes into the kitchen, yells back over her shoulder, "Don't say anything till I get back."

I hate this instruction. People are always giving it so that whoever is left in the room has to sit in stupid silence. A month later she returns.

William downs the water in three gulps, puts the glass on the end table. He's wearing his usual uniform of jeans, a work shirt under his black leather jacket, and black boots. His large hands with their small nails are splayed on his muscled thighs. Color is seeping back into his face.

"Tell," Kip says.

"It happened at Megan's."

"Megan Harbaugh's?" She owns a jewelry and very chic home-furnishing shop on Greenwich Avenue, and is my oldest, dearest friend.

He nods. "Rick's been eyeing this silver ring and his birthday's coming up, so I went in to see how much it was. Megan was behind the counter and I realize now she was trying to signal me with her eyes but I didn't get it then. Anyway, there were two guys in the place, both facing her. After I went in, said 'Hi,' like some unsuspecting moron, one of the guys . . . the bigger of the two . . . turns around and points this . . . this *gun* at me. Jesus, those are scary things. I'd swear it was a cannon if I didn't know better."

"Poor William," Kip says, takes his hand in hers.

"And then?" I encourage.

"Well, he tells me to put up my hands and not to move. I did."

"Good," I say.

"Tells Megan to empty the cash register . . . they must've come in just before me because nothing had started yet. I couldn't believe it. I had no idea a holdup could be so frightening. Truth is, I never thought about it before. Who does? This happens to other people."

I nod, recalling how often I've heard clients say this.

"Anyway, when they were both facing Megan, and I don't know why I did it, I opened the door and ran like hell."

"You turned your back on a man with a gun?" I ask, astonished.

"I did. Can't explain it. I knew it was risky but somehow it seemed *more* risky to stay."

"Then what happened?" Kip asks.

"I ran down Greenwich to the phones on Sixth and called the police. By the time they got there the burglars were gone."

"Robbers," I correct.

Both Kip and William look at me as though I've lost it.

"Burglars are housebreakers," I explain. "Robbers hold up people and stores. Armed robbery is what it was."

"Were you an original quiz kid?" Kip says.

"People are always getting the two confused," I answer lamely.

William says, "It doesn't seem like the appropriate time for a grammar lesson, Lauren . . . and don't bother telling me this isn't about grammar."

I'm properly chastened.

"Did the *thieves* get anything?" Kip asks, glancing at me under long lashes.

"No. When I ran out they split."

"And Megan?" I ask, frightened of the answer.

"A mess. I mean, she's a wreck. Who wouldn't be?"

"Certainly not you," Kip says.

He laughs his deep bass sound, and a light comes back into his eyes like the tail end of fireworks. Sitting up, William arches his back, flexes his long fingers, stretches his legs, looks us over. "Did I wake you? What time is it?"

"It's about nine-thirty," Kip says, trying to make it sound like the middle of the night but failing. We look at each other, remembering why we were in bed, why we'd fallen asleep.

"Oh," William says, suddenly understanding. "I'm sorry."

"No, it's okay. Really." Both Kip and I are slightly embarrassed, eager to bypass this part of the conversation. Although we don't hide our relationship from anyone, we're not into sharing the sexual specifics of our lives. Nor would William want us to.

"So where's Rick?" Kip asks.

"He's working on a script with Susan."

Rick is a sitcom writer. Susan writes screenplays, with an occasional foray into the world of laugh tracks, and is another close friend. She and her husband, Stan, and Kip and I spend many evenings together. "Want me to call him?" I ask.

William doesn't answer, fusses with his mustache.

"It's perfectly normal for you to want him," Kip states.

Coming from Kip, who's a therapist, this seems to reassure William. "Yes, call him."

As I punch in Susan's number I wonder why Meg hasn't gotten in touch, and decide to phone her after this call.

"Hey, it's Lobes Laurano, private dick," Susan says. Sometimes she calls me Lobes and I call her Tony and we talk to each other like gangsters. I don't know why. It's one of the things we do. But tonight I can't play, and ask for Rick.

"Why are you speaking in hushed tones? Somebody die? Ooops, better not ask Lobes that one. Seriously, something wrong?"

I tell her. She says she'll tell Rick. After I hang up, the phone rings immediately. "What?" I say, thinking it's Susan.

It's not. It's Peter Cecchi (pronounced *Check*-key), my friend on the force. "Lauren," he says in a style I recognize as serious business. "I thought you'd want to know. It's Megan Harbaugh...."

"I already know."

"You do?"

"It's an odd coincidence, but you know our friend William..."

"No," he interrupts. "I know about William and the attempted armed robbery. That's not it. It happened after that. Jesus, Lauren, I don't know how to tell you." I can't remember ever hearing him sound like this.

"Tell me what?" But even as he says it I know what Cecchi's going to tell me and I can't stand it.

"Somebody shot her. Megan's dead."

Chapter
Two

I'D KNOWN MEGAN HARBAUGH longer than anyone except my parents. We met in the first grade. She was already the tallest kid in the class, and I was the shortest. I'm not sure if it was her natural caretaking instinct, or whether she simply liked me, but Megan became my friend right away. Friend and protector.

We were a curious duo. Besides the almost eleven-inch difference, she was as light as I was dark, her practically white hair framing a choirgirl face, with bold blue eyes that sunk into your soul if they happened to catch yours.

Even at six she was funny. And fun. After school we played together because it turned out that Meg lived only a block and a half from me in South Orange, New Jersey. Sometimes I've thought the only good thing about the state was that Megan was born there.

Five of us made up our neighborhood crew. Danny, Bobby, Joan, Megan, and me. Meg and I were the leaders . . . actually, she was but because of our closeness it seemed like I was a leader, too. We played all the regular games kids play: cowboys and Indians, cops and robbers, house, school, store. In winter we made igloos and rode our American Flyers down my hill. Bikes got us around the rest of the year. Meg always wanted to go a little farther than we were supposed to, push the boundaries that extra block. Whatever she did, I did. It wasn't that I didn't have any ideas of my own — it was that hers were usually better, more exciting.

When we were about ten and we played without the other three, we invented a game called Evol. It was "love" spelled backwards and we were convinced that no one knew what we were talking about when we mentioned it in front of our parents. I found out later they all knew. The game was a form of house but with some sexual overtones. Meg was always the husband because of her height. We never did more than kiss, and chastely at that, no open mouths, but we'd allude to the going-to-bed part; it was like a fade-out in a movie.

As younger kids we'd all played "you show me and I'll show you" but this was not like that. This had a story, a plot almost, and it was continuous like a soap opera. I guess we played that at least three times a week until we were twelve and graduated from grammar school.

In junior high the boys went wild over Meg. And she over them. I pretended to feel the same way about boys but I never did.

Practically from the first day of seventh grade Meg and her mother became enemies, locked in a battle over boys that was really a sex struggle. Meg matured early in our sixth-grade year and when we got to seventh her breasts were large and fully developed. She looked more like sixteen than thirteen.

When it first happened to her she walked hunched over so no one could see but it didn't do much good. The sixth-grade boys knew and they made her life hell. Not so with the boys in ninth grade . . . their perspective was different and Meg began walking up straight, taking pride in her breasts, small waist, hips. She didn't flaunt them, she just acknowledged them and couldn't understand her mother's hysteria whenever a boy came around or called. What started as acrimony between the two became a full-fledged war, one almost thought, to the death.

Meg had two older sisters, Rosie and Lorraine, but they'd developed slowly and didn't date until later. Still, Rosie tried to win Meg more freedom and eventually wore down their mother. But that first year in junior high was a nightmare.

The boys wouldn't quit; even some from the high school came around. Meg was constantly being grounded but she sneaked out, met guys in the park, and went on joyrides with some of the older ones.

She told me everything. Much more than I wanted to know. I became the repository for her escapades, her life. Sometimes it felt as if the telling of it was more exciting to Meg than the actual doing. She said she had to tell someone about her boyfriends and I was it. I feigned interest, enthusiasm, but the truth was, I didn't get it, couldn't identify. Our relationship was pretty much a one-way street for a while because I couldn't tell her that I was madly in love with a ninth-grader named Vilma Smith who had no idea who I was.

No matter what her mother and father (he battled her too but not as vociferously) thought was going on, Meg didn't have intercourse until we were in high school. We were sophomores and Meg was dating a senior named Larry Chambers and I was dating a sophomore named Jim Betsch while I was really hopelessly in love with a junior named Anne Kiernan who hadn't the vaguest idea that I lived.

Meg got pregnant. Larry found out about an abortionist in Pennsylvania, and Meg and I, Larry and Jim drove down one Saturday while our parents thought we were spending the day going to Point Pleasant on the New Jersey shore.

Jim had tried to get me to have sex with him but I wouldn't, and as we drove in silence I'd occasionally give him a look that said *See what can happen* and he'd gaze at the floor, apparently admonished.

The abortion was a horrible experience. The usual doctor wasn't there and his substitute tried to blackmail Meg into having sex with him before the procedure. But Meg started to scream and we all ran into the room. The doctor calmed everybody down and Meg insisted that I stay with her, which I did.

He didn't give her any anesthesia and her nails bit into my hand, drawing blood. She had a washrag in her mouth but the guttural sounds she made were primitive and unforgettable.

It was the first time I'd seen so much blood. I had to monitor my breathing and actively tell myself not to faint. After it was over the doctor told us to go in another room and instructed Meg to lie there for at least an hour. He gave her several sanitary pads that she pinned inside her panties. While she rested I kept talking because Meg was afraid to fall asleep. She was convinced she'd die if she lost consciousness.

Of course she didn't die but she was in a lot of pain and slept from Saturday night until Monday morning, when she forced herself to go to her summer job waiting on tables. Within the first hour she began to hemorrhage.

The whole thing was a mess: Meg in the hospital, me being grilled by her parents and mine, Larry and Jim getting the third degree from their parents. But nobody talked. Still, it was clear to the doctors what had happened and they told the Harbaughs.

The strange thing was, Mrs. Harbaugh acted almost pleased about what had transpired. Not that she was glad Megan was in pain or enjoyed seeing her suffer, but it was almost as if she felt vindicated about her years of fighting with her daughter, proud of her prescience.

My mother thought Hildy Harbaugh's reaction was "unnatural." It was then that Mother sat me down and told me that should I ever become pregnant I must feel free to come to her and my father with the news. Fat chance! First, I didn't think it too likely that I'd get pregnant, having no interest in sex with boys, and second, my parents would be the last people I'd tell. My pregnancy would give my mother a fantastic excuse to drink and my father would fall apart, making it *his* tragedy, not mine.

Fortunately, my parents weren't dumb enough to try to keep me away from Megan, and when she came out of the hospital we were closer than ever. Still, there was always that secret I had that made me feel slightly separate from my best friend. But how could I tell her? As it turned out, she told me in our senior year.

"Laur," she said one day in her bedroom while painting her toenails a deep purple, "you don't do it with Warren, do you?" Warren was my current boyfriend and Meg was dating Jack Carroll, who went to Villanova.

I'd noticed (and had been grateful) that she never had

asked me to tell her the intimate details of my sex life but I assumed it was just Meg's preoccupation with herself—although she wasn't like that in general. So when she posed this question about Warren I was flustered. I didn't want to lie but I was afraid if I told the truth, one thing would lead to another. In my senior year I was in love with my phys ed teacher, who I was convinced was in love with me, but nothing had happened between us. I stammered around and then Meg cut right to it.

"You don't really like guys, do you?" She blew a plume of Lucky Strike smoke over my head.

"I like them," I said defensively.

"Yeah, but not, you know, like that."

"Like what?" I asked, stalling, my heart smashing in my chest like a demolition ball.

"Sexually." Meg stared at me, waiting for an answer, the brilliant blue of her eyes radiating intelligence and love.

I knew then I couldn't dodge the issue any longer but I was unable to get out the words.

"You dig girls, don't you?"

I felt like I was going to die. I *wanted* to die. I prayed to die.

"It's okay," she went on. "I don't judge you for it. I don't really understand it, I mean why you'd want to make it with a girl when there are so many neat guys around, but, hey, if that's your bag, Laur, it's okay with me."

"It is?" I was stunned.

"Different strokes for different folks," she said.

"But Meg, I'm a freak."

"No you're not. You're just a lesbian."

The word ricocheted round the room, puncturing me in several places while it made its tour. *Lesbian.* It was ugly, degrading, and embarrassing.

"I hate that word," I whispered, staring at the flowered carpet in her room.

"You like *dyke* better?"

"Ugh." I started to cry.

"Hey, what's this for?" She put down her nailbrush, moved across the pink spread of her bed, and put her arms around me. We'd hugged each other often over the years but now I felt self-conscious, stiff. It wasn't lost on Meg, nothing ever was. "Ah, Laur, don't close up on me. I've known for years, it doesn't make a bit of difference."

Sobbing, I said, "What do you mean, you've known for years?"

"Just that. Want me to name them?"

"Who?"

"Your crushes."

"What?"

"Let's see," she said matter-of-factly, "in fourth grade it was Miss Teare, fifth Miss Geisel, then in sixth it was Nancy Donahue from high school who we used to see at the movies Friday nights. In seventh it was Vilma Smith, Joan Brigham, and Laine Beirs. Eighth was Marilyn . . ."

"Stop," I shouted, feeling like an enormous fool.

"Okay. Calm down."

"How'd you know?"

"I dunno. I just did. I mean, you *did* talk about them a lot, you know. And when you talked about your boyfriends, well, there was less life in your voice. I kept waiting for you to tell me but you never did and I guess I decided today you never would, and it's a drag having this stupid thing between us like some humongous hideous creature, know what I mean?"

I certainly did. "But don't you care that your best friend's a . . . a . . ."

"Queer?" She laughed then, throaty and lusty and full of life.

"That's even worse," I said.

"Face it, there's no good word."

She was right, there wasn't and there isn't. After that I told her all about my crushes, my loves, and she counseled me and tried to get me to act on them but I wouldn't. I kept on pretending that I was heterosexual.

And then, when I was seventeen and in the last month of my senior year, an incredible thing happened that would change me forever. While we were parked at Washington Rock, Warren was murdered and I was raped, beaten, and left for dead. But I managed to crawl my way to the road, where I was found.

Megan came to the hospital every day. She always brought me something: a pack of gum; a pen and pad; a paperback book. And she was the first to realize that I felt guilty about Warren's death.

"Laur," she said, "if he hadn't been there with you he would've been there with someone else."

"But he *was* there with me and it wasn't even real."

"So if it was real would he be any less dead?"

"It might've been worth it," I said stupidly.

"I think I'll forget you said that. None of it was your fault, get that through your dumb head. You're lucky you're alive."

It was true.

The other person who came to see me in the hospital was Jeff Crawford. I thought he was a cop but he turned out to be with the FBI and he recruited me. Now I had another secret I shouldn't tell Meg. But I didn't want to go through that again, though I didn't see her as much because we went to different colleges. I told her about it on our first trip home at Thanksgiving.

"You're kidding me," Meg said, pursing her full mouth so she gave herself a prim kind of look.

"I'm not. But you're the only one I'm telling. And you have to keep it a secret, Meg, really."

"Hey, have I ever told about your dykehood?"

"God, I wish you wouldn't talk that way."

"Laur, you have to stop being so uptight about it. Have you met anybody in school yet?"

"No."

"Then you're just not looking. There are loads of lesbos at my school."

I never did meet anyone at school. It was true that they were there but I was too afraid of being kicked out of school and the FBI.

After I graduated from college and became a full-time agent I met Lois, my first lover. Megan was the only one I told.

"Thank Christ," she said. "I thought you were going to die a lesbian virgin. How was it?"

Lois and I had a totally clandestine affair and, although I hated sneaking around, I was very much in love and finally felt fulfilled. Two years later, on a case, I accidentally shot and killed Lois.

By then Meg and I were both living in New York City. She was teaching and hating it, and after the accident and I'd quit the FBI, I sat in my apartment watching television and barely eating. Even chocolate didn't tempt me. I was a zombie, unreachable, bitter and filled with horrendous guilt. I thought I might go mad. It was Megan who nursed me back to sanity.

At first she just sat with me and watched the tube, held my hand, brought me stuff I wouldn't eat. She let me cry and rage all I wanted but one day she let me have it.

"Okay, asshole, this has gone far enough. I'm sick to death of your self-pity and guilt and I refuse to watch one more sitcom. You have to get a job and you have to start seeing people."

"I don't know any people," I said. What I meant was gay people because Lois and I never socialized for fear of losing our jobs.

"Well, *I* do."

She introduced me to a bunch of lesbians and through her I met Jenny and Jill, who own Three Lives Bookstore. We became good friends and eventually they introduced me to Kip. I always felt if it hadn't been for Meg I would never have met Kip, and it's probably true.

But I'd done my share of helping Megan cope with life, too. When she wanted to quit teaching I backed her up, and I'd seen her through three husbands (the first, David Schmutzer, raised ferrets, was forty years older than she, and lasted six weeks before the marriage was annulled) and many lovers. When she decided to learn jewelry making, I was there to argue for her with Nick Benning, her second husband, who thought that it was a stupid idea and that she had enough to do raising two kids.

After she left him and talked about opening her shop I encouraged her and even lent her some money. The shop became a success; Meg paid me back.

Her third husband, Ray Davies, was much younger than Meg and she had a true passion for him. It ended badly. Davies had an affair with a woman his age, but Meg never wanted to talk about it, which was unusual for her.

And during the years when Blythe, her daughter, treated Meg as though she were beneath contempt, someone to avoid at all costs, I listened, sympathized, and predicted a friendship for the two in the future, which finally happened.

When her son, Sasha, got hooked on cocaine, I led her to a twelve-step program and supported her decision not to see him until he was clean.

And recently I listened to tales of the new one. But this was different because she was so secretive about her current lover. She called him Topic A and steadfastly refused to introduce us. The only thing I could figure out was that he was married and Meg knew how I felt about women dating married men. She *did* tell me that things weren't going too well.

"I don't know, Laur," she'd said the last time I saw her, "sometimes I think you had the right idea. I love women, I really do, but I just can't sleep with them. Men. Can't live with them, can't live without them." And then she laughed that full lusty guffaw that always made me smile. I didn't know I'd never hear it again.

Chapter
Three

WHEN I HANG UP the phone and tell Kip and William that Megan was murdered, Kip takes me in her arms. I want to cry but can't.

"Oh, Lauren," whispers Kip. Megan has become Kip's friend too but she doesn't have the history. Still, I know this is an incredibly painful loss for her.

"I can't believe it," I say. And I can't. My mind won't allow me to process the information, the truth. I reject it, as if I have a choice.

William pulls himself together and wraps his long arms about both of us. He, too, is a friend of Meg's. "Jesus," he whispers, "they must've come back."

He means the robbers. It's possible, but something makes me doubt it. Still, it would be a crazy coincidence if it were anyone else. Why hadn't I asked Cecchi? And what in hell did it matter? Dead was dead, no matter who made her that way.

Dead, murder, killed, death. The words rattle round in my head like alien beings. I cannot link them with Meg. There've been too many deaths in too short a time. It's as if I'm on overload. Suddenly I feel I'm acting like my father, making this *my* tragedy, not Meg's. My heart gives a sickening thud. Who will tell Sasha and Blythe?

I ask Kip.

"I suppose the police will," she says.

"We have to go to them, Kip." These children have been

part of my life since they were born, and part of Kip's for the last twelve years.

She nods her agreement and the three of us come out of our group embrace. Kip and I head upstairs to change into street clothes. When I look back at William I see that he's slumped on the couch, his head in his hands; his shoulders heave and he cries in the silent, dry way some men do.

Rick has returned and he and William have come with us. We go to Blythe's first, as it's closer, but she isn't home so we hail a cab to take us to Sasha's. After hearing the address five refuse us. The sixth one reluctantly agrees only after a deposit of twenty dollars is made.

Sasha lives on 108th Street in a tenement. His phone number is unlisted so we are arriving without warning and have no idea if the police have been here yet, whether we'll be the couriers of death or simply consolers.

Rick's still upset about William's brush with extinction, not minimizing Meg's. This is natural.

Rick, who battles with his weight, is in a thin period and wears a bright blue sweater and tan slacks. When he's in his fat phase he dresses in black and William calls him the undertaker. Shorter than William, Rick has an almost cherubic face, cleft chin, deep brown eyes, brown hair shot with gray. And he has an infectious laugh. But no one is laughing now.

We get out of the cab. It's close to eleven o'clock. The neighborhood feels frightening and I wonder if that's brought on by prejudice because its inhabitants are mostly Hispanic and African-American.

This is an exceptionally warm September night and people are stoop sitting as though it's midsummer. Small children play on the sidewalk and I can't help worrying that they're not in bed at this hour. As usual I feel grateful that I have no kids. I would've been overprotective, like my parents.

Sasha's building rises twelve stories, its form bleak against a bright moonlit sky. We make our way through the suddenly silent people on the steps, who don't make it easy for us. Four whites at eleven o'clock can only mean trouble to them.

I'm relieved to see that Sasha's name is next to a bell. He could've moved and Meg probably wouldn't have known. *Meg.* The reason we're here slams my mind like a brickbat and I almost reel. Kip takes my arm, sensing my fragile condition. I smile wanly, press the bell. We wait. Nothing happens.

I walk to the top of the stoop. "Do the bells work in this building?"

Laughter is my answer.

"Please," I implore, "do they work?"

"Ain't nothin' works in this buildin'," a woman says.

"Doors're open, jus' go in," adds a young man.

"Any of you know Sasha Benning?" He has his father's name.

No one knows him. No one tells the truth. These people see me, and probably Sasha, as the enemy and they're not about to help us. At first I feel anger, then I realize that in a sense, because of the color of our skin, we *are* the enemy. Who can blame them?

Rick says, "Let's just go up."

Sasha's on the eleventh floor. As we go inside I guess that the others know instinctively, as I do, that even if there's an elevator it's not going to work.

As if we're in a horror movie the walls appear to fester with peeling, putrid paint, perhaps once green, now a nameless color. Smells so vile I can't identify them gag me. I've inhaled the stench of decomposing bodies and this is similar.

By the fifth floor we're all complaining.

"I'm too old for this," William says.

"Please," I say, "you're all younger than I am."

"Big deal, she's forty-three and I'm forty-one," says Kip.

"For this I came out to my parents?" Rick says.

We laugh, but our levity takes an uneasy turn and dies, as we collectively remember why we're here. The rest of the climb is made without comment; only the occasional grunt or puff rends our silence. As we pass doors we hear sounds coming from within: music, television, real voices.

Finally, exhausted, we make it to eleven, walk down the

dimly lit hall until we reach 11G. Sasha's. I knock. We wait. I bang harder. At last, from far away, something, someone stirs. Perhaps two weeks later, a male voice asks who we are. I recognize it as Sasha's and answer him. The clicks and clangs that signal normal New York life resound, as he unbolts.

Sasha stands before us, disheveled and unkempt. I haven't seen him for some time and he looks worse than I remember. He has long, unwashed blond curly hair. Below his dark eyes are smears that resemble makeup gone awry but are actually part of his unhealthy-looking skin. He's twenty but appears thirty. Maybe forty. He wears an old gray stained sweat suit; his feet are bare and filthy.

Sasha looks at me as if he's never seen me before, glances around, takes in the other three. I try to tell myself that I've awakened him, and I refuse to listen because I know that he's stoned. The deplorable task that I'm here to execute rises to the surface of my mind like a swimmer gasping for breath. But perhaps he already knows. Perhaps the police have been here.

Sasha blinks rapidly, says "Lauren" in a husky voice.

"Can we come in, Sash?" I ask.

"Well, uh . . ."

"We don't care what it looks like," I anticipate.

He shrugs sluggishly, opens the door wider, steps back and lets us enter. None of us is a stranger to him although he's met William and Rick only a few times. I remind Sasha who they are and they nod at one another.

The apartment is a nightmare. Food containers, dirty plates, bunched bags, soiled clothes cover every surface like old quilt pieces waiting to be connected. Sasha looks around helplessly, giggles.

"Sorry," he says. "Just push stuff on the floor."

No one wishes to sit and we all make odd noises in the backs of our throats. Sasha lights a cigarette from a crumpled pack he finds amid the junk.

"I already know, Lauren," Sasha says, as if he's talking about the outcome of a baseball game. "The police were here. They said she was held up in the store and they killed her." He sounds matter-of-fact but he looks stricken, wounded beyond repair. Although he and Meg'd been estranged I am sure Sasha loved her. I want to take this boy in my arms as I did many times when he was a child. I changed his diapers, fed him, took him out to play. But he's no longer a child and he's drugged and dirty so I retreat.

Kip says, "What would you like to do, Sasha?"

"Do?"

"Do you want to come home with us tonight?"

I'm astonished and horrified at the same time. This is incredibly generous of Kip but I can't imagine having him in our house in the condition he's in.

He shakes his head no.

I experience relief.

William and Rick give him their condolences.

"Have you been here all night?" I ask him routinely.

He looks at me, shocked. "Why?"

Guiltily, I look at the others, whose faces clearly express disapproval of my question. "I just wondered."

"You think *I* killed my mother?"

"No, no, I don't," I amend quickly.

"The pigs asked that but I didn't expect you . . . ," he trails off.

"Have you talked to Blythe?" I ask.

"No."

"Where is she?"

"Home, I guess."

"No, she's not. You don't know where she is tonight?"

He shrugs.

"Sashie?"

We all look toward the sound of the voice. A young woman with spiked lavender hair, wearing a long T-shirt that says BUTTON YOUR FLY, stands in the doorway. She sucks her thumb.

Sasha glances at her, then back to us. "This is . . . eh . . . Tamari."

Oh, *please*, I think, but say hello.

She doesn't respond and continues sucking her thumb.

When she does take her thumb out of her mouth she says, "Sashie, get food, okay?"

Even in his condition, Sasha seems embarrassed. "Go back to bed, Tamari. I'll be in in a minute."

"Tamari hungry," she says.

I know intuitively that Tamari isn't speaking this way because she's a foreigner.

"Please," he begs.

"Tamari not sleepy."

I can't help it: "Tamari shut up and go to bed!"

Tamari's eyes widen, the thumb drops from her mouth, and she says, "Bitch!" But she goes.

"Sorry," I say to Sasha.

He shakes his head as if to convey that Tamari has nothing to do with his life and it doesn't matter what I say to her.

After an uncomfortable silence I say, "If Blythe doesn't want to, do you want me to make the arrangements?"

"Arrangements?"

Now I feel annoyed with him. Why does he have to be drugged out? "What are you on, Sasha? And please don't insult me by saying 'nothing.' "

Kip touches my arm and I realize I've been shouting. Rage is flooding me, and I become aware of wanting to slap Sasha's face. Quickly I understand that it's Megan I'm angry with . . . for being dead. As long as I'm angry I can't cry.

Sasha doesn't answer me.

"If Blythe won't, I'll take care of the funeral arrangements if you want."

"Oh. Yes, that would be good."

Rick says, "You need anything?"

He tells us no and after Kip urges him to call us, she gets his phone number and Blythe's. I say we'll be in touch.

William and Rick have gone home. William is still shaken from the earlier encounter with the robbers, and Kip and I decide it'll be better for us to see Blythe alone. Besides, we're back in our own neighborhood, unafraid.

Bedford Street is a far cry from 108th. The building is a

four-story brownstone. Although there's a stoop, no one is sitting on it. The outside door is locked but the bells are accessible from here.

I look at my watch. It's ten after one. As I press the bell a cab pulls up in front of the building and a woman gets out. She sticks her head through the open passenger window for a second, withdraws, and the cab leaves. As the woman comes up the steps I see that it's Blythe.

"Lauren," she says, surprised. After the initial shock her face changes, reflects suspicion. "What is it? Kip, what is it?"

It's I who must tell her, not Kip. I've told people that other people are dead before but I can't remember doing so with such intimate knowledge of the deceased and survivor.

"Blythe, your mother . . ."

"Oh, shit," she says angrily, "did Meg send you here? I can't believe it, she'll try anything to get her way. So we had a fight, so what? Goddammit. I can't believe she's sending emissaries at one in the morning."

"Meg didn't send us," I say. I hadn't known they'd fought and idly wonder why Meg didn't tell me.

"Blythe, your mother's been killed," I say bluntly, because there's no good way to herald death, and perhaps because what Blythe's just said about Meg makes me want to punish her, although I don't like to admit this.

In the dim illumination from the two lights above the front door I can see Blythe's expression change from anger and arrogance to horror. She sways and both Kip and I grab her.

"What," she says, not as a question but a statement.

"Let's go inside," I say.

Her keys are in her hand. I take them from her, make a guess, and insert the right one in the front door lock. We follow her through the foyer, another door, and then we enter her first-floor apartment. When she snaps on the light I see that her place is as elegant as Sasha's is crude. I haven't been here before because she hasn't invited me. After all, I'm just her mother's old friend, someone she's known her whole life whom she hasn't any interest in socializing with. I can understand this. And I don't mind because I don't particularly like

Blythe as an adult. She's spoiled and sulky and has a mean streak.

When I look around I wonder where this twenty-two-year-old woman has gotten the money for such decor. It's done in an Art Deco style and everything is black and white.

Blythe slumps onto the black velvet couch, looks at us with questioning blue eyes. She's quite beautiful even though she's in shock. Her long blond hair touches her shoulders, turns under. *Meg's hair.* Her unbuttoned raincoat reveals a lavender silk blouse and gray silk slacks. Open-toed shoes match the blouse.

Kip sits on a black velvet club chair and I place myself next to Blythe. "I don't know much, but early in the evening she was held up by two men. They weren't successful and then later, somebody shot her."

Blythe sucks in air as though she's been punched. "I don't understand."

This is a common response when a person is informed of another's death. Kip has told me that what they really mean is that they refuse to believe it.

I put my hand over hers and tell her again. "Someone murdered your mother, Blythe."

"Why?"

"We don't know. Maybe the robbers came back or another robber did it. Maybe it was personal."

"Personal?"

"Yes. Maybe someone had something against Megan."

"Everyone loved her," she says like a bewildered child. "We fought but ... I ... I loved her."

"What did you fight about?"

She waves a hand as if it were inconsequential. Now is not the time to press her about this. Besides, she begins to cry. I take her in my arms and she sobs into my shoulder. Kip moves to the other side of Blythe, a hand on her arm, waiting to help Megan's kid through Megan's death.

Chapter
Four

KIP AND I DROOP OVER the kitchen table. We'd gotten to bed at four-thirty and it's eight-thirty now. Kip has patients, and later I hope to meet Cecchi to learn what I can about Meg's murder.

Kip says, "I know what you're going to do, Lauren, don't think I don't."

"Do?"

"Don't play dumb."

"But I *am* dumb. I haven't the vaguest idea of what . . ."

"Oh, please." She slaps margarine on a muffin. Margarine is what we use now because of my cholesterol count. I hate it.

"Kip, I really don't know what you're talking about."

"I'm talking about Megan's murder."

Megan's murder.

The words sound harsh, metallic, yet real to me for the first time. At last I cry. Kip rises and holds me as I unburden myself of grief I've been shepherding like a stubborn old dog.

"I can't believe it," I say, sounding like so many clients I've had.

"I can't either," she whispers. I detect an ineffable sorrow coming from her, and I know that Megan's death has launched the specter of her brother Tom's dying from AIDS. His diagnosis came about a year ago and, since then, he's had two hospitalizations. Now he's back on top, his T cells in charge. Still, Kip worries, as do I.

After a while my tears abate, my heart accommodates despair.

"I have to do it," I say to her.

She knows I'm referring to our conversation before I'd begun weeping.

"You don't *have* to, Lauren."

"She was my oldest friend."

"I know but the police can handle it."

"They don't know Megan like I do. They don't care."

"Cecchi cares."

"I have to help."

She pushes my hair out of my eyes, strokes my cheek. "Darling, I'm not suggesting that you shouldn't help, tell Cecchi anything, everything you can. I'm only concerned that you'll try to do this on your own."

I pray that she doesn't ask for a promise.

"I'll work with Cecchi," I say, which is true.

"Good."

My evasion has succeeded. "What's your day?"

"Patients from hell," she says. "Needy Ned, Bigmouth Michelle, Tortured Tomato. And that's just this morning."

Kip and I use code names for our respective clients. The three she's named are some of her worst. Tortured Tomato, for instance, is a woman in her forties whose husband always refers to her as a "hot tomato." She finds this unbearable but after three years of therapy still can't tell him so. It's like that in Kip's business. Not all patients, of course. Some are simply neurotics. Kip's specialty is hypnosis but not every case warrants it, nor does every client want it.

"Do you think we should cancel the party?" Kip asks.

"Party?"

"Our twelfth-anniversary party. I thought you might not feel like it, under the circumstances."

It's a dinner party for lesbian couples who've been together over five years. Meg wouldn't have been coming anyway. "It's weeks away," I say, as if this explains everything.

"Okay. We can always cancel, I guess."

"She wouldn't have wanted us to."

"You're right, she wouldn't."

Tears threaten both of us but we swallow them.

Too brightly, Kip asks me, "And your day?"

"I have to help Blythe make funeral arrangements and then . . . I'm not sure."

"Oh, please stay out of this case, Lauren. This is what I was afraid of."

"Don't be."

"Okay," she says sarcastically, "glad that's settled."

I try to appease her but nothing works. When I leave the house we're speaking but there's distinct disharmony.

I'm to meet Blythe at the Lorenzo Funeral Home on Bleecker at ten. It's nine twenty-five and already hot and muggy. The radio said it would reach the nineties again. More record-breaking weather. Who cares? Crisp and sparkling, sunny and warm, Megan is still dead. Thud. I don't want to be doing this. I want to be sitting in a dark movie house; calling Bulletin Boards with my modem and computer; reading magazines.

On Seventh Avenue a young man walks toward me. He's dressed in bright blue spandex pants that end at his knees, and a purple, yellow, and pink spandex top. On his feet are huge high-top black sneakers. His yellow hair, the color of egg yolks, is pulled back into a ponytail. He carries a Mets baseball cap by the bill.

"Excuse me," he says as I draw even with him.

I mustn't judge him by his garb. Will this be a nut or someone with a legitimate question? Encounters with strangers in New York City often produce this consideration. "Yes?" I ask, hopefully.

The man, with brown eyes like shelled almonds, seems startled that I've stopped; then appreciatively he smiles and before the corners of his mouth are fully turned up, I know I've made a big mistake.

"I need to know," he says in a husky voice, "whether the Mets are going to win the Tony this year."

"The Tony?"

"Or the Oscar, for that matter." He puts his cap on backwards.

"The Oscar?" I'm not a big sports fan — Kip holds that honor in our house; she watches everything but basketball and hockey (I've come upon her watching *golf*) and the Mets are her team. But even *I* know that the Tony and Oscar have nothing to do with baseball. The big question is, do I answer him in kind, excuse myself, or set him straight? The last is always the most tempting, and usually the most futile. While I deliberate, he says:

"Of course there's the Emmy but I don't think that counts as much, do you?"

"No, not as much," I find myself saying.

"I don't mean to put the Emmys down," he assures me, "but the other two stand for more. Television is, well, television."

"It is that," I say and try to move around him. He blocks my way. Oh, boy!

"You can see by my cap that I'm a Mets fan." He turns the hat around, pokes his ponytail through the opening in back. "Are you?"

Here's the dilemma: if I say no, I'm not a Mets fan, this might incite him, trigger something nasty. But should I say yes, he might hold me here for hours giving me stats, or reflect on which of the other teams might give the Mets competition for the Pulitzer! I decide to risk delay.

"I don't know anything about baseball." I hold my breath.

"Baseball?" he asks incredulously. Then he shakes his head in disgust and moves around me, muttering the B word over and over.

I'm free! I almost skip down the street, as though I've won the lottery. My first thought is of telling Kip about this, my second, Meg. And the elation I feel at outwitting the nut fizzles like dying steam from a kettle. *You will never tell Meg anything again*, I say to myself. *Never.* Sorrow engulfs me, and before I realize it I find myself in front of Megan's shop on Greenwich Avenue.

Besides the usual yellow tape announcing a crime scene,

there are things on the sidewalk: flowers in vases; cards; various icons. The last time I'd seen anything like this was when the actor Charles Ludlum died of AIDS, and the sidewalk in front of his Ridiculous Theater was strewn with countless outpourings of love and grief.

I bend down to a bouquet of yellow roses and read the card:

> *Dearest Megan:*
> *We love you and will miss you forever.*
> *Jim & Sally*

On a card next to a vase of red tulips:

> *Megan:*
> *You will be missed and never forgotten.*
> *Rocco and his brothers*

> *Meg:*
> *There never was anyone like you and*
> *there never will be again. No one can take your place.*
> *A part of us dies with you.*
> *Jane & Arlene*

This is accompanied by a huge bunch of daisies.

I sob. There are dozens more cards but I can't bear to read them. I lean against the building, unable to stem my torrential tears. I knew Megan was well liked in the community but I'd had no idea to what extent she was loved and revered.

I feel the presence of another person and look up.

He's young. To me he looks about fifteen but I know he's probably older because he wears a doorman's outfit. I assume he's from the building on the corner of Tenth. He has an odd blond beard that starts from his sideburns and goes under his chin like the strap of a helmet. His pale blue eyes appear to be an accessory to his uniform. I can tell he's embarrassed, unsure of what to do or say.

I take him out of his misery. "I'm okay," I say.

"Ya sure?"

"Sure."

"I mean, I can call somebody. Ya want I should call somebody, 'cause it's ethical for me to do that, ya know?"

Whom would he call? I wonder.

"I'm really okay."

"There's a phone on the corner there, and my authenticity would make it legal."

What is he talking about?

"I think ya should let me call somebody, lady. Under the circumstances, it's my duty to persist in this."

I'm startled as someone touches my shoulder. I turn to see a woman, eyes filled. She looks vaguely familiar, in her late thirties, with light brown hair like watch springs and skin as white as bond paper. She wears a green shirt, jeans, and brown sandals.

"You okay?" she asks.

I nod, snuffling.

The doorman says to the woman, "I was wanting to call somebody but your friend wouldn't expedite matters."

The woman says, "It's okay now, Harry. I'll take care of her."

"Ya need any help I'm corroborated to indulge."

"Thanks," the woman says, and leads me toward the curb and up a little from Meg's store.

"I feel like everybody's speaking in another language today," I say.

She smiles. "That's just Harry. He wants to improve himself so he reads the dictionary but he doesn't know when to use what words. Were you a friend of Meg's?"

"Yes. You?"

"Yeah. I have the boutique up the street." She points back toward Seventh Avenue. "Cicero's."

Now I know why she looks familiar.

"Been there four years. Held up seven times."

I don't know what to say. The woman hands me a tissue. I thank her, wipe my eyes, blow my nose, stuff the wet wad in my pocket.

"We all tried to get Meg to invest in an alarm system but

she said she'd been there forever and nobody ever bothered her. We said there was always a first time but it didn't matter what we said, you know what I mean?"

I smile, remembering.

"Stubborn."

"Yes."

She holds out her hand. "I'm Arlene Kornbluth."

We shake. "Of Jane and Arlene?" I motion toward the daisies.

"Yeah," she says shyly, warily.

I understand her trepidation; gay bashing still goes on. "It's okay. I'm Lauren Laurano of Kip and Lauren."

Arlene gives me a puzzled look and then I remember that the name Kip doesn't define gender.

"Kip's a woman," I explain.

She grins, more relaxed now, and pumps my hand enthusiastically. We will always be a minority, and meeting others who're the same is like being part of a secret sorority. We may not become fast friends but we have a certain sensibility that many heterosexuals can't have. There are things that are a given, like oppression; we understand without words.

"How'd you know Meg?" she asks.

I tell her.

Her face reflects my pain. "Jesus. I'm sorry. This must be a nightmare for you."

"Yes. Yes, it's a nightmare." I hadn't realized it indeed has that quality and part of my problem is, on some level, I expect to awaken.

"It wasn't them, you know."

"Excuse me?"

"It wasn't the assholes who held her up earlier. They were black. The shooter was white, had light brown, blondish hair."

"You saw who killed her?" I'm astonished.

"I got a glimpse. I was inside my shop but I heard the shot and ran out. I saw the guy come out of the store and race toward Charles, turn the corner." She takes a deep breath. "I found her. Megan."

Now it's my turn to be horrified, sympathetic. I put my hand on her arm, squeeze. So the police, therefore Cecchi, knew it wasn't the original robbers who shot Meg.

"It's crazy, isn't it?" she asks.

"What is?"

"That Meg should be held up twice in one night after *never* being held up before."

It is crazy and I'm not sure this is what happened. "Yeah. Crazy." I look at my watch. "Have to go now. I'm meeting Meg's daughter to make arrangements."

The word *arrangements* reverberates, as if it's a tolling bell.

"The daughter, huh? A lot she cares."

"Why do you say that?"

"I thought you were Meg's old friend," Arlene says suspiciously.

"I am. Was. I only wondered what Meg told you about Blythe to make you say that."

"It's not so much what Meg told me. I saw things, you know?"

"Like what?"

"Attitude. Blythe has a real attitude." She laughs, then quickly covers her mouth as if she's done something inappropriate.

"What?"

"I shouldn't be talking."

"No, please. I want to know."

"Well, Jane, that's my friend, and I have a little joke about Blythe. We say: 'Blythe gives good attitude.'"

I liberate a limp smile. "Anything else?"

"Hell, what do I know about kids?" But this doesn't stop her. "The thing is, not that Meg said this, but it just seemed to me Blythe only came around when she needed something."

"That doesn't mean she didn't love her." I recall Blythe's statement the night before. "Mothers and daughters have their dances. Remember what you were like with your mother when you were Blythe's age?"

"No, I don't," she says, clipped. "Mine dumped me when I

was eight months old. Don't know who she was, don't care."
Arlene looks angry and I know she cares a lot.

"I'm sorry."

"About what?"

"Your mother leaving . . ."

"I just told you, I don't care," she says testily.

"Right. Well, I'll see you around."

"See you at the funeral," she says, as though talking about
a party. I watch her, envy her long legs, as she strides back
toward her shop.

I take a last look at the scene in front of Megan's store.
The urge to cry chokes me but then I'm distracted by my
reflection in her window. Yeah, short all right, I think, as if I
might have grown somehow. I have dark brown hair that I
wear to my shoulders and in this light I can see that the gray
is coming in fast. I look like my father: classic Italian nose,
high cheekbones. But best, and the thing that drives Kip and
my friends nuts, is that I don't have to watch my weight.
Who knows why, but I can eat what I want while everyone
else is on a diet. Still, I have this cholesterol thing now and
some of my eating is done in secret, as though I've got a
problem.

At the corner of Greenwich and Sixth I cross. Dalton's has
revamped and become what they call a superstore. This
means they have *everything*. But one woman's everything is
another woman's nothing. Besides, I have my loyalty to
Three Lives.

I head downtown. The peddlers are not yet set up for
business, but their tables are erected, which lately they seem
to use for beds. I pass two men, each of whom lies on his table
either snoring or drooling. At the bank that surrounds the
recessed subway entrance, homeless people have positioned
plastic lounging chairs so that the site resembles a cockeyed
beach. It shouldn't be like this. If I know it, why doesn't
George Bush know it?

As I pass Blockbuster Video I glance in their windows. The
hot videos are still *Dances with Wolves* and *Sleeping With the
Enemy*. The second one, I know, is because of the incompetent,

overpaid Julia Roberts, who I'm convinced is really Eric in drag. Have you ever seen them together? Think about it.

At West Fourth Street, while I wait for the light to change, I look across the avenue and down toward the Waverly Twin movie theater. My old sugar gauntlet is gone. Only Mrs. Field's Cookies remains. Gone are David's, Ben & Jerry's, even the Burger King, although it didn't have much to do with sugar. On the corner where Fourth, Sixth, and Cornelia meet, there's a new ice cream and sandwich place. It lacks pizzazz and I give it two months.

Though it's not yet ten, a basketball game is going on at the court on Third Street. I stop to watch. This is serious stuff. These guys play hard. Most of them are African-Americans, but two of the ten aren't. I spot one I know: Fortune Fanelli. Fanelli's a private eye, too. I wonder when he's going to quit playing with these men, because he's getting a little long in the tooth to keep up the pace. Naturally, no women ever play here. Kip once asked if she could and the guffaws greeting her request could be heard on Fourteenth Street.

I'm stalling and I know it. Though it's true I'm not a sports fan, I enjoy watching the spectators who line the metal fence and yell their lungs out as if their lives depended on the outcome. I force myself to leave because I know that on this day I'm using it to avoid dealing with death.

Chapter
Five

THE LORENZO FUNERAL HOME has been in this spot for sixty-five years. What can I say about it? Except for some signed celebrity photos, it looks like any other funeral parlor. I can't help wondering when and under what circumstances these people gave their autographed pictures to Lorenzo's.

A beefy man wearing a dark gray suit approaches me. His black hair lies limp across his dome and his face looks like the back page of the *Daily News.*

"I'm Fabio Lorenzo, how can I help you?" he asks in a high fluty voice that doesn't fit his image.

"I'm meeting someone here to . . . to pick out . . ."

"The container," he supplies.

No one says what anything really is anymore. Missions become *sorties,* handicapped are *physically challenged,* pets are *animal companions,* instead of a mistake, *friendly fire.* And now a coffin is a goddamn *container.* It's as if sanitizing the language will ease the pain of reality. It doesn't work. Still, I nod in assent.

"Would you care for some coffee while you wait?"

"No thanks."

"A brownie?"

Uh-oh. "Brownie?" I say as if I've never before heard the word.

"My wife made them."

Homemade brownies. I try not to eat chocolate before noon like an alcoholic trying not to drink before five. And there *is* something gross about eating a brownie at five after ten in the morning. "If your wife made them I can hardly refuse," I say.

He laughs lightly and shows me tobacco-stained teeth like tarnished tiles. The plate of brownies is on a mahogany table. They're studded with walnuts and slathered with a thick mocha frosting. Lorenzo offers me the plate. In the split second I have I look for a small one, I really do, but there aren't any that I can see, so following the proper route taught me by my mother, I take the one closest, which amazingly turns out to be the biggest. This is not my fault!

Lorenzo hands me a small white paper napkin. "Are you related to the deceased?"

My mouth is full. Guilt grabs me by the throat and I almost choke. Stupid. Because Meg's dead I shouldn't be eating a brownie?

"I'm her . . . I was her oldest friend. We've known each other since we were six."

"Ahh," he says, nods, and closes his eyes for a moment, as if this gives special sanction to our relationship.

"May I ask what the deceased died of?"

I'm surprised by the question. Blythe said she'd call the place and make the appointment. I assumed she'd explain. "Didn't her daughter tell you?"

"Daughter?"

I pop the last of the brownie in my mouth, chew, swallow, wipe my lips. "Weren't you expecting us?"

"No."

"But I thought she'd made a ten-o'clock appointment. She said she'd call me if she couldn't get one. She didn't call so I assumed. . . ."

"I'm sorry but no one called to make a ten o'clock. I have an eleven, though."

"What's the name?"

Lorenzo turns to his desk, flips open a green leather-bound book, runs his finger down the top part of the page. "Cross, Aleen. That's the deceased. My appointment's with her husband, James."

"No. The name's Harbaugh. The deceased. The daughter's Blythe Benning."

He shakes his head and suddenly his hair resembles a badger's tail. "No one by that name's called me."

"Is there anyone else she could've talked to?"

Lorenzo gives me a supercilious smile. "Had anyone else taken the call, I'd know. There'd be a record. We don't run a slipshod business here, Miss . . ."

"Laurano."

"Ahh," he says again, noting my Italian name as if this somehow makes us best buddies. "Miss Laurano, we keep track of things here. Otherwise. . . ." He shrugs, rolls his eyes, and raises both palms upward, indicating, I suppose, chaos.

For a moment I imagine hundreds of people fighting about the same appointment, people struggling over the *containers*, dead bodies rolling on the floor. I want to laugh but instead I say, "Yes, I can see that." I bite my upper lip with my bottom teeth because the urge to laugh, to lose it, is extremely close to the surface.

"So there's no chance that the Benning woman called," he assures me.

There it is again. The Benning woman. Would he say "the Benning man," had it been Sasha? No way. I've never heard anyone say something like "the Rose man," for Pete, or "the Gotti man," for John. Were they Sally Rose and Jean Gotti, you can be sure they'd be called "the Rose woman" and "the Gotti woman." Why is this? How did it start? Inherent in the expression is disdain; it's definitely a pejorative reference.

So, "the Benning woman" didn't call. "May I use your phone?"

"Certainly."

I take the slip of paper out of my purse, careful not to let Lorenzo see my Smith & Wesson .38, and punch in Blythe's number. On the fourth ring the answering machine picks up. It's an annoying message, one of those with a fanfare of rock music, then Blythe, after saying the usual, giving us instructions on how to spend our day and ending with more music.

After twenty-six hours I hear the beep and leave my message asking her to get in touch with me here, my office, or home.

As I hang up the phone I wonder *why* Blythe didn't call, didn't show up here. And I also wonder what I should do. Is it my place to pick the casket? Megan's body won't be released from the morgue for a few days anyway.

"I guess I'll come back," I say.

"Do you wish to schedule?"

"Schedule?"

He sighs. "We're a very busy place, Miss Laurano. You should schedule when the wake will take place."

Wake. Would Meg want a wake? And why is it called a wake . . . the person's anything but a-wake. I feel lost, little, as if this is too much for me. I need Kip's help or . . . Megan's. If I were arranging for someone else's funeral and Kip couldn't be with me, Meg would. It's as if a part of me is gone . . . a hand or leg . . . my heart. Tears push their way into my eyes. I don't want Lorenzo to see this because I know he's inured to expressions of grief and that my sadness will be meaningless to him, therefore somehow making Megan's death meaningless.

But, of course, her death *is* meaningless. It's her life that was meaningful. I have to stop this.

"I'm not sure I should schedule anything without a member of the family."

"Tentatively," he suggests.

"I suppose I could do that. All right, how about Monday?"

"And why not pick a tentative container while you're here?"

"No, I don't think so." I have no idea what the kids want to spend, what Meg would've liked, although I can guess about that.

"As long as you're here," Lorenzo points out. I wonder why he's so eager since business is obviously booming. He indicates a recessed walnut door.

Meekly, I follow him as if I have no will of my own. Inside the cream painted room, the lighting is soft. The containers are arranged in rows, going from wood to metal and lined in synthetic to satin. The price on the one nearest to me is astronomical. Suddenly I realize that although many of my friends have died of AIDS and other illnesses over the last five years, I've not been the one to go through this process. This is my first experience dealing with a funeral home, funeral director, containers. I don't like it.

Lorenzo gives me a rehearsed rap on each, starting with the least expensive, which he describes derisively, and ending in a crescendo with the steel, satin-lined, five-figure number. If it were up to me I'd buy the cheapest one because I don't like to be taken for a chump and what does it matter, anyway? But it's not up to me.

When I look at Lorenzo he's smiling, lizardlike.

"I can't," I say. "I just can't." I hurry through the door into the lobby. "I'll be back," I yell over my shoulder, and push open the heavy glass doors to the street. New York City air has never smelled so good.

On my way to meet Cecchi I take a swing by Blythe's apartment. I lean on the bell but there's no answer. I feel uneasy, as if there's something I should be doing, something I'm forgetting. As I'm about to leave, the front door opens and a man comes out dressed in gray jogging clothes.

He's probably in his forties, good-looking in a conventional way, his brown hair thinning, but combed straight back so that it won't be so noticeable. Around his neck he wears two keys on a string. As he has no pockets, I assume they're to his apartment.

"You need help?" he asks as though he's challenging me rather than offering assistance.

"I was looking for Blythe Benning. I guess she's not home."

He shrugs and starts down the steps.

"Excuse me," I say.

"Yes?" Large brown eyes look me over.

I feel uncomfortable. "Do you live here?"

"Why?"

"I just want to know."

He grins, generous lips moving to the right side so that the smile is crooked. "I didn't think you were asking me because you *didn't* want to know."

"Right," I say, feeling put in my place. "Do you know Blythe?"

"Sure. This is a small building." He comes toward me, puts one foot on the step like he's standing at a bar. "Who're you?"

I tell him and ask his name.

"Jason Lightbourne," he says. "What's up?"

I reach into my purse, pull out my wallet, flip to my P.I. license, and hold it out to him.

He leans in, looks, then laughs. "You gotta be kidding."

"Why?"

"For one thing you're a shrimp." Now he's laughing in my face.

There's practically nothing I enjoy more than a good laugh at my expense, particularly when it has to do with my height. My first instinct is to use judo on him, toss him over my shoulder like a sack of apples. But I know I can't do this because the man is laughing.

"My height has nothing to do with it," I say as calmly as possible. He must see that my eyes belie my words.

"Don't get in an uproar, okay?"

"Mr. Lightbourne, last night Blythe's mother was murdered and today I was to meet her at the funeral parlor at ten. She never showed up."

"What's this got to do with me?"

I would laugh if it weren't so pathetic, so discouraging about the human condition. The Me Decade is supposed to be over but it'll never be over. Was it always this way, only we didn't know because there was no Oprah, Donahue, Geraldo? Did Betsy Ross, for instance, really make the flag for self-aggrandizement? Did Ben Franklin worry about his image?

"Mr. Lightbourne, it doesn't have anything to do with you," I say wearily.

"Right."

"Don't you even care that Blythe's mother was murdered?"

"Well, sure I care," he says, looking back at me, scowling. "I hardly knew the lady, okay? Met her maybe . . . three, four times. As for Blythe, we're neighbors, good neighbors, but not best friends or anything."

"Ever see anyone with her?"

"Like who?"

"Like I don't know, that's why I'm asking you."

"You mean a guy?"

"Man, woman, I don't care." I'm not even sure why I'm asking these questions.

"She isn't a nun, if that's what you're getting at." He smiles at his description as though it's highly original.

"Meaning?"

"Sure I see her with people. And she sees me with people, what's that supposed to prove?" Impatiently, he looks at his Movado wristwatch, and his diamond ring catches a chance sunlight speck that makes me blink.

He's wearing the watch on his right wrist. "You a lefty?"

"That a crime?"

I sigh. Why does everyone respond the same way?

"When you met Meg, Blythe's mother, was she with anyone?" I wonder about Topic A.

"Let's see, maybe. It was pretty casual. There was a party at Blythe's once, she might've been with someone, I'm not sure."

If she was, and if Topic A was married, as I suspected, then he wouldn't have been with her.

"When did you see Blythe last?"

"Can't remember. A few days ago, maybe. Yeah, we were both taking out the garbage at the same time."

"Did you talk?"

"Sure."

"About what?"

"We talked about rats."

"Rats?"

"Yeah, rats in the streets."

"You didn't see her last night, then?"

"Oh, yeah, wait a minute. I did, but we only said hello. She was with a date. I guess he was a date."

This must've been the person who brought her home in the cab. "Can you describe him?"

"What for?"

"For fun, Mr. Lightbourne," I say.

"I don't have time for fun."

"I'm sorry to hear that. Please describe him."

"Let's see. Tall, thin, blond hair, nothing special."

Big help. "Had you ever seen him before?"

He thinks. "Don't remember."

"How was he dressed?"

"I don't know," he answers, irritated.

"A suit, jogging clothes, shorts ... anything you can recall."

Lightbourne shuts his eyes to convey concentration, opens them. "A jacket and slacks, can't remember if it was a suit or not."

"Handsome?"

"Sorry, I wouldn't notice something like that."

I almost laugh. Insecure heterosexual men never fail to express a version of this. I want to say, *Yes, Jason Lightbourne, I know you're straight*, but I don't.

"Ever see her with this guy before?"

"Let's see. No, I don't think so. This was a new one."

"So you kept track of whom Blythe went out with?"

"Hey, wait a minute, don't go implying anything here."

"Like what?"

"Like ... like, I don't know. Like I spied on her or something. I didn't *keep track* of who she went out with."

"You ever go out with her?"

"No."

"If you should see Blythe will you tell her to call me?" I say, handing him my card.

He steps back from me as though I'm offering him a contaminated crack needle. "I don't have any pockets."

I tell him I'll leave it on the top step and he can pick it up when he returns. He agrees, then says: "It probably won't be there when I get back. They'll steal anything, even a dumb card."

When I turn the corner I take out my pad and write Lightbourne's name in it. Next to it I put: "Major Asshole."

Chapter
Six

A NEW CAFÉ, Donatello's, appeared on the scene this summer. They'd been working on it for the last two decades, but finally it opened on Waverly Place near the south side of Seventh Avenue, about thirty seconds from my house. It's got clean green awnings and is large, as cafés go. The best thing about it is a slab of mousse cake with a cream sauce. But I intend to abstain today because I've already had that brownie and it's still not noon.

In warm weather there are tables outside, and this is very warm weather. I can't believe how hot it is and I can never understand why anyone would want to sit outdoors with the dirt and street noise when you can sit inside with air-conditioning and a relatively quiet environment.

Peter Cecchi is at a table near the window. I pull out a chair and join him. We greet each other and he signals for a waitress.

Cecchi is a looker. A tad shy of six feet, he has currant-colored hair with white streaks in all the right places. His craggy face has a strong nose and sad brown eyes that have seen things no human being should ever have to view. Cecchi's an elegant dresser. He wears an expensive gray suit and pale pink shirt with a striped silk tie.

There are many reasons I like Cecchi: he couldn't care less that I'm a lesbian; he's an Italian-American from the same background as mine (no Mafia; no undershirts at the table); and he doesn't try to arrest me every time there's a crime.

Cecchi is secure in his gender and abilities and I don't threaten him in any way. His wife, Annette, who is an assistant to a Broadway producer, is also a good friend of ours. By choice they have no children.

The waitress, who wears her tar-black hair in a style suited to the forties, places a cappuccino and a slice of the mousse cake in front of me. I look at Cecchi, who's smiling.

"I ordered ahead," he says, proudly.

I hold out my arm and tap my watch.

"So what's a few minutes early?" he responds, knowing my noon rule.

"It's more than a few minutes."

"So, forty-five, who's counting?"

"Kip."

"You mean if you eat this cake at noon it's going to do less to your cholesterol count than if you eat it now?"

Cecchi's such a sensible man. And clearly I have no choice, as the last thing I want is to hurt his feelings. "Thanks," I say and tuck right in.

He clears his throat twice and presses his lips together, then says, "Did I tell you how sorry I am about Meg? I know how you feel."

I know he knows; he's lost friends and partners. I nod, acknowledging his condolence.

"So you saw her kids," he states.

I tell him about the meetings with both Sasha and Blythe and add this morning's fiasco. He writes Lightbourne's name in his pad and tells me that he and his partner, Meyers, interviewed Blythe at about four this morning.

"She seemed pretty wiped out when I saw her," he says, "but she mentioned something about meeting you this morning. So why do you think she didn't show up, make the appointment?"

"I don't know. And it worries me. She was always spoiled and irritating but a responsible kid. When she was younger, sometimes it seemed like she was running the family, taking care of Meg and Sasha. So this thing today isn't like her."

Cecchi turns some pages in his notepad. "She works for

Nichols and Thompson, an ad agency on Fifth and Thirty-eighth. Think she went there?"

"Would she go to work the day after her mother was killed?"

"You know her better than I do." He looks at me over the rim of his cup.

"Got a quarter and the number?" I ask.

He gives me both.

"Nichols and Thompson," states a woman's voice. I wonder when men will start answering the phones at big companies.

"Blythe Benning, please."

"I'm sorry, Ms. Benning isn't in today."

"Thanks," I say and hang up. Standing by the phone, I realize I haven't told my mother. Meg was like a second daughter to her. I know because she told me often enough, compared us all the time. It was amazing that I didn't resent Meg, having her perpetually presented as an archetype of perfection, at least until the abortion thing came out. But even then my parents didn't turn against her, they just stopped saying that they wished I were more like Meg.

Meg's parents moved away from South Orange years ago and didn't stay in touch with my family, so there is no chance my mother will hear of it through them. But what about the media? It would be terrible if either of my parents learned of Meg's murder that way. I know I should call but as I don't have a quarter handy I use this excuse to avoid talking to my mother. She probably won't be up yet anyway, sleeping off the night before.

Back at the table I tell Cecchi what I've discovered.

"So," he says, "she's not home and not at work and she doesn't make the funeral parlor appointment or meet you." He takes a swallow of his cap, foam flecking his upper lip, then disappearing as if by magic. "I don't like it, Lauren. I don't like it at all."

"Me either."

We stare at each other, not speaking, not needing to. A dozen scenarios play on the screen of my mind. None of them is good. I tell myself that I'm being negative and there's bound to be a simple, logical, temperate explanation. So why don't I believe myself? I scrape the plate with the edge of my fork for the last of the sauce.

"If she doesn't show up in twenty-four I'll put an APB on her."

I feel like I'm in a bad dream: Meg is dead and her daughter is missing and suddenly I'm crying. I look down, shade my eyes with my hand. "I'm sorry."

"No, no, go ahead."

I know that Cecchi is not a man afraid of tears. Still, I hate crying in public places. He shoves a napkin into my other hand.

"I'm okay now."

"Sure?"

"Yes." I wipe away my tears. "Cecchi, I spoke to Arlene Kornbluth this morning."

"She tell you what she saw?"

"The robbers didn't shoot Meg, did they?"

"Kornbluth could be wrong. Anyway, we picked up the guys who tried to rob Meg."

"That's great."

"Lineup at two. William's coming down. Want to be there?"

"Does Barbara Bush wear pearls?"

"They say they have alibis that check out for nine-twenty, the time she was shot, but not seven-thirty, when the holdup took place."

"Seven-thirty?" I ask, confused.

"Yeah. Why?"

"I thought . . . I don't know, I somehow had the idea it was later than that. The robbery." I don't want to say more, I don't even want to say this.

"Seven-thirty," he repeats.

Obviously the robbery investigation was well over by nine-twenty or Meg wouldn't have been in the store alone. And if the robbery took place at seven-thirty, where was William between then and when he knocked on our door at nine-fifteen? Had he mentioned the time of the holdup? I recall how upset he was, as if the thing had just happened. But it was two hours later. My detective's heart panics.

I go home for lunch to talk about William with Kip. While I wait for her to finish with her last client of the morning, I bite the bullet and call my mother. We go through a knee-jerk opening and I try to assess whether she's started the day's drinking. She sounds sober to me. I know that what I'm about to tell her will give her the reason to start if she hasn't. Of course, she never *needs* a reason.

"I have something terrible to tell you."

"So glad you called," she says sarcastically.

"I think you'd better sit."

There's a long silence, then she says, "Has something happened to Kip?"

"No."

"Thank God. And you're all right?"

It doesn't go by me that she asks about Kip before me. But I'm consoled because I'm on the phone and Kip isn't, so her concern comes in a natural sequence.

"I'm fine. It's Meg."

"What about her?"

"She's . . . she was murdered in her store."

"Oh, my God," she says, as if I've punched her, the words expelled rather than spoken. "When?"

I tell her what I know. She keeps asking questions for which I have no answers. It never matters that you tell a person you've given them all the information you have; they somehow don't believe it or think they're going to ask the one thing you've forgotten.

"I've told you everything I know," I say for the third time.

"Hold on," she instructs.

I hear her lay down the phone, the refrigerator door open, and I know what she's doing. Getting ice. She's very civilized and never drinks without it. I imagine I can hear her at the liquor cabinet in the dining room (which I can't). But I do hear the clip of her heels go and come back into the kitchen, a pouring sound, ice cubes clinking.

"There was someone at the door," she lies.

I've learned not to contradict her, to ignore the drinking, to understand there's nothing I can do. But I've also learned that I can remove myself from the situation. I want to hang up now and say so.

My mother screams at me: "What's wrong with you, Lauren? Don't you have any heart? Can't you imagine what this means to me?"

To *her*. It wouldn't occur to her that Meg's death would have any effect on me or that the real tragedy here is that Meg is dead.

"You are so selfish," she continues yelling. "Megan was like a second daughter to me and she's been murdered and you want to hang up? I don't understand you, Lauren."

No, you don't, I want to say. You don't understand anyone because you're so self-involved. But I don't say it. Instead, I ask her to stop screaming.

She slams down the phone.

Shaking, I replace mine in the cradle. Why do I let her get to me this way? I wish I could be more like Kip, who doesn't allow her mother to inflame her. Of course Carolyn's not a drunk. Still, like all mothers, she can sometimes be irritating and Kip manages to endure it without falling apart. She wasn't always so insouciant regarding her mother. I remember times when she'd sulk after a conversation with her or slam things around. But no more. I guess Kip's more mature than I. I *hate* that!

The phone rings. I'm sure it's my mother and I vow to try. After all, she's not drunk yet. But when I pick it up I hear my father's voice:

"This is the worst thing that's ever happened to me," he says.

What can you say to people like this?

He asks me more questions I have no answers for and then he says:

"Lauren, I want you to come home."

"Come home?" Is he finally going to admit my mother's drinking problem? I wonder.

"This is what I've been talking about for years. Your room is still here for you."

Appalled, at least now I understand. My father's view of the world is that it's a totally dangerous place. There's no room in his conception of life for fun or joy. It's all dark. Not only did he go berserk when, after college, I moved to New York, he becomes almost apoplectic on the subject of my career.

"Daddy," I say, "do you realize that I'm forty-three years old?" So why am I still calling him Daddy?

"And how old was Meg?" he counters.

I sigh. "Where will Kip sleep?" I ask, facetiously. "My room has a single bed."

"We'll get a double."

"I see. So you want Kip and me to sell our house and come live with you and Mother in my old room?"

"What's wrong with that?" he says, defiantly.

"Maybe I can get a cheap office in Newark," I muse.

"NEWARK? Are you crazy? Don't you know it's like Beirut there?"

"And I suppose Kip could see patients on the porch," I continue.

Kip enters the kitchen on this note and raises an eyebrow at my statement.

My father says, "This isn't funny."

"No, it isn't," I answer seriously. "It's not funny at all. The thing we're all losing sight of is that Megan's been killed. Meg's dead." Even as I say this the words feel like bricks in my mouth.

"Yes. Yes, that's the thing," he says, sounding sad. Then: "You're not going to get involved in this, are you?"

"The police are handling it," I say, evasively.

But he's too smart for that. "Is Kip there? I want to talk with Kip."

"She's seeing a client."

"Tell her to call me," he orders and hangs up.

For the second time in ten minutes I'm left with a phone in my hand like some hideous growth. I put the receiver down and turn to Kip.

"He wants you to call him."

"Why?"

"To discuss the movers."

"Movers?"

"Yes, he thinks we should move into my bedroom."

"What are you talking about?" She goes to the refrigerator and gets out one of her frozen meals. I say *her* meals because they are. Recently, Kip's found out she's allergic to all kinds of foods and has begun to make her meals so that she can be sure of what she's getting. It's very annoying to both of us, for different reasons. I have no one to share pizza with, for instance. God, now I sound like my parents!

She pops her lunch into the microwave. "I should've canceled everybody today," she says solemnly. "I mean, what am I doing working the day after a friend dies?"

I go to her, put my arms around her. This is one of those times that I wish I were taller than Kip, so she could put her head on my shoulder, the way I can on hers when I need comforting. I do the best I can, stroke her back, kiss her neck.

Slowly, she pulls back. "How're you holding up?"

I start to say "Fine" and before I know it I'm crying again. And so is Kip. We wail together like wounded animals; the discordant sound engulfs us. Our bodies slump into each other, giving and getting solace. Eventually, when we pull back from our waists, still holding each other, we see a wet face, red eyes, lost hope.

The microwave signals life with its dissonant beep and we hug again, then Kip retrieves her lunch.

I don't know why but I don't tell Kip about William and the discrepancy in time. I do tell her about Arlene Kornbluth and that a man was seen running from the store. I also tell her that Blythe stood me up and I can't find her.

Kip sits down at the table with her container of rice and beans. "Aren't you going to eat?"

"I'm not hungry." This is true but I don't say why, so she touches my hand as if my appetite has disappeared because of Meg's death. I feel like a swine. Before I can confess, Kip says:

"I guess there's no point in arguing again about your working on this case."

I sit. "No point."

"Everything happens at once," she says enigmatically.

I wait for an explanation.

"Tom called. He and Sam are coming to New York."

"When?"

"Couple of days."

I can't help thinking: *Will Megan be in the ground by then?* Tom and Sam didn't know her though they'd met once or twice. They have their own apartment here but we'll want to see them, and I can't imagine being cheerful.

Kip says, "They're coming to see some doctors."

"Has something changed?" I ask, alarmed.

"No. It's precautionary. You know everybody believes the best doctors are in New York. And I think they want to see friends, too. I told Tom about Meg. He said to tell you how sorry he is."

"I don't know how up I'll be for entertaining."

"They'll understand. You don't have to put on an act for them."

"True." I love Tom and Sam. They've been together since college — I guess staying power runs in the family. But at the beginning of their relationship, Sam required them to have an "open marriage" and that's probably when Tom contracted AIDS. It's tempting to blame Sam, since Tom never wanted that arrangement, but we don't because what's the point? Sam won't be tested. If he tested positive it wouldn't determine who gave it to whom, but if he tested negative he would be somewhat off the hook, so I don't understand why he won't do it. Perhaps he doesn't *want* to be exonerated.

"You glad they're coming?" Kip's only seen her baby brother once since the diagnosis and that was more than six months ago.

"I am. Of course, I wish . . . I wish *everything* were different." She sighs, accepting things the way they are.

"Kip, do you think Topic A could've killed Meg?"

"It hadn't occurred to me. What does Cecchi think?"

"I haven't mentioned Topic A yet."

"You'd better."

"Yeah, I will, after the lineup. Maybe one of the robbers did come back."

"I thought you said Arlene Kornbluth told you the shooter was white."

"Well, we all know about eyewitnesses."

"True. Did you see the paper this morning?"

"No."

"Get this."

I know that what's coming is something Kip can add to her S.A. campaign. For the last year she's been ever-vigilant on Sleaze Alert.

"A man is suing Ben and Jerry's for making him fat."

"No."

"Disgusting."

Kip actually keeps a file on these things besides offering an almost daily rant. The ones that stand out are — murder as a solution to anything; example: the woman who murdered her child's friend's mother so that the friend would be too grief-stricken to compete with her daughter for cheerleader. Twelve-step programs that have gone too far; example: F.E.O.T.P.L., For the Empowerment of the Psychiatrically Labeled. People having ghosts write their tell-the-truth books and making appearances on talk shows; example: Michele Launders, biological mother of Lisa Steinberg. The newly created sections in bookstores for true crime; The Donald; and anything about the Iran-contra affair.

"I mean, God, Lauren, you should sue every place you eat in the city for raising your cholesterol!"

Does she know about this morning or is this merely a sleaze example? I study her face.

"Why are you staring at me like that?"

"Like what?"

"You were sitting there staring at me."

"I think you're beautiful," I say, which I do.

"Lauren, that's not why you were staring at me. What is it?"

"I had mousse cake this morning," I blurt.

Now *she* stares at *me*.

"What?" I ask.

She shrugs. "I refuse to be your food police. If you want to pump fat into your veins, be my guest. So I'll be a young widow."

I could kick myself. Why the hell did I tell her? "I'm not going to die of mousse cake," I say, defensively.

"I don't want to talk about it," she says.

"Good." Why *doesn't* she want to talk about it? Doesn't she care about me anymore? "I had a brownie, too," I add in a particularly puerile manner.

Saying nothing, she finishes her disgusting little meal, rises, puts the container in the sink, drips soap into it, and fills it with water.

"I have to go back to work," she states.

Clearly she's lost interest in me. Almost twelve years down the drain.

"Who's on your docket?" I ask, as if everything is normal between us.

"Lorna Doone, All About Alfie, and a new one."

Lorna Doone is so named because she continuously binges on Lorna Doone cookies. All About Alfie is a womanizer.

"Could be worse," I say.

"Could be. So long," she says and goes through the kitchen door to her office.

It's over. There's no doubt about it in my mind. What a fool I was to think we'd make the long haul together. We'd even talked about the book: *Oldest Living Lesbian Couple Tell All.*

The door opens and Kip sticks her head in the kitchen: "If you have one more smidgen of fat today I'm leaving you."

She loves me!

Chapter
Seven

AT ONE-THIRTY I knock on William and Rick's door.

"Who is it?" William asks.

"Veda Pierce," I answer. This is Mildred's daughter, played by Ann Blyth in the forties film.

"Is Kay Pierce with you?"

Veda's sister. "No, she's dead." Kay dies in the movie. "Open the door."

He does. "Veda," he declares, "you're so short."

"Very funny." I waltz by him into the apartment.

Rick, in sweats, is on the NordicTrack, a torturous device that simulates cross-country skiing. As usual, I wonder why anyone would want to simulate it when the real thing is so awful. He's huffing away, and I find that hearing this, looking at it, make me want to take a nap.

Their apartment is laid out exactly like our first floor but the room Kip uses for her office is their bedroom. Her waiting room is William's study, and Rick uses what we jokingly refer to as our Entertainment Center for his study.

They have decorated it in what they call early eclectic. The main aim is comfort: overstuffed chairs, comfortable couches. On the walls they have a collection of Hudson River School paintings, worth plenty.

William, in a dark blue Gap T-shirt, jeans, and loafers, looks haggard, as if he hasn't slept all night. There are deep circles under his blue eyes. I look at his hair. Would anyone call him a blond? His hair has blond streaks, it's true. But this doesn't make him a blond, or blondish, as Arlene Kornbluth described the shooter, does it? And what am I thinking about my friend? Still, I'm compelled to ask.

"What color does it say your hair is on your license?"

"License for what?"

"Driving."

"I don't have one."

"He doesn't drive," Rick says, panting and stepping down from the misery machine.

I'm astonished. How could I know William so long, think I know him so well, and not know this about him? "How come?" I ask.

Rick says: "He's afraid."

"Of what?"

"Merging."

"Where am I going to drive, to the Cineplex?" asks William.

"But you grew up in Connecticut," I offer as a sensible reason.

"I never drove," he says. "Didn't want to. I liked being driven." He smiles, his eyes jaunty as he savors his dependent role.

"How could I not know this about you?"

"One doesn't know *everything* about one's friends, does one?" he asks.

"Driving's so basic."

"To what?"

"Oh, William, you know what she means."

"Forget driving. What do you call your hair?"

"You mean like Steven or Pierre or . . ."

"William!"

He laughs as though he's been a bad boy. "I like the idea of giving my hair a name. What do you think of Alphonse?"

"Will you stop. What *color* is it?"

"One can't believe you've known one all these years and you don't know what color one's hair is. This is much worse than not knowing that one doesn't drive."

When William uses the "one" form of speech it's because

he's being funny or is frightened. I opt for the latter. "Do you consider yourself a blond?"

"Light brown with blond streaks," he says.

"Rick?"

"Same. No, I wouldn't call William's hair blond."

William says, "Would you call it Rose Marie?"

Ignoring William, Rick says, "Why do you want to know, Lauren?"

Now what? I can't tell them the real reason, and I don't want to discuss William's time gap in front of Rick. I look at my watch. "We'd better go, it's getting late."

"You're going with him?"

"Of course. What are friends for?"

"Then I don't have to go," Rick says, unable to hide his delight. "I have a deadline." Rick always has a deadline.

"Don't give it another thought. C'mon, William."

As we start for the door Rick says, "So why did you want to know about his hair?"

"I'll tell you later," I say.

William says: "Perhaps Milton would be a good name for my hair."

We don't speak on the stairs but once outside I say to him: "Will you get serious now?"

"I'm always serious."

"I mean it, William."

"Okay. What?"

"What time did the holdup take place?"

"I thought you'd never ask," he says dryly.

"I'm asking."

"About seven-thirty. Yes, I know, I didn't get to your apartment until nine-fifteen. Is that why you were asking about my hair? Do you actually believe that I killed Meg?"

"Of course not." So why *was* I asking? Sometimes my profession pollutes the most sacred things.

"Then why did you want to know about the color of my hair?" he persists.

"Forget your hair. Where were you for those two hours?"

"Well, I was with the police for a while."

"And then?"

"Lauren, I'd really rather not go into it."

"You're going to have to go into it with the police, so you might as well tell me." We turn the corner onto Bleecker.

"Actually, I don't see how that follows."

"Why are you being this way?"

"What way?"

"Exasperating."

William looks at me, gives me a withering smile. "Chill, okay?"

I feel enormously hurt. He's never spoken to me like this and has always told me everything. At least I thought he did. But then I assumed he drove, too. I wonder how well we ever know anyone. Kip comes to mind at once. Do I know her the way I think I do? Even after these years together there are still little surprises, but that's what makes it fun, alive. It's secrets I'm thinking about. Does Kip have *secrets* from me? Obviously, William does.

At Tenth Street we silently turn toward the Sixth Precinct. On the corner a small man, hair disheveled, a face like a dried apricot, asks us for money. I don't have my usual bags of change with me today and William seems disinclined to give as we move around this person.

He begins to yell: "You fucking plebeians. No class. What's the world coming to? Fuck your heinies."

William and I look at each other and at the same moment say: "Heinies?"

"Yeah, heinies," the man says, defiantly. "You bourgeois cowards."

We continue walking. "I haven't heard that word since I was a kid," William says.

"Me neither."

The momentary bonding over, we fall silent. I feel as if I'm walking with a stranger.

We sit in Cecchi's small office. It's a depressing place: dim lighting, gray metal furniture, paint peeling like burned skin. William has picked out the two suspects from the lineup.

Cecchi says, "Glad we got those bastards. I think they figure in some other holdups, too. Got a couple more witnesses coming in later. But even if they can't I.D. them, you'll be a great witness, William."

William's face pales. "Witness?"

"When they go on trial. Unless they plead guilty."

"Oh. Right," he says.

I may not know *everything* about William but I do know when he's worried, scared.

"By the way," Cecchi says, "where were you between the time we let you go and Meg was killed?"

"I was with Lauren and Kip," he says facilely, as if he's been lying to the police all his life.

I'm stunned and distressed because I know Cecchi is going to ask me to corroborate this. I can't recall ever lying to him, but on the other hand, William needs my alibi and instinct tells me it's got nothing to do with Meg's death.

"That's right," I say before Cecchi actually asks. "Remember, when you called I told you William was with us and . . ."

"Yeah, but that was later, almost ten."

"Well," I say smoothly, "he'd been there since about . . . oh . . ." I realize that I have no idea what time the police let him go and that what I say now could be crucial. Appalled, I recognize that I'm thinking like a criminal. I shrug, grin stupidly, hoping William will fix the time.

He does. "About twenty of nine."

"Yes," I say. "It must've been around then."

Cecchi gives me The Look. I've seen him give it to countless people who he suspects are lying. But I don't let it get to me because I'm ready for it. Brazenly, I look into his droopy brown eyes.

"How do you know?" he asks me.

"I'd just finished using my modem and I always note the time on my computer," I say.

"Kip was home?"

"Yes."

Cecchi picks up the phone and William and I glance at each other without moving our heads. After tapping in the number, Cecchi waits, still giving me The Look. Eventually, he says: "Kip, this is Cecchi, give me a call soon as you can."

I know Kip will be in session for the rest of the day and won't pick up her messages until later. Still, I have to get to her before Cecchi does.

"Why'd you call Kip? Don't you believe us?" William asks indignantly.

"Just doing my job," Cecchi says. He stands up. "Thanks for coming in, William." He extends his hand. William shakes it. Cecchi gives me a curt nod, turns back to the papers on his desk.

He knows.

I feel like hell.

As casually as possible, we walk silently out of his office, through the station, to the street, until we turn the corner.

"Okay, Clyde, what the hell is going on?" I ask him.

"*Clyde?*"

"Of Bonnie and."

He chuckles.

"It's not funny."

"Then why're you saying something funny, like Clyde? Don't answer. Let's get a cup of coffee."

William leads me to the Pink Teacup on Grove Street. Until a few years ago it was on Bleecker but it's been in the Village longer than I can remember. African-Americans run the place and it's probably the only spot in the Village that serves things like grits, collard greens, and hush puppies.

The restaurant is one medium-sized room that's usually bursting with people, but at this hour it's nearly empty. We take a table for two against the wall.

A woman with crimson lipstick and dreadlocks stands with one hip jutting out. "Know what you want?"

"Have any iced coffee?" I ask.

"I can pour some over some ice."

"You mean it's actually hot?"

"Uh-huh. Hot coffee. Ice cubes. Iced coffee," she tells me as if I'm a dunce.

"Fine."

William says, "I'll have an iced coffee and a piece of pecan pie."

Pecan pie doesn't tempt me, and I feel virtuous because I don't ask about any other desserts.

When she's gone, William says, "I suppose I should say thanks."

"But you're not going to?"

He laughs. "No, I'm going to. Thanks."

"Oh, Christ," I say, remembering. "I'd better call Kip." I leave a message: "Don't call Cecchi back. Should he come by, you must say that William got to our place last night around twenty of nine. Figure out a reason you remember. I said I'd just been using my computer. I'll explain later. Erase this tape." I hang up and try to imagine what "the teller of total truth" is going to make of this.

Our coffee and William's pie have arrived.

"Did you get her?" he asks.

"Machine. I left a message."

"What if Cecchi gets hold of the tape?"

"William, do you realize we're behaving like criminals?"

"I *am* a criminal," he says, pops a piece of pie in his mouth.

"What's that supposed to mean?"

"There are certain things one does that make one a kind of criminal."

"Don't you think you'd better tell me what's going on?"

"I do. First, one did *not* have anything to do with Meg's death. You do believe that, don't you, Lauren?"

"Of course I do." And I do.

"What I'm about to tell you may shock you. However, I implore you to have an open mind."

"Don't I always?"

"No."

This shocks me. I pride myself on being nonjudgmental and I could get into this with him, but whatever he has to tell me has priority. "I'll try to be open now," I say through clenched teeth.

William swallows some of his iced coffee. "This isn't very cold."

"Want to get more ice?"

"Never mind. Oh, God," he sighs. "You have to promise not to tell anyone."

"Anyone like who?"

"Rick, Kip, and Cecchi."

"William, you know I can't promise that."

"Then I can't tell you."

I swing swiftly from irritation to fury. "You're being impossible. Do you realize you made me lie to one of my best friends?"

"*I* made you lie? I *never* asked you to lie."

"By inference you did. William, you'd better tell me."

"Or what? You'll spank?"

"I'm not kidding around."

"Can you promise not to tell Rick?"

I ruminate and finally decide that I don't have to tell Rick. "But I'm not going to lie to Kip."

"Cecchi?"

"It depends on what it is."

He drums his long fingers on the table. "Oh, all right. You can imagine what it was like, I mean, being in the store with these two burglars, Meg looking terrified, them waving guns around."

"I thought only one of them had a gun."

"Them waving gun around," he amends ridiculously. "I was terrified."

"I know this part."

"The background's important."

"I know the background."

"I want to make it vivid for you so you'll understand."

"Just tell me what you did when you left the police and before you came knocking at our door."

"That's all you want to know?"

"Yes."

"I scored some coke."

Chapter
Eight

═══════════════

THERE'S AN INSTANT when I don't think I've heard him correctly, quickly followed by the knowledge that I have, but wish I hadn't.

"Cocaine?"

"No, Coca-Cola Classic. Very hard to get. I made a big score."

"Don't, William."

"Sorry. Okay, this is what happened. After the holdup and the police, I was upset, scared. So I scored some coke and it made me crazier. I should've known that's what would happen. I didn't. That's it."

"That's *it?*"

He nods.

I'm astounded by this revelation. "What do you know from scoring coke?"

William looks at me as though he's never seen me before. "Lauren, I know a lot about it."

"What are you saying?" I like to stay in denial as long as possible.

"I'm saying that I use coke," he answers simply.

"And Rick doesn't know?"

"And Rick doesn't know. Right."

"Are you addicted?"

"No."

I know enough about addiction to know William might not know, or admit, he's addicted. Part of me feels frightened, the other furious. I guess I feel betrayed. This is absurd because William owes me nothing, has no allegiance to me regarding drugs or anything else. Yet, there's friendship, and what that means. Are my standards too high? My principles indefensible? Because we're good friends does that mean William must tell me every facet of his life? Do I tell him everything? Still, I can't shake the feeling of betrayal, as if he's broken a basic tenet.

"When did you start?" I ask, not actually caring about that aspect, but not knowing how to proceed.

"About a year ago."

"Do you do it a lot?"

"Not really."

"I don't know what *not really* means."

"Look, Lauren, are you going to make a federal case out of this? Of course, I suppose it *is* a federal case, isn't it? Anyway, it's no big thing except I don't feel like telling Cecchi, getting involved in some drug mess."

"But you *are* involved in a drug mess."

"No, I'm not," he says, defensively. "I get the strong feeling that I need an alibi for the time of Meg's death. And the only one I have is scoring coke. I don't want to tell the police that."

It makes sense. I understand. So why do I feel my soul's swindled?

"Why are you looking at me like that?" he asks.

"Like what?"

"As if I'm a pariah. What would've been the point of me telling you about my coke . . . coke . . ."

"Habit," I supply.

"It's not a habit," he says fiercely. "I use it in a purely recreational way and can knock it off anytime I want."

"But you don't want to?"

"Not until now. Now I think I'd better. At least until everything blows over."

"Until Meg's murder *blows over?*"

"Don't make it sound like that."

"*You* said it, William."

"I didn't mean it to come out that way. I'm devastated

about Meg's death. I know we don't go back the way you and she did, but I loved her, I did." He puts both hands over his face, his shoulders heave, and I know he's crying.

I wait. Drink my coffee. I don't try to comfort him. I run my feelings by me. Disappointment. Betrayal. Anger. I have no right to disappointment, William's not my child, my lover. He's my friend and has every right to do what he wants, including taking drugs. But I hate drugs. If he's addicted and wants to quit, that's something else.

He pulls a blue bandanna from his pocket, wipes his eyes, blows his nose. "I should've stayed with her after the police left. If I'd stayed maybe she'd be alive." His eyes fill again.

"Or maybe you'd be dead, too."

He waves away the idea as if it has no bearing on anything. "You don't understand."

"What don't I understand?"

"Nothing. Never mind."

"Tell me."

"Forget it. I don't know what I'm talking about anymore."

And we're back to secrets again. I know that he's keeping something from me. But I don't press him because, incomprehensible as it once may have been, I want to get away from him.

"Let's get the check," I suggest.

"You hate me," he says.

"I don't hate you." And I don't.

"What, then?"

"Let me absorb this, okay?"

"You won't tell Rick?"

"No. That's between you and him."

"Cecchi?"

"No. Not now. Not unless it becomes essential."

"What about Kip?"

"Yes. I have to tell her, William. I've involved her in a lie and I owe her the truth." Besides, I need to talk about this with someone and Kip is the person I want to discuss it with. But I don't go into this with William.

As predicted, the temperature outside has reached the

nineties, and people have proliferated like dandelions at the wrong time of the year.

"What're you going to do now?" he asks tentatively.

"I'm not sure. I'll see you later."

Hesitantly, he bends to see if I'll kiss him as usual. I do. We turn in opposite directions. I have the park in mind so I make my way west along Bleecker to Sixth Avenue, where I turn uptown.

I'm an emotional wreck. Shattered. It's as though two friends have died instead of one. How will I ever trust William again?

I turn right at Washington Place. As I approach my friend Susan's building, I toy with the idea of giving her a buzz (she never minds) but decide I'm not fit company . . . and what if she strains our friendship in some unexpected way? I can't imagine how, but an hour ago I would've staked my life on William being drug-free. So what do I know about anybody?

I grasp that I feel like a fool, as if his drug taking has more to do with deluding me than hurting himself, and I'm ashamed of my egocentric thinking. I stop walking. Okay, Laurano, I say to myself, pull yourself out of this self-indulgent muck and do something productive. Perhaps a chat with Nick Benning, Meg's second husband, is in order. I walk back to Sixth and hail a cab.

The driver, a man in his late fifties, with a face like a cold potato pancake, keeps up a sonorous soliloquy.

"I was born in St. Vincent's, darlin', you know what I'm sayin'? I'm a real New York City cab driver. These guys coming over, the Chinks and Pakis . . . the TLC don't care you have a heart attack, they don't know where an emergency room is, you know what I'm sayin'? They just want the six hundred bucks for the license. Anybody can be a hack now. It's all goin' to hell. The whole ball a' wax.

"You like cats? I found this black kitten on the street behind a wheel of a car, threw it in my cab and been with me ever since, never took her to a vet, nothin'. I don't believe in that cuttin' and stuff. Cat's like a dog. Follows me everyplace. You got cats?

"Used to work for Julie at Measure Movers, never did know what that name meant. Julie, he's a millionaire now, looks like a street person. A street millionaire. Still wears shoes no socks, drinks in the Bistro, know where that is? This street millionaire bought the warehouse for twenty-five large, sold it for a mil and a half."

"I'll get out here," I say at the corner of Madison and Thirtieth. He continues talking as I step out of the cab. I close the door, glance through the window at him, and see that his mouth is still moving. Does he know I'm gone?

I confess, I don't understand people who love to hear the sound of their own voice. I already know what *I* know, so I find it much more interesting to hear what others think. Even the driver . . . well, maybe not.

I look around. This is a part of New York City that I find arid. Though there are apartment dwellers here, the area connotes business life. Bleak buildings brace themselves like standard-bearers waiting for something, anything, to begin. The occasional grocery or newsstand, tucked between staid structures, emits only the slightest sparkle. On weekends the neighborhood resembles an end-of-the-world movie.

Sycamore Publishing resides in a moderate sixteen-story job with a marble-floor lobby. On the building directory I find that the company is on the sixth and seventh floors. I get on a waiting elevator and push six. Of course it doesn't move, because it's programmed to remain there a certain amount of time, after the first passenger boards, before closing its shiny doors. And I'm the first. In moments other people get on. One is a skinny delivery boy carrying cardboard boxes and wearing the ubiquitous baseball cap turned backwards.

Two more are women in their fifties, neatly groomed, who continue a conversation they've been having.

"So since he's PVS I can understand why Harriet wants to do it," says one.

"I can *understand* it but I wouldn't want to be in her shoes."

"No, me either."

I'm desperate to know what PVS is. What would these women do if I asked? What *could* they do, other than tell me it's none of my business? They can't call the Nosy Police. What will the other passengers (the car's half-full now) think of me asking them? Do I care?

No. "Excuse me," I say to the kinder-looking one.

She recoils as if I've slapped her, so frightened to be spoken to by a stranger. Narrowing her eyes, she says: "Yes?"

"I know this is none of my business," I say, and try a dazzling smile but note immediately that it's not working. The women have moved, their backs to the wall. I wish I'd never begun this. But I can't stop here, say "Never mind," say nothing. I must go on. "Would you mind telling me what PVS is?"

Both their mouths drop open as though I've asked them to show me their underwear.

"This is outrageous," the woman I haven't addressed sputters.

No one else in the car is speaking.

"I'm sorry," I say. "I don't mean to . . ."

"You were listening, eavesdropping on our conversation," says the one I've asked, as appalled as the other.

"Well, it was hard not to hear you," I say weakly.

"Even so." And there's a sound in her voice that strongly suggests I buzz off.

Finally, the doors shut and the elevator starts to move. I pray the women are getting out before me. It takes a month to get from the lobby to the first floor.

They don't get out. Others do, glancing at me as if I'm insane, cautiously moving around me. The doors close. I weigh the risk of asking again; then at the third floor the women do get off.

But before the doors close, the first woman says, "PVS is persistent vegetative state. Now I hope you're ashamed."

On the contrary, I'm delighted to have gotten an answer, and can't wait to tell Kip this acronym that's obviously a new expression for someone in a coma. Harriet, I guess, wants to pull the plug.

By the time I get to six, the remaining passengers, treating me as though I'm a serial killer, have moved into the corners of the car and stare straight ahead. I get off and have to restrain myself from doing something *really* bizarre, like saying good-bye to them.

Nick Benning is an editor at Sycamore. I haven't seen him for years and wonder if he'll meet with me, especially since I don't have an appointment. Appointments are de rigueur in New York.

The waiting room of Sycamore Publishing is large and furnished with comfortable-looking chairs covered in a beige nubby fabric. A large white U-shaped creation is the front desk. The woman behind it has black hair twisted into a braid that sits on top of her head like a slaughtered snake. My eyes go immediately to her lips, slathered with a blood-red lipstick. I assume that's where I'm meant to look but don't know why. I say who I am, ask for Nick, and get what I expected:

"Do you have an appointment?"

This is always asked in the same manner, as if you're subversive, a burner of the American flag, at the least.

"No, but if you'll tell Mr. Benning I'm here . . ."

She gives a long, condescending sigh, picks up the phone, punches a few buttons, cocks her head to one side and her ruby lips to the other.

"Mr. Benning, there's a person here to see you, a Miss Laurano. She doesn't have an appointment." I see her tongue make a bulge in one cheek as if to say, *Now you'll see, asshole.* But slowly the tongue is removed from the cheek, head straightened, eyes widened. "You will?" She replaces the phone in its cradle. "He'll see you," she says, with a grudging respect. "His secretary'll be out in a moment."

"Thank you," I say, as though I've not noticed any of her behavior. I feel it's the best revenge.

A minute or so later, a large woman wearing a garment similar to a piano cover appears in the waiting room and introduces herself to me as Romona Verona and, with dark eyes, dares me to say something. I don't.

"I'm his secretary," she says, as if she's referring to the president of the United States.

I follow her through a thickly carpeted hallway to the third door on the left. Romona Verona knocks once, opens the door, and announces me: "Ms. Laurano."

"Thank you, Romona." Nick, seated behind a huge walnut desk, stands up and comes around it to greet me. He extends both arms, ready to give me a bone-crushing hug. There's no way to avoid it.

I don't actually hear crunching but I imagine I do. When he lets go I see that his eyes are red-rimmed, ready to discharge tears. "It's terrible," he says in a temperate tone, "just terrible." He smacks my back three times, with what are intended to be supportive pats, but are really the expression of someone unfamiliar with giving affection. I remember that this was one of Meg's complaints about him.

He guides me to a blue chair in front of his desk, seats me, and makes his way back to his chair, tents his hands under his chin, trying, I think, to look like the flower child he once was.

When he finally speaks he shocks me. "I have to tell you, Lauren, I'm not surprised that Meg was murdered. Not surprised at all."

Chapter
Nine

MY IMPULSE IS to get up and walk out. Nick's implication is that there was something about Megan that would invite murder. I'm not sure if I can bear another disillusionment today. Even as I think this I recall Meg's descriptions of Nick during their seven-year marriage: cold, calculating, irresponsible.

"Why do you say that, Nick?" I ask, gripping the walnut arms of my chair.

"I know you think you knew her but you didn't. Not really. She showed you one side of her. Only one side." He opens a silver box on his desk, withdraws a cigarette. "You don't smoke, right?"

"Right." I know there were many sides to Meg, like everyone. And I'd seen lots of them.

Nick runs a hand, from front to back, through his light brown hair. I note that it would be difficult to consider him blond. Still.

"What do you mean, she only showed me one side?"

His handsome, craggy face reflects my question as though he's a contestant on a quiz show. "Ah, Lauren." He shakes his head. "The woman was a monster."

I feel angry, and chalk his charges up to being dumped by Meg. All these years later and he's still carrying a grudge. Although I know what he says is biased, colored by his palette of emotions, I'm not ready to leave.

"That's quite an allegation," I say calmly.

"Guess it is. Let's not forget, you never lived with her."

"And you lived with her a long time ago."

"At least I kept up with my children," he offers as an endorsement for his claim.

Nick had to be taken to court three times for lack of child support and almost never saw Blythe and Sasha. And what is he suggesting, after all? I ask.

Blowing a haze of smoke between us, he says, "It's real simple, Lauren. Meg was a bitch."

"That tells me nothing." I'm furious that this man, whom Meg shed more than fifteen years ago, is maligning her now. Now that she's dead. "If she were such a bitch and monster why were you on the verge of tears when I came in?"

"She's my children's mother," he says smoothly.

"You just implied that things weren't that wonderful between Meg and the children."

"This is true. Even so . . ." He shrugs.

"Not good enough, Nick."

His face grows hard like the facade of a cliff. "What's that supposed to mean?"

"It means you're talking in circles, implying things with no verification or example. Why the hell do you want to sully her memory like this? Is it because you couldn't have her, because she left you? If you have something to tell me about Meg, then tell me."

"You won't believe it. You were always her champion."

"It's true that I loved her, but if you can prove something I . . ."

"Prove? How the hell do you prove a woman's a liar and a con?"

A liar and a con? I find it incomprehensible that we're speaking of Meg. William's veiled allusions to some secret about her briefly haunt me. "Nick, please tell me what you're talking about."

"Didn't you ever wonder how Meg supported herself in such a grand style?" he asks. His almost closed eyelids give him a sinister appearance.

"I didn't think she lived particularly high."

"What about those vacations: to the islands, and the one she took last year to Europe?"

I hadn't given it much thought because I was involved in a case at the time of the European jaunt.

I think of Jenny and Jill. They own a bookstore but manage to travel a lot. There's nothing inherently corrupt in this and I tell Nick so.

"You see," he says, "you won't believe it."

"You're not telling me anything. Meg's rent was low, she never spent a lot on clothes, why shouldn't she have money to travel?" I know that in the last year the store wasn't doing well.

I stare at him.

I hold my breath.

I don't want to ask.

I know I have to.

"Are you suggesting she was doing something illegal?"

"Yeah, *Detective*, that's what I'm suggesting." His upper lip curls into a snarl.

"So what was it?"

"The truth is, I don't know the particulars, I just . . ."

Relieved, I stand up. "You know, Nick, you're as slimy as ever. Always ready to lay blame at Meg's feet. Now you want to blame her for her own murder. No way. And where were you last night when she was killed?"

Blood rushes to his cheeks, making him look rouged, clownlike. He bolts up, knocking over a vase with daisies in it. "I don't have to answer that. Who are you working for? Nobody, probably. You know what I think, Lauren? I think you were always in love with her. Why else would you be so fucking blind?"

"Don't try to turn this around."

"I told Meg more than once I thought you wanted her."

"I'll bet you did," I say. "What are you so mad about, Nick? And why won't you tell me where you were last night?"

"I already told the police. I don't have to tell you anything. But for the record, I was with Blythe."

"Really?"

"Yeah, really."

"Until what time?"

"About eleven."

This doesn't jibe with the time Blythe arrived home. Whom had she met after seeing her father? "You know where Blythe is now?"

"No. Should I?"

"Have you talked to her since she found out?"

"Yeah, matter of fact, I have. She called me after you left."

So they could have arranged an alibi for him. What am I thinking? That Blythe would give her father a false alibi to cover the murder of her mother? And was Nick really capable of killing Meg? What would be his motive?

"You've never married again, have you?"

"That a crime?"

If only once someone would respond differently. "Why not?"

"You know something, Lauren ... it's none of your goddamned business why I didn't get married again. Maybe once was enough. Maybe the thought of ending up with another malcontent like Meg made me wary. Maybe I never met the right one. What's it got to do with anything?"

"And maybe you never got over Meg," I suggest.

"Maybe *you* didn't."

"Listen, Nick, because I'm a lesbian doesn't mean that I lust after every woman I know. I've been happily married to Kip for twelve years. And besides, I *never* thought of Meg that way. So don't try to turn my feelings for her into something they never were. Friends. That's what we were. Old friends." On the verge of tears, and not wanting him to see, I walk toward the door. "If you hear from Blythe tell her to get in touch with me."

"Meg called you a dyke behind your back," he says.

It almost stops me but I make myself keep going, open the door, shut it behind me, and force myself to walk briskly past Romona Verona to the waiting room, where I push for the elevator.

I'm devastated. He's managed to shake my faith in my

friend and for that I feel guilt. Conflicting emotions cause my stomach to roil, and sweat beads my face like seed pearls.

Which is worst, that Meg might have been involved in something illegal, that she called me a dyke, or that she wasn't who I thought she was?

I don't believe she maliciously called me a dyke. Perhaps in jest. I can imagine that. And what illegal thing could she have been doing? Meg? It's ridiculous. Or is this response to do with my ego? Am I unable to admit that someone I loved could be anything but who I thought she was? William comes to mind again.

If he could be taking coke for a year without me knowing or suspecting, then wasn't it possible that Meg was doing something I didn't know about?

When I finally admit that it *is* possible, my confidence cracks like a cheap vanity mirror.

I've spent most of the day and evening looking for Blythe but she's nowhere to be found. Sasha doesn't answer his phone. Arrangements for the funeral are still unmade.

It's after midnight, and Kip and I lie as far away from each other as possible in our king-sized bed. Unable to sleep, we're not speaking either. She's reading Blanche McCrary Boyd's latest novel and I'm reading Marilyn Wallace's newest mystery. Except that I'm *not* reading. I'm staring at words. This has nothing to do with the quality of the novel, which is very good, but rather that I'm unable to concentrate. I wonder if Kip is really reading.

From the corner of my eye I try to get a look at her but it's impossible and I'll be damned if I'm going to turn my head.

I turn my head.

"What?" she asks immediately.

"I didn't say anything."

"You were looking at me."

"I wasn't looking at you . . . I *glanced* at you."

"Oh, excuse me, I didn't know we had to be so damn literal."

"Well, we do," I say stupidly.

"So why were you *glancing* at me?"

"No reason."

"That's absurd."

"I wondered if you were really reading."

"Of course I was. No, I wasn't."

"Me either."

"I know."

"How do you know?"

"You haven't turned a page in five minutes." She rests the book on her covered thighs.

"You've been turning pages," I accuse her, as though this is a punishable offense.

"And I have no idea what I've read. Look, Lauren, you know I can't go to sleep this way."

It's a rule we made at the beginning of our relationship . . . we would never turn out the light if we were angry with each other. And we're plenty angry. The trouble is I don't know how to make up. I haven't changed my position and I doubt whether she has. Lying is the topic. Cecchi and Kip haven't connected yet but she refuses to lie for William.

"What d'you want me to say?" she asks.

"I don't want you to *say* anything."

"You just want me to do what you want."

This is true. "William's your friend," I remind her, perhaps for the hundredth time.

She sighs. "Don't."

"But it's the point, Kip."

"Lying is the point."

I close my book and turn toward her. "You're such a WASP."

"What in hell is that supposed to mean?" Facing me, her brown eyes are like burnished baubles.

"All these rules."

"What rules?"

"Ethics," I state, as though it's a filthy word.

"What does that have to do with being a WASP?"

"Everything." I feel myself growing more immature every

second but I'm unable to halt the deterioration of my personality.

"You know," Kip says evenly, "no one ever thinks this, but calling somebody a WASP that way is a form of prejudice."

"Oh, please." Brilliant.

"It is, Lauren. You're saying it in a pejorative fashion."

This is how I meant it but I can't say that. "We're getting off the subject, which is why you won't give one of your dearest friends an alibi so he won't be dragged into some awful coke nightmare."

"Lauren, he's already in a coke nightmare. I just don't choose to compound it."

"No, you choose to betray him."

"Oh, no you don't," she says, sitting up straighter. "William lied and you lied. He didn't even have the decency to tell you ahead of time what he was going to do; ask you if you were willing to lie to Cecchi. And neither of you asked me. You assumed that I'd do your bidding."

"*Bidding?*"

"Yes, bidding."

"Bidding. What kind of word is *bidding?*"

"A perfectly good word."

"Archaic."

"Isn't."

"Anyway, that's not the point."

She stares at me. "What *is* the point?"

We look at each other blankly, realizing the new phenomenon has happened again. Our memories are not what they used to be and sometimes it's alarming. Like now. I don't remember how we got to *bidding* and I can see that she doesn't either. "Never mind that, let's get back to the original argument," I say, throwing the ball firmly into her court.

A smile cavorts around her lips, then quickly vanishes. "Okay," she says. "Let's."

Back in my court. *Bidding*, I think furiously. *Bidding, lies, William.* "We were talking about your refusal to help William," I say serenely, as if I've always known.

I see the light of remembrance in her eyes. "We were talking about you wanting me to do it your way. You wanting me to lie to Cecchi to give William an alibi."

"Exactly."

"And we're right back where we were earlier."

"So what're you going to do, tell Cecchi that William didn't get to the house until about quarter after nine?"

"Yes, Lauren, I am."

"You are such a prig," I say.

"And you're a fascist."

"You could ruin his life."

"I doubt that."

"What about Rick?"

"What about him?"

"Well, how do you think he's going to react when he finds out about William using cocaine?"

"I have no idea and neither do you and that's not the issue."

"It's part of the issue."

"Lauren, listen. We're enabling William if we lie about the time and everything."

"But it's already in place."

"That doesn't make it right."

"Oh, fuck right."

"I can't believe you sometimes," she says.

"Ditto."

"You're impossible."

"And you're not?"

"We're not going to get anywhere with this." Kip turns away, picks up her book.

I feel myself spiraling from frustration into anger into rage.

"What in hell am I going to tell Cecchi?" I yell.

She looks at me; a superior expression skips across her face but then she has the decency to hide it. "That's what this is *really* about, isn't it? You know you did the wrong thing and now you're worried Cecchi will also think you did the wrong thing."

I hate her.

I've never hated anyone more than I hate her right now. Briefly, I entertain ideas of disappearing her. What I hate most is not just that she's right, but that I have to admit it. I toy with denial, flirt with refusing to acknowledge her rightness, but I know it's stupid and that she's got my number.

"I loathe you," I say.

She laughs, puts the book on her night table, and opens her arms to me. "C'mere," she says.

To go or not to go into those comforting, loving arms?

"Lauren?"

I go. There's no turning back now. She kisses the top of my head.

"Cecchi will understand," she soothes.

"No he won't. He'll never trust me again."

"Not true. But I think it'd be better if you tell him yourself rather than having me expose your lie."

"And what about William?"

"Tell him what you have to do."

"Oh, God. What if he never speaks to me again?"

"He's not going to do that. I'm sure somewhere he realizes the position he put you in."

"But I promised."

"It was a dumb promise and I know William knows it. The two of you could tell Cecchi the truth."

It's a suitable plan but I'm not positive William will go for it. "Maybe I should call him now." He's always up late and the phone doesn't ring in their bedroom so it won't wake Rick.

"Good idea," she says.

Reluctantly, I remove myself from her embrace, pick up the phone, and push the button that automatically dials William's number.

I'm shocked when Rick answers.

"What're you doing up?"

"I couldn't sleep," he says, a definite frost in his voice. "You want William?"

"Are you all right?"

"No," he says. "Here's William."

William takes the phone and says, "I know."

"What?"

"We have to tell Cecchi the truth."

Relief floods through me like sun on a winter day. "Yes. What's the matter with Rick?"

He doesn't answer.

"You told him?"

"Yes."

"Oh, God. Is he mad at you?"

"One could say that."

"I'm sorry, William."

"Me, too."

We plan to meet first thing in the morning and go see Cecchi, and then we hang up. I worm my way back into Kip's arms.

"Rick's mad at William," I tell her.

"I can understand that."

"William's not an addict," I say defensively.

"Who said he was?"

"I know that's what you think."

"No, you don't. Matter of fact, I have no idea if he is or isn't."

"I feel terrible for him. For them both."

"So do I." She puts her hand under my chin and tilts my face up to hers.

When she kisses me I don't immediately respond, still thinking of William and Rick's predicament. But then her warm lips captivate me, her tongue touches mine, explores, and I feel it as though she's penetrating my being.

I slip my arms around her, slide on top of her, gently move my body against hers. Our breasts are pressed into each other, our legs entwined. She slides a hand over my back, fingers trailing like feathers. I forget my friends upstairs for the moment and concentrate on Kip. Kip. Right now there is only Kip.

Chapter
Ten

AT NINE IN THE MORNING, William and I meet with Cecchi at the coffee shop at Waverly and Sixth Avenue, a cop hangout, and tell him the truth. Cecchi explains to William that he has no interest in his drug taking or buying. He's not the DEA. But, if he has to prove his whereabouts at some point, he'd better have his dealer back him up. William's not thrilled about this and I can't blame him, though it's unlikely that this will be necessary.

When William leaves, Cecchi stares at me.

"What?" I say.

"I can't get over you lying to me like that."

I shrug. "He took me by surprise. And he's my friend."

"What am I, chopped garlic?"

"It's different."

"Because he's gay?"

"Of course not," I answer, annoyed. But for a moment I wonder if it *is* true. I've known both men about the same length of time. Although Kip and I often spend evenings with Cecchi and Annette, who always treat us as though we're just another married couple, there *is* a difference. With the Cecchis I'm aware of them accepting me, as though it's an indulgence, and with Rick and William I never think about it because I don't have to. A subtle distinction, but a distinction.

"Don't get hot under the collar, Lauren. I just wondered."

"Sorry." And I am. It's not his fault, he's a product of his culture, and God knows he tries, with women's issues as well, and that's more than can be said about most men, straight or gay.

With a piece of bagel Cecchi scoops up the last of his scrambled eggs and pops them in his mouth. His eyes look sad and I hope I haven't hurt him.

"I would've done the same if it'd been reversed," I say.

He nods but I'm not sure he believes me. I'm not sure *I* believe me.

"The body's going to be released this afternoon," he says suddenly.

Body. It takes me by surprise. This is Meg's body Cecchi is referring to and I'm not ready to accept her as a body.

"You made the arrangements?"

"No." I remind him about Blythe's not showing up.

"So where's it gonna go?"

It. I have the impulse to ask Cecchi to stop talking about Meg this way, but I curb that because I don't want to appear timorous or he might stop confiding in me. The real problem is the answer to his question: where's it going to go?

"I guess I better take care of things at Lorenzo's," I say. I swallow some cold coffee.

"Sorry you're stuck with it."

"We have to find Blythe," I say.

"Found her."

"Why didn't you tell me?" I ask, confused.

He shrugs. "I'm telling you now."

I realize then that he'd known William and I were lying and had decided not to tell me anything more about the case until I told him the truth. Who could blame him? I try not to feel wounded. "Where was she?"

"She'd been at a girlfriend's place."

It makes sense. Still, why did she stand me up at the funeral parlor? I need to speak with Blythe.

"She went to work today."

"Really?"

"Yeah. And her story checks out. She was with her father the night of the murder."

"Until eleven," I say.

"Yeah, until eleven. Why?"

Obviously, there's a lot Cecchi hasn't told me. It's hard not to feel offended, though I'd lied to him and probably deserved his decision not to inform me of the particulars.

"She was with someone else after that," I offer.

"So what?"

"I just thought you should know."

He smiles. "You trying to make up for not telling me about William?"

"I guess." Along these lines it occurs to me that I could tell Cecchi there's some possibility Meg wasn't the person we all thought she was. But it seems like disloyalty to repeat what hasn't been proved, and there's enough betrayal blemishing this case. However, I definitely must mention Topic A.

"You want some hot coffee?" he asks.

I nod and he signals Ruby, our waitress.

She arrives at the table with the glass pot as though it's an extension of her hand. "So, who wants?"

"Both."

"You on a big case, Cecchi?" she asks.

"I'm always on a big case."

Ruby is the quintessential older New York waitress: eyes that can no longer be surprised, a thick square body, and hair so sprayed into place it looks like cement.

"It's that girl on Greenwich Avenue, huh? The one who had the store?"

Girl, I think, and remember when Meg was one. Wasn't it last week?

Cecchi says, "Yeah, Ruby. You knew her?"

"Nah. She wasn't the kind come in here. Not that I hold that against her, mind. But when I seen her picture in the paper I recognized the face from around the nabe."

Ruby always addresses everything to Cecchi, even if I ask her a question, because to her I don't exist. Cecchi's the cop, the man, the everything.

"Funny thing, though, I seen her with some weird-looking types."

"Like who?"

"Didn't know them but they were cheesy characters. Don't fit with her, that's how come I noticed."

My detective's heart snags on a thump.

"You think of anything else about her you let me know, Ruby, okay?"

"Sure, Cecchi, you know me, Ruby Packard on the case." When she laughs yellow teeth flash like candy corn. Silently, she moves away on white waitress shoes.

Cecchi says, "Wonder who she saw with Meg?"

It's hard to believe that Meg would be romantically linked with someone whom Ruby would describe the way she did, but I know I have to tell Cecchi about Topic A.

When I'm finished he says, "You have no idea who he is?"

"None."

"But I thought . . ."

"We *were* good friends," I interrupt, not wanting to hear him say the inevitable. "I think she was ashamed of him in some way."

"So then he could've been one of the guys Ruby saw her with?"

"No. Yes. I don't know."

"Okay, what aren't you telling me?" he sighs.

"He was probably married."

"So?"

"What do you mean, so?"

"So he was married, so what? Why would that keep her from telling her best friend?"

Why is it that I feel my standards are on the line?

"I have a problem with women dating married men."

"Oh, yeah. What's the problem?" he asks ingenuously.

Now it's my turn to sigh. I explain.

"In other words," he says, "she didn't want you to judge her."

"Mmmm."

"I can see that. Well, this puts a new light on things. We have to find this guy."

"I guess we do."

"I'll get Ruby to give me more detailed descriptions. What're you going to do?"

"It's too early to go to the funeral parlor." The truth is, I'm not officially on this case. I have to face it: for the moment I'm unemployed. "I guess I'll go to my office. Haven't been there for a few days."

As we pay our check, Jason Lightbourne comes in and I almost don't recognize him because he's dressed in a snappy suit and tie.

"If it isn't Dickette Tracy," he says to me.

I grunt and introduce him to Cecchi.

"We've met," Cecchi says.

Of course. But just to get on Lightbourne's nerves I say, "He saw Meg at a party with a guy."

"I said, I *thought* I did."

Cecchi says, "I'd like to hear more about that, Mr. Light-bourne."

"I have an appointment. I just came in for some coffee."

"While you're waiting," Cecchi says.

Lightbourne shoots me a lethal look and I smile back at him all innocence and say good-bye to both.

The weather is cooler than it's been and I wear a green corduroy jacket that's the perfect weight. I walk down Waverly toward Sheridan Square. None of the shops is open yet except the liquor store. At the square, the two benches outside the little park are inhabited by three men and a woman. Two of them are passing a bottle back and forth. All look drunk, dirty, homeless. Only one is over forty.

It's getting worse. The homeless, the jobless, the filthy streets, and, of course, the crime. Why do I stay here? Kip and I could sell the building, though it's not a good time, and move to the country, buy something spectacular and never have to worry about money again. She could open a practice almost anywhere but what would I do? Do they really need private investigators in High Falls, New York?

"Hey, sister," the woman on one of the benches calls to me.

"What?"

"Got a cig?"

"Don't smoke."

"Fuck you," she says.

Nice. Is this why I stay here? I'm verbally abused by strangers at least once a day, hit up for money on almost every block, and assaulted by sounds and smells that would drive any sane person screaming for refuge elsewhere. So who said I was sane?

When the light changes I cross Grove, pass a newsstand where I can't help noticing a headline that says "JFK SAYS 'TEDDY IS BREAKING MY HEART.'" Briefly, I wonder whom JFK has said this to and decide it was probably Elvis and James Dean.

I cross Seventh Avenue and go into Smilers to get a coffee.

A rotund man, in his thirties, wearing a work shirt open to two buttons above his waist, chest hair spilling out like a raccoon's coat, is explaining to the bored counterman why he doesn't want mayo on his sandwich.

"Dairy. Mayonnaise is dairy. Dairy kills."

Oh, boy.

"So whatcha want on it, then? Butter?"

"Butter?" the man says as if he's been offered arsenic. "Are you stupid?"

The counterman narrows his eyes in a threatening way. "What'd you call me?"

Here we go. I wish that there were something I could do to defuse this but I know better.

"I didn't *call* you anything. I *asked* you if you were stupid."

I can tell that the counterman can't see the subtle distinction here, because he looks at the other people as though someone might explain. No one says anything. He licks his lips. "So what'd you ask me?"

"I asked if you were stupid."

I can't believe the customer has repeated this. More people have come in and are lining up, grumbling.

The counterman says, "Listen, shithead, get the hell outta here before I call a cop." His face is turning red.

"What?" The customer makes his hands into fists and props them on his hips.

"You deef?"

"Deef?"

"Yeah, deef."

The customer breathes as if he's in labor. "Just give me my turkey, lettuce, and tomato on a roll."

"Listen, fag, I ain't givin' you nothin'. Get outta here. Next."

It's my lucky day as I'm next. To speak or not to speak? I don't get the opportunity.

"You fucking moron," the customer shouts.

"Suck my dick."

I never understand this: he disparagingly calls the guy a fag and then he wants him to go down on him! Does this make sense?

"I wouldn't suck your filthy dick if it was the last one on earth."

"You'd suck a duck's dick." The counterman walks toward the break in the counter, ready to defend . . . what, his dick?

The customer pumps up his pecs but moves toward the door. "Butter is dairy, you fucking asshole," he shouts; the cords on his neck bulge like telephone wire.

The counterman, taller but slighter than the customer, gives him a push. "Out, cocksucker!"

"Eat me," the customer yells and pushes back.

They can't get off the subject. There ensues a scuffle, and the words *cock* and *dick* are thrown back and forth as if there are no two other words in the language. When the customer is finally ejected, and the counterman returns to his place, I realize I cannot order from this man who's called the man a fag. In fact, I can never come in here again.

I say to him, "Sir, you have a childlike grasp of the English language, you're homophobic and one of the dumbest people I've ever encountered." I turn to leave.

"Fucking dyke," he yells after me.

"Absolutely," I say. "As much as I can."

I go into Tiffany's and order a coffee and doughnut without incident. At my building, next door, the super is mopping the floors.

"Hi," she says.

I return her greeting. Her name's Kim Alpert and she's six feet tall. She wants to be a stand-up comedian and spends her nights going from club to club trying to get a break. Kip and I went to see her once and she's not bad.

"Anything new?" I ask, looking up at her.

"Got a gig in Great Neck Saturday," she says. "A bar mitzvah." She rolls her eyes. "Better than nothing, I guess."

"Sure. Anyway, you need the experience."

"Yeah. That's what I tell my mother but she doesn't get it."

"Mothers never do."

"I could discover the cure for cancer, she'd go, 'Yeah but do you have a date for Saturday night?' "

I laugh and wish her luck.

My place is on the second floor. I have the usual sign on the door advertising my profession and name. It always startles me to see it. I know it's not like it's in lights on Broadway, but to me it's still remarkable that I have this career and an office of my own. I shove my key in, but when I go to open the door it doesn't. I realize immediately that I've locked it, which tells me it was *un*locked. I'm not a P.I. for nothing.

I place the bag with my container of coffee and chocolate-covered doughnut on the floor, extract my .38 from my purse, and turn the key back, unlocking the door. Slowly, I turn the knob and ease it open. When it has cleared the lock I kick it wide and stand in a combat pose, my gun held in front of me in a two-handed grip, a clear view of my one room.

Sitting in the client's chair is Ray Davies, Meg's third husband.

I lower my gun. "What a coincidence bumping into you here."

"Yeah. Weird, huh?" Grinning, he stands up. Davies is a slender man, almost delicate. He wears a pink shirt, cuffs rolled up, navy slacks, black tasseled loafers. His hair hints at thinning, the brown sideburns a trifle too long. Deep-set gray eyes sparkle although I detect despondency in the way he stands; his slight form sags like laundry on a line. He's handsome in a rugged way, all right angles. Ray Davies is now thirty-one years old, and one of Meg's worst mistakes. He offers me his hand.

I take it and notice the smoothness of his palm, the lethargic squeeze.

"How'd you get in?"

"I have my ways."

I give him a withering look, go outside, pick up my paper bag, and return to my desk. Facing Davies, I take out my coffee and doughnut, offer him nothing.

"You look good, Lauren."

"What do you want?"

"Don't be a hardass," he says.

"Why not?"

He laughs. "You're right, why not? Hey, babes, I know there's no love lost between us but I think we have something in common: Meg."

"Meg? Are you kidding, Ray? Seems to me when you found your new girlfriend we stopped having even Meg in common."

"Whoa." He runs his hand over the top of his hair as if he's trolling for fish. "That wasn't my fault."

"Really? Whose fault was it? Mine?"

"Hey, babes, let's not argue."

"What do you want, Ray?"

"Same thing you want. I want to know who killed Meg."

"The police are working on it." I open the lid on my coffee and a wisp of moribund steam escapes.

Davies grins again, his thin lips a slash across his tanned face. "Po-lice," he says. "Gimme a break. They aren't gonna do squat and you know it."

Do I? Cecchi will keep on it but what will happen when a new case comes along and he's pulled off this one? I say nothing.

"That's why I'm here. I want to hire you."

I almost laugh. "Hire me? With what?"

"Cold cash," he says and pulls a huge roll from his pants pocket. There's a hundred on the outside but I know the rest might be ones.

"Where'd you get that, Ray?"

"It's legal."

Ray had never done a day's work in his life when he met Meg, and didn't bother doing any during the eighteen months he was with her.

"Are you going to tell me you have a job?"

"Nope."

"At least you're honest about it."

"I won it in AC. Craps."

I feel a momentary pang of envy. Kip and I love to gamble, especially craps. The first time we tried it was in Reno after studying several books on our train trip there. We noticed at once that the tables were surrounded mostly by men, and when Kip threw the dice for the first time and they landed on a different table from the one we were playing at, all the men picked up their chips and left. Humiliated, she refused to throw again, but we won over a thousand dollars between us.

"How much did you win?"

"Well, now, babes, that's between me and my accountant. Let's just say I got enough to finance an investigation."

I don't know what to say. This is what I want, someone to hire me to investigate Meg's murder, but do I want it to be Ray Davies? He'd lied and cheated during their whole silly marriage and he'd broken Meg's heart.

"I know what you're thinking, babes," he says.

"Really?"

"You're thinking, why does this guy, who lied to Meg and played around on her, care about finding out who killed her? Am I right or am I right?"

"You're right."

"Thing is, Lauren, what you never got was that I was in love with Meg."

"You had a funny way of showing it."

"Young and foolish. But I've since recognized the error of my ways, so to speak."

He'd been twenty-six when he and Meg were married, almost twenty-eight when they split.

"What happened to your girlfriend? She was younger and even more foolish than you, if I recall." I knew this much from Meg.

"She was younger all right. But I don't think I'd call her foolish. Shrewd and mean is what I'd say."

It sounds as if Davies got his and I'm glad. Meg was devastated when it happened. Kip and I had spent many late nights with her during that period, trying to give her comfort, but she was inconsolable for months so we just let her grieve. Then one day she was over it, almost as if it had never happened, and she never mentioned Ray's name again. It was strange the way she bounced back but we didn't probe, glad to have the old Meg in our lives again.

"I don't get it, Ray."

"What's to get, babes? I want to find her killer, that's all."

"So much so you're willing to pay me three hundred a day plus expenses?"

"Yep."

"It could take weeks, months."

"Go to it. You want an advance?" Davies stands up and peels off bills. They're all hundreds.

"Hold it," I say. "What's in this for you?"

He looks wounded, like a child whose mother's just denied him an ice cream cone.

"That stings, babes," he says.

I'm silent.

"Why d'you got it in for me so much, huh?"

Nothing.

"You figure I caused Meg a lot of pain, right?"

"Something like that," I say.

"I won't deny it. But I was young and stupid."

"I won't argue with stupid," I say. "Twenty-eight is old enough to know better."

"I guess," he relents reluctantly. "But, damn it all, *she* came after me." He holds up a hand to head off my riposte. "What's a randy twenty-eight-year-old gonna do when a squeeze like that one comes along? You probably wouldn't a' been able to resist her yourself."

"Put a sock in it, Ray."

"You never cheated on Kip?"

"No."

"Well, you oughta hold off judgment, then. You don't know what it's like when that kind a' temptation falls in your lap."

"I didn't say no one ever tempted me, Ray. I said I never cheated on Kip."

His eyes light up as though I've admitted adultery. "So you know, then."

"What I know is that you don't do it if you're married. Of course you shouldn't have been married to Meg in the first place."

"You think she was too good for me?"

"Too *old* for you. And, yeah, too good for you."

"You're right. But I loved that lady more'n life itself. Look, I know it's probably hard for you to understand, but sex and love sometimes just aren't the same thing."

As always I wonder if this is true for women. Perhaps for the younger ones, although I suspect we *are* different. If no drugs or alcohol is involved, women need to at least call it love.

"I know," Ray says, "I was thinking with my dick, excuse my French, but Jesus, Lauren, that girl wouldn't leave me be. I know you probably can't see the appeal, it's always different when you know somebody real good, like that."

Suddenly I feel like Ray and I are in two different plays. "Like what?"

"Well, hell," he says, "the way you know Blythe."

Chapter
Eleven

BLYTHE.

I remember so clearly the night Megan came to our door without calling first (something she never did) and Kip and I took her in.

"Oh, kids," she said. "The little bastard's done it now."

"Done what?" We guided her into the living room, one of us on each side.

"I can't believe it," she said, crying.

We waited patiently until she could speak, glancing at each other from time to time, feeling terrible for Meg yet tacitly, and arrogantly, acknowledging that we'd been right about Ray Davies.

"You know what the little shit did?"

"What?"

"He . . ." She shook her head and cried some more. I went for tissues while Kip continued to try to console her, then when I came back Kip left to make a pot of tea. Meg always loved tea.

I held Meg, waiting for Kip to return and Meg to stop crying so she could tell us what had happened. I wrote a dozen or so scenarios in my head. The two leaders: Ray stealing her money and having an affair.

When Meg did pull herself together, we all had tea and some Pepperidge Farm cookies (chocolate) and she told us.

"You never could stand him, could you, Laur?" she asked.

I shrugged. What was the point?

"I know you both hate him," she stated.

"*Hate*'s too strong a word," Kip answered. And it was. We simply thought Ray Davies was a number-one loser and that Meg could do a lot better.

I was getting impatient and prodded her. "What did the little shit do?"

"He's having an affair," she muttered.

"With whom?" Kip asked.

She looked at us, one at a time, as if making an assessment, bit her top lip hard, closed her eyes but didn't answer. It was then that I should've known. Meg had never been taciturn but we had to beg for details.

"Is it someone you know?" I asked.

She shook her head.

"How'd you find out?"

Again, she shook her head, wouldn't answer.

Kip said, "It's someone very young, isn't it?"

She nodded, and the tears were accompanied by sobs.

Later, when Kip and I reviewed it, we talked about how the age factor had gotten to Meg and wondered why she hadn't expected it. We certainly had.

"Humiliating," Kip said.

"No matter how old the person is."

"But in this case, much worse that she's young."

Meg never would tell us how old the other woman was, saying the *exact* age wasn't the issue. And that's when I should've known again, because if it wasn't the issue, why wouldn't she tell us?

She'd kicked Ray Davies out and, a few weeks later, told us he was no longer seeing Madame X, and that he'd begged her to take him back, but she wanted no part of him.

Meg had gotten over Davies in a relatively short time. Still, there was always something about the whole thing that bothered me, but I couldn't pin it down. Now I knew.

"Blythe?" I say to Davies. "Your affair was with Blythe?"

"Hey, babes, I thought you knew, you two being confidants and such. Wow. Hey, it wasn't anything, you know. The kid just wouldn't leave me alone and, like I said, I was thinking with my dick in those days."

"And you're not now?" I ask sarcastically.

A sly grin, like a snake in slow motion, splits his face. "Hell, I try to use the old bean." Fist clenched, he raps his head twice.

Davies makes me sick. But what makes me feel worse is that Meg lied to me by omission. I want this twerp to leave. Still, if he wants to pay me to go after Meg's killer I'd be a jerk to turn him down. It's not the money, it's the legitimacy. Even Kip would have to sanction me being on this case. I think.

"Let me get something straight," I say. "When you were with Meg and Blythe was, what, seventeen . . ."

"Eighteen," he contradicts indignantly, and takes a pack of crumpled Camels from his pocket.

"No," I say. "You can't smoke in here."

"Jesus, Mary, and Joseph," he mumbles and puts the pack away. "You always were an uptight broad, you know that?"

How am I going to work for this man? I ask myself.

"Ray, if I'm going to take the case we have to get some things straight, make some ground rules."

He stands, turns the chair around, and straddles it, arms across the top of the back. "Shoot." Mr. Man.

"First, I'm not a broad. Nor do I want you to call me babes."

"Whatcha want me to call ya, Ms. Laurano?" He cackles long and annoyingly.

"Lauren."

"Lauren," he repeats as though it's a new foreign word. "Hell, *Lauren*, I call everybody babes."

"But not me," I instruct. "Not ever again."

The skin near his eyes crinkles and I know he thinks he's adorable. "Well, what if I forget, call you babes by mistake?"

"Don't forget," I say bluntly.

"Jeeze Louise."

"And don't call me Louise either."

"Huh?"

My humor's lost on him, and I recall that lack of had been one of Meg's complaints. "So Blythe was eighteen when you had this . . . thing with her?"

"Right."

"Was she living with you and Meg then?"

"Hell, no," he says, appalled. "Think I'd do something like that?"

"Like what?"

"Well, in the same house and all."

"You mean it was okay to sleep with your wife's daughter, *your* stepdaughter, as long as you lived separately?"

He stares at me as if I've thrown him a difficult riddle to solve.

"Well, hell," he says.

"Some people would call it incest."

"Shit. Incest? She wanted it."

"That's what you all say."

"Who all?"

"Perpetrators."

"What are you talking about, bab — . . . Lauren?"

"Ray, you were her stepfather. You were married to her mother."

"That doesn't automatically make me the bad guy. And it doesn't make it incest. Blythe was a big girl. She was living on her own, working. It's not like I went creeping into some little girl's room after my wife was asleep or something. Don't try to make me out to be a pervert or perpetrator."

If what he says is true, he has a point . . . a small one.

"What's this got to do with anything now, anyway?" he asks.

"Probably nothing. Where were you when Meg was killed?"

"You kidding me?"

"No."

"You think *I* wasted Meg?"

Here it is again. The only thing that ever changes is the verb: wasted; murdered; killed; offed; punched her/his ticket.

Now I have to say my boring line: "I don't know what I think yet."

And he says, predictably: "If I killed her would I hire you to find out who did it?"

My line: "It's possible."

"Well, hell, I didn't."

"So where were you?"

"Home with my wife."

"You got married again?"

"Third time," he says, as if it's an achievement.

I sigh. "So I assume she'll give you an alibi."

"Damn right."

"What's her name?"

"Melinda."

I write it down. "Address?"

"Same as mine."

"Well, I don't know yours, Ray."

"Oh. Yeah, that's right. We live on Staten Island. Got a real nice place there. A house."

"Address?"

"Six twenty-two Westervelt Avenue."

He continues with the phone number and adds that two other people were at his house that night. I get their names and numbers as well. I don't believe Ray's guilty but I need to rule him out.

"There's just one thing," he says. "Melinda's, well, she's kind of a jealous type, you know?"

"And she'd be upset if she knew you were financing this investigation?"

"Yeah."

"I'll call your friends."

"Thanks."

"Something else, Ray. Do you have any ideas, suspicions about who killed Meg?"

"If I did," he says, puffing out his chest, "I wouldn't hire you."

"Of course," I say wearily. I tell him I'll start immediately and for him to call in once a day. I can't believe it when I shake hands with the little worm, but now he's my employer and I don't have a choice.

When he's gone I take a bite of my doughnut. It tastes like a poor grade of paper. But I know it's not the doughnut, it's me. How I'm feeling. Or how Ray Davies has made me feel about Meg.

Why hadn't she told us about Blythe's being the one Davies had the affair with? Or at least me, if she felt uneasy about Kip. Didn't she know I'd sympathize? God. Didn't she know how much I'd feel for her? Didn't Meg trust our friendship enough for that?

But maybe that wasn't it. Maybe it had nothing to do with me and Meg. Maybe it was wanting to protect her daughter, even under those circumstances. You'd think she'd want to expose Blythe, let everyone know what an insufferable, corrupt little brat she was. And who could blame her? Betraying Meg that way. But then I realize that that was the very thing that had kept her silent; something I'd never understand firsthand. Mothers and daughters. I'm a daughter but not a mother and I never will be. Never wanted to be.

Would my mother protect me if I humiliated and betrayed her somehow? I know in my gut, even though she's a drunk, she would.

I acknowledge that mother love is special, different from other kinds of love, but I can't *know* what it's like. I can't feel that connection of another being coming from my body, truly part of me.

Still, I can empathize. I can forgive my darling Meg for lying to me. What I begin to accept, though I don't completely understand, is that essentially, I *didn't* know the friend I thought I knew so well.

And it hurts; it hurts like hell.

So I'm employed. The first thing I do is to phone Blythe. She takes my call.

"I know I should've come or called but I couldn't face it," she says to me about her no-show at the funeral parlor.

"Meg's body is going to be released this afternoon," I tell her without artifice.

Silence.

"Blythe?"

Not even breathing noises.

"Blythe, are you still there?"

"Yes," she says in a small voice. "What are we going to do, Laur?"

I hate it that she calls me Laur. Only Meg was allowed to do that.

"We have to arrange for a funeral."

"Can't we just have her cremated?" Blythe asks this as if she's talking about someone else's dog or cat.

I don't react because the important thing is to get this worked out. "Did she want to be cremated? I never heard her say that."

We'd had those conversations that everyone seems to have past the age of forty, when you realize you're not going to live forever. Meg had never expressed a wish for cremation. But she had wanted to have a party.

Blythe says, "I don't know what she wanted, I just thought it would be easier."

Easier. Well, what should I expect from a woman who slept with her mother's husband even if she was only eighteen? Hell, eighteen is old enough to know better. Of course, maybe what Ray told me isn't true. Still, Blythe's present behavior is unacceptable. I feel myself growing impatient and angry. Through my teeth I say, "Blythe, she didn't want to be cremated. Besides, that has to be arranged for as well."

"Could you do it? I have a ton of work piled up here from missing yesterday."

I resist hanging up on her. "All right."

"And, Lauren, you don't have to go all out, know what I mean?"

I fear that I do, but I say, "No. What?"

"I *do* know that Mother thought funerals were rip-offs." This is true. "So?"

"Pine box," she barks out, unabashed.

"She discussed this with you?"

"Not exactly. But I know that's what she'd want."

I know this too. I also know that it isn't for Meg that Blythe suggests this. It's to save money for herself. I prove it.

"What about the party?"

"Party?"

"Meg wanted a party at the Plaza."

"Really? I didn't know that. Well, it seems like a big waste of money and she never mentioned it to me. The funeral's enough."

"She told me that she wanted a party."

After a long silence, Blythe says, "But not me."

And I know this means that she's not about to spring for it. Well, Kip and I will and not invite the little shit.

"I really must hang . . ."

"I saw Ray Davies today." I cannot let her go unscathed.

"That bastard," she says. "What did he want? Thinks he's in the will or something?"

"No." I can't ethically reveal to her that he's hired me. "But he was very upset about Meg's murder."

"I'll bet."

More than you, I want to say but don't.

"Let me know . . . let me know what you arrange, okay? 'Bye."

And she's gone; like that. Why am I so surprised at Blythe's behavior? I've always known there's something missing in her. Meg adored her and was completely blind to Blythe's innumerable faults. Neither Kip nor I felt we had the right to point them out, but now I'm sorry I didn't. This is stupid. What difference would it have made?

I start a series of phone calls, beginning with Mr. Lorenzo, realizing it isn't necessary for me to go there again. I remind him who I am, tell him the coffin I want (not the pine box but something modest because Meg *did* think this stuff was bull), and then just before I'm ready to hang up he hits me with a roundhouse.

"Will you be bringing the clothing?"

"Clothing?" Of course, clothing.

"You want her interred in something, don't you?"

Do I? God, these decisions are tough. I think of Meg in her coffin . . . naked. "Yes, I'll bring something."

"By the way, you don't need the undergarments," Lorenzo explains.

After we hang up I sit staring into the middle distance. Major question: What difference does it make to Meg if she's naked or not in her coffin? Major answer: It doesn't. So why do we dress our corpses? Because we don't really believe they don't know. Or we think they can still feel. When I conjured Meg naked in the casket I thought she'd be cold. It's so dumb I almost laugh out loud but I feel too awful. Awful about Meg. Awful about me. Awful about death.

I pull myself together and make the other obligatory calls: morgue, cemetery, headstone maker. When this is finished eight years later, I look at my watch and see that it's lunchtime. I decide to go home to have it with Kip. I need her support to get me through the next step . . . going into Meg's apartment and choosing the clothes in which she'll be buried.

Chapter
Twelve

WHEN KIP COMES INTO THE KITCHEN, where I sit at the table drinking a diet cherry Coke, there's a peculiar expression on her face. Actually, it's less peculiar than horrified.

"What?" I ask. "What's wrong?" I start to rise.

She holds out a hand to stop me. "I can't believe it." There's a solemnity to her tone that scares me.

"Believe what?" Another death?

"I found a gray hair," she says dramatically.

Has she gone crazy? She's been turning gray since she was thirty-five.

"You have hundreds of gray hairs," I say, bewildered.

"Oh, Lauren, sometimes I wonder how you can be a detective." She pulls out a chair, sits, props her elbows on the table, and holds up her head as if it weighs two hundred pounds.

"What's that supposed to mean?"

"Why the hell didn't you tell me?"

I feel exasperated. "Tell you what?"

"About the gray hair."

"Kip, you have . . ." Oh. Now I know what she's talking about and I can't control a chuckle.

She snaps to attention. "You think this is funny?"

I shrug.

"You've seen it, haven't you?"

I don't think there's a way I can win here: damned if I have and haven't mentioned it; damned if I haven't and am accused of inattentiveness. I opt for truth. "Yes, I have to confess, I did see it," I say, feigning seriousness.

She stares at me as if she's looking at an escapee from Creedmoor. "And you didn't tell me?"

"No. As you well know, I didn't tell you."

"Why not?"

Why not? "Lots of reasons," I say lamely.

"Like what?"

"Well, when I first saw it, it wasn't the time to mention it . . . I mean, it would've been inappropriate." I smile salaciously but get no response.

"And then?"

"Then I . . . well, the truth is, I forgot until the next time I saw it, which was also an inappropriate moment to mention it."

"I can't believe this." She gets up and goes to the fridge, takes out her special nonyeast bread from Balducci's, slaps it on the cutting board, and picks up the bread knife.

"You can't believe it was inappropriate or that I forgot?" I ask her stiffened back.

Thunnnk thunnnk goes the knife as she cuts two slices.

"I can't believe either."

"What was I supposed to do while I was making love to you, stop and say, 'Miss, excuse me, miss, but you have a gray pubic hair here!'?"

She's still, almost as if she's not breathing, and then, slowly, she turns to face me. "Why would you call me miss?"

We both laugh. I get up and take her in my arms.

"I can't believe it's happened," she says. "Why don't you have any? You're two years older than I am."

"I don't know why. I'm sure I'll get them . . . someday. I think you tend to take after your mother with these things."

"And your mother?"

It was terrible, totally inappropriate, but I *did* know the answer, because my mother continued to undress in front of me until I left home, and insisted on telling me that my father called it his black forest. She also told me that Bill Bishop called Ginny Bishop the bald eagle.

"Well?" Kip asks.

I tell her.

"Your mother doesn't know the meaning of the word *boundaries*, does she? Wait a minute. Stop the presses. What did that mean, 'the bald eagle'?"

"Just what you think."

"Ginny Bishop went bald . . . *there?*"

"Apparently."

"Oh, my God. You mean some women actually go bald?" Her eyes widen like a startled cat's.

"Ever hear of a merkin?"

"No."

"They're like little toupees."

"Oh, stop it." She goes back to making her sandwich.

"It's true, I swear. They had them in the Middle Ages."

"This isn't funny."

"Want me to get the dictionary?"

"No." She wheels on me. "I want to know if I'm going to go bald."

"How should I know? Ask your mother."

"Great idea," she says, falsely perky, and picks up the receiver of the white wall phone, while holding down the thingamabob on the other part. "Hello, Mom, this is Kip. Fine. Just fine. You? Good. Listen, I called because I wanted to know if your *venus mons* has gone bald. It hasn't? Swell. Thanks, Mom. Love you, too." She slams the phone back in the cradle.

"*Venus mons?*"

"What the hell do you expect me to call it to my mother?"

"But *venus mons* is so . . . so . . ."

"There's no good word and you know it. Anyway, *venus mons* is accurate. And I'm not about to subject my mother to slang or vulgarisms."

"Kip, you're acting nuts."

"Just because you have a mother who doesn't know where she begins and you leave off doesn't mean that we all talk to our mo—"

"Kip. You-weren't-talking-to-your-mother. You were pretending, remember?"

"Oh." She comes to the table with her food. After a moment, she says, "Well, it's the beginning of the end, that's all."

"One gray hair and it's the beginning of the end? C'mon, get real; Meg'll never have *any* gray hairs." I know it's a cheap shot.

She chews her sandwich, swallows, and says, "You're right. I'm sorry."

"You don't have to be sorry. I'd probably feel the same way."

"But in the grander scheme of things . . . well, as you said, Meg."

"Yeah." I want to tell her the latest developments, William's confessing to Cecchi about his time discrepancy and the coke, Blythe's attitude, the funeral, and, most of all, Ray Davies's hiring me. "Can we leave your gray hair now?"

"Please."

"Honey, before we do, I know it must be a shock and I'm sorry I didn't tell you, okay?"

She nods. "Thanks, Lauren."

"From now on, no matter what's happening, I'll stop whatever I'm doing and give a gray-hair count."

"Very amusing, miss," she says playfully and laughs. "Don't you dare."

We kiss across the table. Then I fill her in on everything that's happened.

"Ray Davies? Ray Davies has hired you?"

"The very one."

"Why?"

"He says, because he loved her." Now I tell her about Blythe and Ray. "Do you think he's telling the truth?"

She takes another bite of sandwich, says nothing.

"Kip? You hear me?"

She nods.

"Well, do you think he's telling the truth about him and Blythe?"

"Yes," she says softly.

"How come? I mean, why wouldn't Meg have told us it was Blythe if it was true?"

"She did tell me," Kip says, wary.

Whoa! What is going on? "She told *you?*"

"Yes. She didn't want you to know."

"My oldest friend in the world gets dumped by her husband for her daughter and doesn't want to tell me but tells my lover?"

"What can I say, darling?" Kip puts her hand over mine, strokes it.

"But why? I mean, why would she tell you and not *me?*"

"She had to tell someone and she just ... I don't know, honey, she thought me being a therapist ..."

"Meg taught me how to use Tampax, for Christ's sake."

"I know, honey."

"You know why, don't you?"

"It was ... she ..."

"Tell me, Kip."

"She was afraid you'd judge her. I know that hurts you, Lauren, but ..."

"Judge her? Judge her? After all I'd been through with that woman? I can't believe this shit." I push back my chair, take my Coke can, and fling it into the recycle bag like a good New Yorker. "When? I ask you, *when* did I ever judge Megan Harbaugh?"

"What's the difference now? Talk about in the grander scheme of things."

I know this is true but I can't stop. "Did she tell you when I ever judged her? Huh? Did she?"

"Laur-en, stop."

"No. I want to know. Did she?"

"Okay. Meg thought you *always* judged her."

"WHAT?"

Kip shrugs. "She did. I'm sorry. That's what she said."

"NEVER."

Kip is silent but she has that look that says *There's more to this.*

"What? What else?" I ask.

"Nothing." Kip takes her plate to the sink.

"Nothing? Puh-leeze, give me a break. Don't you think I can see it written all over your face?"

"Lauren, you may not have judged her but that's how you made her feel."

"But you and I often talked about Meg."

"So?"

"So did I judge her?"

"Yes."

"You're crazy, Kip. I never judged that woman. I loved her like she was my sister."

"I know you did. Don't get so upset."

"Don't get upset? This from a therapist? And by the way, just why didn't *you* tell me about Ray and Blythe?"

"Because I promised Meg I wouldn't."

"I knew you were going to say that." Furious, I push past her and slam out the front door.

I can't believe what I've learned. My dearest friend thought I judged her, told my lover an incredibly important thing, and my lover didn't tell me because she promised my dearest friend she wouldn't. This makes me physically sick. A pain worms round in my gut like a miniature chain saw. Before I know it I'm in Donatello's, sitting at a table with a cappuccino and a large piece of chocolate ganache cake.

I reach for my cap, but when I pick it up I see that my hand is shaking, so I put it back, spilling some onto the table. As I wipe up I realize I'm shaking all over.

It is rage.

I can't remember the last time I experienced the sensation that my body is undergoing an earthquake. It's a bodyquake. Will part of me fall off into the surrounding sea of perfidy and duplicity?

I can't believe that Kip's deceived me this way. True, when the incident with Blythe and Ray happened, Kip and I were together only eight years. Why am I saying *only?* And Megan, who I've known almost all my life, lied to me by omission. I wonder what else I wasn't told . . . don't know about her. It seems that the revelations keep coming in frightening waves. And I am drowning.

Oh, shut up, Lauren. So dramatic.

Yeah, maybe. But why do I feel so bad? I have to sort out my feelings, separate what's true and false, what's causing which pain.

Is it true that I judged Meg?

Do I make judgments about people?

Of course I do, but so does everyone else.

Don't they?

It's only human.

Isn't it?

I flash on something William once said to me: "When you point a finger at somebody, you have three more coming back at you."

So why did he say this to me? I must've been making a judgment. I can't remember the circumstances but it's clear William wouldn't say something like that for no reason. Is this why it took him so long to tell me about the cocaine? And did I judge him when he told me?

I did. I didn't call it that but it certainly was what I did. At the time I'd recognized other flaws in my character but basically it all came back to judging William.

But he takes drugs, I scream inside my head.

So?

I think it's weak and sick and unworthy of him.

God, I'm self-righteous. I look at my chocolate cake. I'm not supposed to be eating this because of my cholesterol level. Is this different from William's doing drugs? Do I judge myself each time I order some delicious fatty dessert?

No. *Drugs are different.*

And Megan lied.

And Kip lied.

But I lied for William. Different. Totally different.

Fuck you, you judge people all the time:

Helen should be doing something else with her life; Susan and Stan should see more people; Rick shouldn't let himself get fat; Boover should be in therapy; Elissa should get into a relationship; Jill and Jenny shouldn't buy a house in the country; Ed should buy a laser printer instead of using his old dot matrix, for God's sake!

Should, should, should.

Why do I *care* what kind of printer Ed uses? Or whether the Js buy a house, or Elissa finds a lover? Maybe their choices, their lives are better the way *they* run them.

Secretly you think you know best!

Maybe I do.

I take a bite of the cake. Sublime. I'm being too hard on myself. In fact, I'm judging myself!

And after all, what have I done? I haven't lied to Kip or taken drugs or done anything.

A perfect person!

Does my lover owe me the truth on everything that she knows? Should she betray a friend because if she doesn't she's betraying me? Has anyone ever told me something and asked me not to tell Kip?

Of course!

And have I told her?

No.

But it was different.

Wasn't it?

My head spins. I'm overwhelmed. I can't answer these questions now. There are things I must do. I finish eating and get the check.

I have to go to Meg's apartment to pick the clothes she'll be buried in. I can't help wondering what else I'll find there. Maybe something else no one's bothered to tell me.

Chapter
Thirteen

MEG LIVES ... lived ... on King Street. This is off Sixth Avenue and is one street below the demarcation between Greenwich Village and SoHo. SoHo means south of Houston. New York City is made up of many neighborhoods, all with names.

Her apartment is in a brownstone. Usually, they're very narrow, but this one isn't. The building's kept immaculate by the owners, who live on the first two floors. Geraniums grow in window boxes.

I climb the cement steps, use my key on the massive walnut door. Inside, I make my way to the top floor. On the wall, next to Meg's door, is a Deborah Kass painting. It's from her latest period and it makes me smile although I've seen it often. I wonder who'll get this, and for the first time I think about a will.

Did Meg have one?

If so, where is it?

Who's the executor?

Why isn't it me?

Am I becoming more and more like my mother, thinking only in reference to me? I console myself that I'm not a raving narcissist by acknowledging that much of what has happened bears directly on my life.

I unlock Meg's door. A stunning silence greets me. In my mind I hear Meg's voice: *"C'mon in, Laur. I'm in the kitchen."*

"That you, Laur? I'm on the phone, be right with you." "Hey, Laur, what's happening?"

My eyes fill, and when I look down the hall it's fuzzy, out of focus. I'll never hear Meg's voice again. I'll never come into her house and see her. This is almost impossible for me to believe. I have to concentrate to understand this concept. This concept? What am I, in Hollywood? You want concept? Here's high concept: Meg is dead. Maybe if I say it repeatedly, like a mantra, I'll come to believe it.

I close the door, lock it, drop the keys in my purse, and put that on a small oak table where she threw her mail. A pile of it rests there, unopened. I pick it up, flick through; it's mostly bills and her checking account statement. The bills are Visa, MasterCard, Discover, American Express, Diners Club, and telephone. I remind myself that I'm here on a case, as well as to do this morbid chore, and that I have to open the mail.

I've done this hundreds of times on cases, but never with someone I knew. Is this betrayal? Am I adding to the dissolute district I find myself living in?

THIS IS MY JOB! And one wonders: what kind of job is this?

I replace the mail to deal with later.

Now I'll take care of the business at hand. *The business at hand?* Have I become a master at euphemisms? Am I such a coward I can no longer be direct, honest, candid even with myself? I'm disgusted.

Shades of purple embellish the living room. A year ago Meg had her colors done and decided to throw out her old wardrobe and redo her place. *"Turns out, Laur, I'm a purple, lavender lady. Always thought I was blue and green but not according to Roz Begun. Fabulous dame, Laur. You should go see her. On second thought don't bother, you'd just think it was crap."*

And I did think that. I judged it. Why? What difference did it make if it made Meg happy? The room is beautiful: plush wing chairs, lavender-flowered couch, matching drapes, another Kass painting over the fireplace. I sit.

Sadness settles on me like fine dust I can't blow off. How many times had we sat in these chairs and endlessly talked about love and life and money and children and ...

Money.

Meg was always complaining about money, never enough, always in debt. So how did she afford two Kass paintings? A new wardrobe? New interior decoration? Like so many other small businesses, with Reaganomics in full bloom, the store wasn't even holding its own anymore. My mind flashes on the credit card bills. She obviously lived on the edge like the rest of Americans. Clearly, Blythe mimicked her mother in chalking up bills. No way could she live as she did on her salary.

I hoist myself out of the chair and go into Meg's bedroom. This is also in shades of purple: the bed covered by a light-colored comforter and a darker canopy; pale purple rug; Laura Ashley curtains that match the sheets.

At her vanity table (so strange she should have one) I pick up her hairbrush, and when I see the golden strands clinging to the bristles, I burst into sobs.

Time passes. I stop. Put back the brush. Move on. Open the closet door. There's a smell of potpourri combined with perfume (Obsession) and something like fresh-mown grass. It's Megan's smell. I'm almost overcome again but steel myself, soldier on the way Kip would. This is when her WASPhood pays off for her, and now, for me.

Meg's clothes hang in the closet in an orderly fashion, so unlike her. Shirts, slacks, skirts, dresses. They're all variations on the purple theme. As I sort through them I notice that many still sport price tags. A blouse for three hundred dollars? I can't imagine Meg spending that on a piece of clothing. I'd known about the new wardrobe because of the change in colors but here were clothes she'd never worn.

I add up the figures but when I get to two thousand I stop. What in hell was she doing? Should I choose one of these unworn outfits to bury her in? No. I try to recall if she had a favorite outfit, but my mind won't focus. I glance down at her row of shoes. Near the end is a black-and-white patent leather pair I remember. *"Laur, I feel like a tap dancer when I wear these. They're my good-luck shoes."* No matter what outfit I choose I'll definitely want them.

As I reach for the shoes, at the back of the closet, I see a large glass jug, half-filled with coins. What a strange place to keep it. On my knees, I use both hands, and pull it toward me. The coins are a strange color, and only when I reach into the open neck and scoop out a handful do I discern that they're not coins.

They're subway tokens.

And this is weird because Meg *never* took the subway.

I look carefully at the tokens in my palm and see at once that they're the current ones. Was Meg hoarding them, anticipating a raise?

"Nothing," I hear her say in my mind, *"can get me to take a subway. I'd rather walk three hundred blocks in a hailstorm."*

So why hoard tokens? Bewildered, I leave the jug there. I pick up the shoes but I'm still uncertain which outfit to select. Finally, I decide on a familiar lavender blouse and purple skirt, both by Liz Claiborne.

Back in the hall I put the clothes on a chair, and start opening the mail. The Visa bill shows that Meg owes fifty-five dollars for a dinner at Provençal ten days before. That's it. I open the next one and it reveals a similar small amount. There's no finance charge, which tells me she's paid her credit card bills on time. They are all alike. Twenty dollars for Tower Records; forty-two for the Gap; fifteen for Footlocker. No interest on any of them.

I feel alarm. If Meg didn't use her credit to the max, where did she get her money? And why didn't I ever notice this? I open her bank statement.

The checks are what one would expect: telephone, Con Ed, rent. And no indication of a withdrawal of cash with a bank card. What does this say to me? Surely Meg used cash. I recall her buying things with it.

"Don't you just love this pig, Laur? See, it's a corkscrew. God, I have to have it. One hundred twenty, it says. C'est la vie!*"* And she'd easily peeled off the money from a wad she had stashed in a buttoned pants pocket. Why didn't I think anything

about it at the time? But why should I? Because she said the store wasn't making a profit. And yet she bought an antique pig for over a hundred dollars.

And that wasn't all.

I recall the number of times Meg insisted on taking me to the movies, buying my popcorn, or picking up the check for coffee and dessert.

And Nick Benning had a point. There was the trip she took to Italy, France, and England last year while I was working on the Lake Huron case. She'd gone for a month. I hadn't questioned where the money was coming from. I'd been so used to Meg taking trips it didn't occur to me that times were different, that money *should* have been short during that period. It was for everyone else. The truth was, I'd been so deeply involved in that case I hadn't given Meg a thought.

What about these books? Besides the packed shelves, there are hardcovers stacked in piles around the living room. I examine a bunch. The top one is a new mystery by Mickey Friedman. Underneath is a new Consuelo Baehr novel. As I take one after another from this stack, and make a new stack, I see that they are *all* new.

I walk around, sort through them. Some have been read, some not. There are lots of current books. But why am I surprised? Over the last year or so Meg gave us many hard-covers. Whenever she came to dinner she'd bring us a new book. I can't believe we didn't wonder about it.

"Kids, you're going to love this book, best thing she's written in years. Don't bother giving it back, I'm running out of room. Pass it on if you don't want to keep it."

The implication was that she'd bought it for herself and so it wasn't really a present. Still, what was wrong with us that we didn't question where the money for these books was coming from? Was it that we didn't *want* to know because we liked getting the gifts?

Were these books here the last time I visited Meg? They were but I hadn't paid attention to them. Meg always had piles of books on the floor and the last few times I'd been here we rushed out to go somewhere. I know she bought her books at Three Lives. I make a mental note to ask the Js about this.

When was it that I'd actually been here for any length of time? I'm astonished when I can't remember. It's been ages. Meg had stopped cooking several years ago, saying she'd burned out on it, and ate out almost every night. *How could she afford that?*

Back in the bedroom I go directly to the antique chest of drawers and open the top one because I know this is where Meg keeps her jewelry in a dumb yellow box. I open it.

All that glitters *is* gold! I'm sure of it. This is not the old Meg-type jewelry: plastic beads, silly pins. There are heavy ropes for the neck, thick bracelets, earrings. But I've never seen her wear any of this stuff.

What is going on?

I replace the box. Methodically, I examine all the drawers, but I find only some unworn cashmere sweaters, nothing to explain this uncharacteristic opulence.

I spend an hour and a half going through everything in the place but I find nothing that gives me clues, tells me a tale.

It's only as I get ready to leave that I realize, besides discovering evidence of Meg's puzzling prosperity, I've not found one thing that reveals the identity of Topic A. How can this be? Had she ended it with him so he then ended her life? Certainly not an unusual occurrence. Or didn't Topic A exist? Did she feel so alone she made up someone? This seems too bizarre. Still, how would I know? And then it hits me: does Kip know? Did Meg tell Kip who Topic A really was?

Carefully, I pack blouse, skirt, and shoes in a tote bag, and leave the apartment, anxious and despondent.

At the funeral home, Mr. Lorenzo tells me that shoes are unnecessary. With the kind of conviction that makes him readily agree, I tell him that he'd better put them on her.

When I leave the funeral parlor, I notice the sound of a car alarm I'd registered when I'd arrived. It grows louder as I cross Sixth Avenue, pass the Lucca, the church on the corner of Carmine, and continue across Bleecker. At the corner of

Leroy Street the culprit car alarm rages on. The siren is deafening and annoying. People are gathered around a blue two-door Alfa Romeo.

A hefty man in his thirties, with bushy brows over pinwheel eyes, gives the passenger door a solid kick with a size-twelve yellow work boot. There's a collective noise from the assembled group that sounds like "Yeah" but I'm sure that can't be true. The offending alarm has not capitulated to the kick.

Two women of medium build, one with pink curlers in her hair, the other, a cigarette dangling from her lips, carry a metal garbage can between them and throw the can at the hood of the car, where it crashes, bounces off, and leaves a large dent. This time I'm sure the sound is "Yeah"!

"Excuse me," I say to an elderly woman, who appears frail in her flowered housedress. She gives me the once-over. "What?" Her scratchy voice sounds like an old 78.

"What's happening here?"

"We're killin' this fuckin' car," she says seriously.

The woman turns away from me and I look back at the car in time to see a scrawny boy, arms like chicken wishbones, wield a two-by-four that turns the windshield into a Byzantine pattern.

There's cheering and clapping.

The alarm continues.

"Excuse me," I say again, to no one in particular.

Several people look at me, hostility clear in their eyes. No one speaks.

"Why don't you call the police?" I ask.

This brings the welcome relief of laughter to all. They turn away from me and someone says, "Here comes Lou."

I follow their gaze.

A diminutive man, twenty or so, sleek black hair shot with premature gray, wearing a black T-shirt and old jeans, comes down Bleecker carrying a red bucket. Whatever is in it is heavy as Lou lists to his left.

"Lou, you got it?"

"Whatcha think?"

"He got it."

"Lou got it."

"Where'd you get it?"

"Don't matter."

"He got it."

"Lou got it."

"Knew he would."

"Where'd he get it?"

"Didn't say."

"You got it, Lou?"

"I got it."

"He got it."

I think I might scream. Instead, I say to the woman I'd spoken to before, "What does Lou got?"

Again she eyes me suspiciously. "Gasoline. Lou got gasoline. Who wants to know?"

I don't think she actually wants an answer because she turns away, back to Lou and the others. It doesn't take long to realize that these people are going to pour the gasoline over the car and light it. They must be insane.

"Wait," I shout, as Lou walks up to the car.

He stops, stares at me, puts the red bucket on the sidewalk. "Yo, whadda ya want?"

"What are you going to do?"

"Kill this fuckin' car."

"You're going to throw the gasoline over it and then light it?"

"Yeah. You got objections?"

"It's a criminal act," I explain, knowing as I'm saying this that they couldn't care less what it is. "Who's the owner of the car?"

"If we knew that, lady, we wouldn't have to kill the fuckin' car, we'd just kill the fuckin' owner."

They all laugh.

"This here is a fuckin' Noo Joisy ve-hicle and it's got to die."

"But the alarm will stop soon," I say intelligently. These car alarms go for about twenty minutes and then turn off.

"When's soon? This pig's been screamin' over four hours,"
he glances at his watch, "and twenty-two minutes."

Maybe it's house alarms that turn off in twenty, I think.

"Go ahead, Lou."

"Do it."

"Lou'll do it."

"He's got the gas."

"C'mon, les' do it."

"Lou's doin' it."

And Lou is. He picks up the bucket and deliberately circles
the car, splashing gas over the fenders, hood, roof, and rear.

"Save some for the tail."

"Lou'll keep some."

"He's savin' some for the tail."

"Don't use it all, Lou."

"I'm not."

"He needs it for the tail."

"Lou's keepin' the tail part."

When Lou's through dousing the car he carefully makes a
thin trail from the back of the car out into the middle of
Bleecker Street. The much-referred-to tail, I presume.

"Okay, everybody move back," Lou says.

"Get back."

"Go back."

"Move it or lose it."

"How far, Lou?"

"Far."

"Get far back."

"You heard. Back."

"This far enough?"

"No. Farther."

"C'mon, girls, back."

"Lou says move it back."

"Back, back."

The men are herding the women and children onto Leroy
Street.

"Listen," I say, "if you light that, the car's going to blow
up."

"Really?" Lou says, sarcastically. "I dint know that. Jou know that, Richie?"

"Nah. Who woulda thought?"

"You can cause a lot of damage," I persist.

"Nah! Damage," Richie says, as if I might be crazy. "Lou, this lady thinks we're gonna damage this fuckin' car."

"Nah, don't worry, lady, we ain't gonna *damage* this fuckin' car, we're gonna *kill* this fuckin' car."

"But if it explodes it could start fires in these stores, blow out windows, hurt people," I explain sensibly.

"Who the fuck're you, anyways?" Lou asks me.

I calculate what my chances are if I take out my license and gun. I hate the odds.

"Huh? Who're you? You live in this block? You own one of these stores? Huh?" Lou is in my face.

"I understand that the alarm's annoying but . . ."

"Oh, hey, people, the lady understands that the fuckin' car's an annoyment. You live here? You from the hood? Huh?"

"I live on Perry Street," I say, to show, at least, I'm not from New Jersey.

"Oh, Perry Street. This one lives on Perry Street. You hear this fuckin' siren over there on Perry? Huh?"

"No. But that's not the problem."

"So what is?"

"What's the problem, then?"

"Lou's askin' her what the problem is."

"She got a attitude problem."

"You givin' me attitude?"

I stand my ground and try again. "I'm trying to point out that if you do this thing the car's going to blow up, the store windows are going to crash, places might catch fire, and some of you might get hurt. Don't you think you should ask the owners of these stores what they think before you do this?"

They laugh.

"We *are* the owners."

I'm shocked. "Don't you care what might happen?"

"What we care about is killin' this fuckin' car. So get out a' the way 'cause I'm lightin' it now." Lou walks back to the end of the trail.

"You got a light, Lou?"

"I got 'em." He produces several large kitchen matches.

"Lou's got 'em."

"He's got 'em."

"Where'd he get 'em?"

"Didn't say."

"He's got 'em."

"I got 'em."

I bite my upper lip with my bottom teeth to not go crazy and scream. But I can't let this happen. So how can I stop it? The only thing I can do is try to find a cop. As I pass the car at a good clip, knowing I can always find some help at the Charles Street Station on Tenth, I see that Lou is striking a match against his jeans. It doesn't light.

I hurry, but keep looking back over my shoulder.

Lou tries again. Nothing. Again. It lights!

Oh, Christ. I run, still glancing back.

Lou leans over and touches the flame to the famous tail, which whooshes immediately on its way to the car. The people, basically unprepared for this, run farther away from the site. As does Lou.

By the time I reach Seventh Avenue the car is in flames. I watch, waiting for the light to change, the explosion to come. People are stopped at the avenue, gawking. The car alarm can still be heard. The light changes. I cross, running. When I hit the west side of Seventh it happens.

The noise is tremendous and the pieces of metal fly in all directions, crashing through store windows, fire catching awnings. People are scurrying away. Miraculously, no one seems to have gotten hurt. I hear the fire engine before I see it coming down the avenue. It takes the turn and roars toward the burning, exploding car.

A man and woman, map in hand, clearly tourists, say to me: "What is it? What happened?"

I open my mouth to explain, realize I can't, so simply say, "Some people killed a car."

They look at me both frightened and confused, but mostly sorry that they've come to New York.

I have to make a decision. Am I going to the police station to report these people, like a good citizen, and get tied up for the rest of the day, probably harassed by Lou and his friends for the rest of my life? Or am I going to stay out of it like a true New Yorker?

Several police cars screech toward the scene. Even at this distance I can see that the people are still there and I know that they'll play dumb when questioned by the police.

No one will know anything.

It will be my word against *all* of theirs. We will go to court. It will consume days, weeks, months. The case will be dismissed. I know it's immoral and cowardly of me but there's no point. To go to the police station and report what I've seen WILL NOT MAKE A DIFFERENCE. WILL RESULT IN NOTHING. MIGHT ENDANGER MY LIFE. I AM NOT A PERFECT PERSON. I HAVE THINGS TO DO. A LIFE TO LEAD. IT WON'T MATTER ANYWAY. THE OWNER OF THE CAR WILL COLLECT INSURANCE. MY PARTICIPATION WILL BE LESS THAN USELESS.

I go to the police station.

Chapter
Fourteen

━━━━━━━━━━━━━━━

I HAVE SPENT the last ten years at the police station reporting what I saw on Bleecker and Leroy. When I walk outside I'm amazed to see daylight. And even more amazed that it's still fall.

Was it worth it? Probably not. But at least I'll sleep tonight . . . unless Lou and Richie firebomb our house. The discouraging part is I don't think anyone is going to bother with Lou and Richie. Of the four thousand cops I talked with, not one seemed interested in what I had to say. The last word was that I'd be called for a lineup if they had any suspects. *If they had any suspects.* I've given them names and descriptions but it's still *if.*

The hell with it. I put it out of my mind and head for Three Lives Bookstore on Tenth Street and Waverly Place. It's a charming place, very like an English bookstore, and was built from scratch by Jenny and helpers. Jill, like me, is not handy with things like that.

When I enter, the store is empty except for Hilary, the manager, who is behind the counter on the phone, and Kari, who's really a dancer, disguised as a clerk. She's leaving soon to go on tour and we'll all miss her.

"Hi," I say. "Jenny or Jill here?"

"They're downstairs having a meeting, but they should be up real soon. Can I help?" Her long black hair is pulled back behind her ears and held by a greenish-brown clip that matches her hazel eyes. Kari has sharp, pretty features and a thin, lithe body.

"Thanks, Kari. I think I'll wait." I know these meetings are usually about staff problems. The turnover is phenomenal. It's hard to live on a book clerk's salary and only the very young can swing it. And with the very young you often get incompetence.

"How's Kip?" Kari asks.

She's newly married so I don't want to disillusion. "Just great," I say. "How's John?"

Her pale skin flushes, as though she's recalling something private. "He's fine." She smiles enigmatically and moves away like the wind.

I look over the new selection of hardcovers. Nothing appeals. But nothing would in my present state.

Hilary puts down the phone. "Hey, Lauren," she says.

Hilary's in her midthirties with blond hair that she treats as a sculpture. I've never seen so many different styles on one person. Today, the left side ends at her chin line and the right side is shaved. She isn't conventionally pretty, but her deep blue eyes and full lips are soft, sensual, sometimes seductive. And even with this haircut she's very attractive. A gentle, lovely woman, she wants to be a writer, but has to make a living. Though I've never read anything of hers, I'm told she's good. I believe it.

She wears striped overalls and a blue T-shirt. From behind the counter, which is on a raised platform, she says, "Sorry about Meg, Lauren."

"Thanks." Why *thanks?* It's what you say; I'm just not sure I understand why. Am I thanking her for being sorry; for acknowledging Meg's death; my grief? Or all of the above?

I say, "As a matter of fact, I came in to talk about Meg with Jenny and Jill, but maybe you can help me."

"Sure. I'll try. What is it?" Hilary has the habit of looking directly into your eyes, which makes you feel you're the only one who matters. This is nice, but can sometimes be distracting.

"Does . . . did Meg have an account here?" Kip and I do and pay once a month.

"No. She used to. Mmmmm. Maybe two or three years ago. I can probably look it up if it's important."

"I don't think so. Are you saying she stopped buying books?"

"God, no. She just stopped running up a bill."

"She paid as she bought?"

"Right. Sometimes she'd spend three hundred a week."

I recall Meg's telling me recently that her store had made only five hundred one week. How did she manage this?

"How often would she spend that much?"

"Actually almost every week. Sometimes two hundred, one fifty, but usually around the three-hundred mark."

I remain astonished. But why? I saw the books in her place. Did I think she stole them, for God's sake?

"Meg was always addicted to books," I say, as if this truth might explain everything.

Hilary nods sympathetically.

"How did she pay?" I ask, not wanting the answer I know I'm going to get.

"Cash money," Hilary says, smiling. "Guess she wasn't hurting the way all the other stores are."

"When she stopped being billed, then she started paying cash?"

"Yup."

I experience a sinking sensation. I don't want to face the inevitable truth about my Megan.

"It was weird," Hilary continues, "because she bought *everything.* I mean, when she was being billed she was careful about what she selected. When she started spending cash, she was sort of indiscriminate: mysteries, garden books, novels . . . just about anything."

"Garden books? Why would she buy garden books?" Meg didn't have a garden.

"Those were probably gifts, now that I think about it. Yeah, sure. The coffee table books she usually had us wrap for her."

I'm about to ask another question when there's suddenly a cacophony emerging from the basement: Jill and Jenny and Theo, their new Welsh terrier. It's Theo who makes the most noise. She races over to me, nails clicking where the floor isn't carpeted, and jumps up, her front paws reaching my middle.

"Theo," I croon. "You're getting so big." She's about eight months old and adorable. Also, at the moment, the focus of the Js' existence.

"Theo, down," Jenny commands.

Theo ignores her.

"Theo, down."

Theo ignores her.

"You're a regular Clyde Beatty," I say.

"Very funny," she says. Jenny's short, about my height, has light-colored curly hair and a cherubic face that belies who she really is. Not that she's not nice, but when she wants to she can have a wicked tongue. She's wearing a striped T-shirt and blue shorts. Jenny loves to wear shorts no matter what time of year.

Jill comes over and gives me a kiss while Jenny struggles with Theo. Jill's in her forties, older than Jenny by a few years. We're all patiently waiting for Jenny to turn forty, as she is the youngest of our crowd and it seems she's been the "kid" forever.

Jill has deep red shoulder-length hair, freckles, and green eyes. She's about five four, an attractive woman. She also wears shorts, and a neat pinstriped shirt, cuffs rolled.

"How're you doing?" Jill asks.

"Theo, down."

"Okay," I say. The Js have already given me their condolences by phone.

"Down, Theo."

"I was just talking to Hilary about Meg's book-buying habits."

"Theee-o!"

"Mmmm. Can't say I haven't wondered about that," Jill says.

"Hilary said she started paying cash about three years ago."

"More like two. I have to tell you, I wanted to say something to you, but I didn't think I had the right."

"I understand."

"Down. Theo, sit."

"Hilary tell you how much she spent?"

"Yes."

"Funny thing is, I'd sometimes ask her about one book or another, if she liked it or not, but seven times out of ten she hadn't read it. I could see, after a while, that my questions embarrassed her, so I quit asking."

"So why was she buying all these books?"

"The usual. But, hell, I don't know how she afforded it. Not that that ever stops a book-buying addict. But her habit went from paper to hard overnight, it seemed."

"Stop, Theo. Sit."

"In the past, when she was being billed, buying less, did you talk about books?"

"Sure. She read everything she bought. We liked a lot of the same mystery writers: Shankman, Carlson, Kelman, Wheat, Piesman. And other books, too. I'd say we had very, very similar tastes."

"Theee-o, stop. Jill, come help me with her. I can't make her do anything," Jenny moans.

Softly, Jill says to me, "Theo's a brat ... just like her owner."

I don't have to ask which one.

"Theo, sit," Jill commands.

Theo sits.

"Now stay."

Theo does.

"How do you do that?" Jenny asks, astonished.

"It's all in the fingers," Jill says, laughing, and comes back to me.

"Do many people pay cash when they buy lots of books?"

"Not many. Some. I can't prove anything, Lauren, but the ones who buy big, with cash, and I'm talking three, four hundred a week, well, I think something's going on. Some are legitimate, just insatiable readers. Others . . . I don't know." She shakes her head slowly as if she does know. "We always check the money out carefully to see if it's counterfeit."

"And?"

"A few times. But never Meg."

"Still, you think her book buying these last two years was odd?"

"Yeah. Hey, that lady used to gobble up books fast as we could get them to her, but mostly in paperback because that's all she could afford. Then, boom, she starts paying cash and doesn't read most of them. I'd call that odd."

I would, too. "Thanks, Jill. You have any ideas about who might've . . . killed her?"

"Nope. I thought it was a robber."

"Maybe. I'm not sure I believe that."

"You think Meg was into something illegal?" Jill asks.

"I don't know what I think yet. Did she ever come in with anyone, a man? Maybe a special man?"

"You mean like a lover?"

"Yeah."

Jill thinks, asks the staff, but no one recalls seeing Meg with anyone. She asks me when the funeral will be; I tell her and she says they'll be there.

"Thanks for everything," I say. "S'long, everybody."

They all shout good-bye. As I open the door I hear: "Theee-o, down!"

"You can't just walk out when things don't go your way, Lauren," Kip says.

"Why not?" I ask childishly.

We're in the living room, each of us on a couch, facing the other.

"You know why not. Oh, why the hell do I answer you? Now look . . ."

"I hate *look*."

"Too bad. I told you why Meg didn't tell you about Ray

and Blythe, and I know it hurt you, but you have to face the truth. You're very judgmental."

"I know," I say.

"Excuse me?"

"You heard me."

"Yes, I did. I'm glad that you can see that."

"Don't push it."

"But walking out on me like that is the real issue here."

"No. The real issue is that you kept that information from me."

"No, it isn't, Lauren. I have every right to keep certain things to myself."

"What else haven't you told me?" I ask suspiciously.

"Whatever it is I'm not going to tell."

"Then there *is* something!"

"God, you can be tiresome."

"Thanks."

"You're welcome."

"I'm going to ask you something very important and you have to tell me the truth. Do you promise?"

"Of course not."

"This has to do with the case, Kip."

"You really are something. If this isn't a form of blackmail, I don't know what is."

"Call it what you want."

"What is it?"

"Did Meg tell you who Topic A was?"

"No."

"Is that the truth?"

"Yes."

"Because he's a prime suspect and we don't know who he is and can't get a lead on him."

"She never told me."

"If she had?"

"This is stupid."

"No, it isn't. If she'd told you, would you tell me now?"

"Yes. I'd tell you now."

"But you wouldn't have told me before?"

"No."

I can't believe this woman. "Why not?"

"Because if Meg had told me who he was, it would've been in confidence. But now, I can see that it would be necessary and important to tell you."

"I still can't get over that you didn't tell me about Blythe and Ray."

"Look," she says, but stops abruptly. "How do you feel about *listen?*"

"Hate it."

"Tough. Look and listen," she says perversely. "I was entrusted with a secret and asked especially not to tell you. What could I do?"

"You could've told me."

"No, Lauren, I couldn't. Maybe if it were reversed you could, but I couldn't."

"Holier-than-thou," I accuse.

"It's the way I was raised, I can't help it."

"Oh, brother. And how was I raised, like a guttersnipe?"

"Guttersnipe?"

"Like a street urchin," I explain.

"I know what the word means. I could really throttle you sometimes. I don't know how you were raised and it doesn't matter. But I was raised to keep something that's confidential, confidential. What if I told people everything you tell me not to tell?"

"That's different."

"No it isn't. And I suppose you have no secrets from me."

"None that involve you," I whine.

"This didn't involve you. You're getting just like your mother."

"Don't make me hurt you," I say flippantly.

"Well, I'm sorry, but that's the kind of thing she'd say. The affair between Ray and Blythe had nothing to do with you."

"But it had to do with my best friend."

"And she didn't want you to know."

"So you had to be Ms. Perfect and not tell me."

"No, not Ms. Perfect. Just an honorable person. Would you love me if I weren't honorable?"

I think it over. I despise her. Because she's right. "No," I whisper.

She doesn't make me repeat it like some people would, pretending not to hear. Instead, she comes over to me, takes me in her arms, and holds me.

"I'm so sorry that things are coming out about Meg that hurt you, Lauren."

I start to cry. They are tears of grief, betrayal, frustration, and confusion. Though Kip's arms are around me and she's making makeup sounds, I feel totally alone. Well, in the end we *are* alone, I think gloomily. Better get used to it.

The doorbell rings.

Kip jumps up. "They're here," she shouts happily.

It's only then I remember that Tom and Sam have arrived from San Francisco. I love them dearly and they're the last people I want to see. I have no choice.

I stand behind Kip as she opens the door. My human heart reels.

Chapter
Fifteen

I HAVEN'T SEEN TOM since he was diagnosed with AIDS almost a year ago. At thirty-four, he's the youngest of the four Adams children, and Kip's favorite. I've always thought of him as one of the handsomest men I've ever met.

I can't believe that this is the same man whom I've known for almost twelve years. When I put my arms around him I fear if I hug hard he'll break like a piece of porcelain.

My eyes meet Sam's. The blue's bleached of life and I know he registers my shock. We both smile falsely, wanting to cry.

After the usual greetings, we gravitate to the kitchen and sit around the table while Kip gets coffee. Tom and Sam are young enough to drink it without having it keep them up all night. I have a soda without caffeine.

"Really sorry about your friend, Meg," Tom says.

I nod my thanks.

"We know what it's like," says Sam.

"Yes, I know you do."

Tom says, "We've lost over sixty people since it started."

Sixty. God. We've seen our share die of AIDS, as well as other things. And now Meg. But the thought of sixty women we know dying of a disease that almost no one wants to deal with is impossible to imagine.

Kip joins us while the coffee brews. She is cheerful beyond redemption. This is the way she can handle it best and I mustn't judge her. Hey, maybe I've learned something.

I try not to look at Tom too much, but that's not the right thing to do either. I can't remember feeling like such an oaf, so out of control.

And then he knocks me for a loop: "Lauren, I know how I look." It's said gently, kindly.

I want to protest. Don't. Instead, I force a smile.

Sam puts his arm around Tom. "We're not afraid to talk about it. Oh, we were. There was a time when we were both in denial, but that's past now. Right, darling?"

Tom nods. "Pretty damn hard to stay in denial when you have to shave every day." He grins.

We laugh lightly.

Still, it's difficult. Tom's skin is the color of fog. His brown eyes are recessed, haunted. The armature of his face shows clearly, cheeks so sunken I'm sure they touch inside. The neck of his plaid flannel shirt fits him, but I know it's at least two sizes smaller than what he once wore. Although he hasn't had chemo, his hair is thin, like light brown threads.

Kip gets up for the coffee, pours them each a cup. When Tom, a lefty, lifts his, I notice his hand, the fingers like pencils, his wedding band loose.

Sam says, "I guess we might as well tell you, we're really here to see a special kind of doctor."

"What do you mean?" Kip asks.

Sam, who looks healthy but tired, runs a hand through his long black hair, strokes his short beard. "Try not to judge, okay?"

Predictably, Kip and I glance at each other. The dread J word, as I will think of it forever.

This doesn't escape Tom, and he asks why we've looked at each other that way.

"It hasn't anything to do with you," Kip says, "and it's too difficult to explain."

I can see they don't quite believe that it's unrelated to them.

"The long and short of it, guys, is that I've been accused of being judgmental."

"Who? You?" Tom and Sam say like some comedy act.

"Crazy, isn't it?" I say.

We all laugh.

This is becoming a nightmare. But it's not the time to ask them if they really believe I am, or when they witnessed this. It's the time for reassurance. "Even though by nature I'm open and accepting, I promise not to start judging now."

"Good," says Sam. "Because we've heard terrific things about this woman."

"What?" Kip asks.

I can tell by the sound in that one word that she's skeptical. Isn't that another word for judgmental?

"Well," Tom says, "her name is Dr. Woo and she uses ancient herbal recipes. A friend of ours, who has Kaposi's, started treatment with her about five years ago and he's still with us."

"And we know of others," Sam adds. "It's hell trying to get an appointment with her, but we have one, day after tomorrow."

They seem to glow, as though they've seen a rainbow.

Everything in me wants to judge this Dr. Woo. The old me would have. The new me keeps her mouth shut, waits to hear more.

Kip asks, "How much does it cost? No, I'm sorry. That's none of my business."

The men smile, exchange a knowing look. Tom says, "It's expensive."

I feel angry. Why is everything to do with AIDS so damn costly?

"Insurance doesn't cover Dr. Woo," Sam says, anticipating our next question. "She's not considered a *real* doctor."

"Is she?"

"Not by AMA standards. She's real enough in her own country."

Tom says, "She's strict as hell. You have to follow her regimen exactly. Not just the herbs but a whole new way of eating. Sort of macrobiotic."

"Not sort of, honey. It *is* macrobiotic."

Kip and I have always referred to this diet as macroneurotic and I realize that that's been a judgment. The good news is Kip did it, too.

"It's hard for me to accept, I guess, because Sam and I have always called it macroneurotic."

Kip and I screech, tell them we have too. We laugh together and it feels wonderful.

"Would you like to come with us?" Tom asks.

"To Dr. Woo's?"

"Yeah."

The invitation is meant to make us feel involved in Tom's illness and though I find it slightly scary, I know I'll do whatever Kip wants.

"What time?" she asks.

I can tell she's frightened also.

"Eleven."

Without a beat Kip says, "I'll reschedule appointments."

"Great," Tom says, smiling, and looks at me.

"I'll be there," I say intrepidly.

Tom reaches out for Kip's hand and mine. We take his. "You don't know how much this means to me," he says, eyes glistening. He lets go of my hand, takes Sam's, and Sam takes mine so that we are all joined.

The moment is incredible. I feel as if I'm part of something extraordinary and I suppose I am. Love pulses through our arms, hands, to each other. At the same time we all squeeze, then let go.

"So," Tom says, "what's the gossip?"

And we're off.

A few minutes after Tom and Sam leave, there's a banging at the door. Then the bell rings. When we hear William's voice we can't help a sense of déjà vu. We run to open the door.

William looks stricken, his hair disheveled, eyes redrimmed.

"What is it?" I ask.

"It's Rick," he says. "He's leaving me."

We gallop up the stairs, me in the lead. Their front door is standing open; presumably William left it this way. On the CD player Michael Feinstein is singing "Old Friend." Rick's not in the living room.

"He's packing," William says.

I look at Kip.

"I don't think we should go in there," she says.

William says, "But he'll be coming out with suitcases."

"He can always go back in with suitcases." Kip believes that nothing, except death and taxes, is irrevocable.

"Shouldn't I tell him you're here?" William suddenly looks like the Incredible Hulk as he's pacing the room, arms dangling.

"Yes," I say, but just then Rick comes out carrying a suitcase and his portable computer in its black bag.

I've never seen him looking so grim. As always, his hair is in a muddle, but his customary smiling face is solemn, grave.

"What's this?" Rick asks. "The Supreme Court?" He sets his bags on the floor.

"Where are you going?" I demand.

"Lauren, I don't think this is any of your business." This stings and I assume I show it because he amends, "I know you mean well, but this is between William and me."

"But we're your friends," I say.

In the background, Feinstein is still singing about friendship.

"So you're my friends. So what? What's this got to do with anything?" He crosses the room and ejects the CD, turns off the CD player, and viciously hurls the disc on a pile of albums. He whirls on William. "And what the hell do you think you're doing, dragging them into this?"

"I didn't know what else to do," he answers lamely.

"Okay. You want to know what's happening here, I'll tell you. This man" — he points to William — "who's been my lover for almost six years, is a cocaine addict and a liar."

"I'm not an addict," William protests.

"Really? Then what were you doing out on the streets scoring?"

"I was upset."

"William," Rick says, furious, "you were trying to score *before* the holdup. You told me yourself."

Kip and I look at William.

He can't meet our eyes, stares down at the rug.

"You didn't know that, did you?" Rick asks us.

Kip says, "I don't think that's very important, Rick. I mean, when and all. The thing is, William needs help and he needs you."

"He doesn't need me," Rick yells. "All he needs is that disgusting stuff he can shove up his nose."

I know that Kip is dying to say that addiction is usually a family disease, but I also know that she's more politic than that.

She says, "You can both get help."

"Fuck that," Rick says. "Why the hell should *I?* It's not my problem."

"It would help you to understand," she says, meaning about himself.

"I understand perfectly. The man's a cokehead and I don't want to live with that."

I feel alarmed. Is Rick really ending this relationship? "What're you saying?"

"I'm saying, he makes me sick and I have to get the hell out of here before I do something I'll really regret."

I look over at William, who's crying silently, tears streaking his cheeks, hiding in his beard.

Kip says, "God, Rick, I'm really shocked by you."

Now Rick looks hurt.

"You're going to walk out on him because you have a problem?"

"*I* don't have a problem. *He* does."

"How come you never noticed?" I ask Rick.

"Oh, no you don't. You're not going to make this my fault." He starts for his bags.

"Wait," Kip says and shoots me a shut-up look.

"Why? Naturally, you're going to take his side. You've always liked William best, don't you think I know that?"

"That's not true," Kip and I say together.

She continues. "We're not taking his side, Rick. It's only that when things happen in a relationship you don't walk out. You deal with it. Don't you know by now that if you leave him you'll end up with someone who has the same kinds of problems? I mean, Rick, haven't you told us that both your parents are pill addicts?"

"Don't try to shrink me, Kip."

"Sorry."

"Anyway, I never said I was going for good."

William exclaims, "You're not?"

"I need ... God, I can't believe I'm saying this ... some space."

"Where are you going?" William asks.

"To California."

"What?" we all shriek.

"Well, it's not like I'm going to Kuwait. I always go to Hollywood to work, so what's the big deal?"

"You have a lover there," William accuses.

"Oh, puh-leeze. This is so typical of you, William, trying to turn the whole thing around. It's not going to work this time. I feel betrayed." His voice catches. "Can't you understand that?"

I can.

Rick picks up his bags, but before he leaves he says to me, "You should too and not because of William."

"What's that mean?"

"Ask him."

Kip says, "Don't go like this, Rick."

I stare at William, who averts his eyes.

"But he'll probably lie to you the way he's been lying to us all, unless I hang around. Well, tough. I have a plane to catch."

As if we're playing statue, we listen to the sound of Rick's feet go down the stairs and the front door open and close. Rick is gone.

No one says anything.

Finally Kip says, "He'll come back, William."

"We don't know that," he says.

Kip says, "I think we do."

"I'd like to know what you've been lying to us about," I request.

William shakes his head piteously, goes to an overstuffed chair, and falls into it with a thud, his long legs sticking straight out.

Kip and I sit opposite him on a couch.

She says, "Do you want help?"

"Help, shmelp," I say. "First things first. What have you lied about?" Normally, I wouldn't behave this way, but for a reason I can't explain I feel whatever he's hiding has something to do with Meg. "It's about Meg, isn't it?"

His chin, which had been resting on his chest, pops up and those beautiful blue eyes look stunned. "How do you know?"

"It's my job," I say for the two hundred thousandth time in response to that question. "Does this have to do with money? Lots of money?"

"Money? No."

"Coke?"

He doesn't answer, then, almost imperceptibly, nods.

I don't want to hear this about Meg. "What?"

William takes a deep breath, sighs. "The night of the holdup I wasn't going into Meg's store to buy a ring that Rick wanted. I was going in to score some coke."

"From Meg?" Kip asks, shocked.

"Yes." He looks up at us. "I'm sorry."

I will myself to press on. "Meg was a dealer?"

"No!"

It would explain about the money. "Are you sure?"

"Of course I'm sure."

"Then what? Meg was a coke addict?"

"She wasn't an *addict*."

I disregard his opinion on this. "But she did coke?"

"Yes."

I look at Kip.

Understanding, she says, "No, I didn't know this, honey."

"The truth is," William says, "I really don't think she did it much. I know you believe I can't tell an addict from an elbow, but she wasn't. She only did it once in a while. The thing was, she usually had some hanging around, and that night the cupboard was bare everywhere. So that's why I went to Meg's."

"But you didn't get it, because of the holdup," Kip says.

"Would she have sold it to you?"

"Of course not. She would've given it to me. Meg was very generous, you know that."

Yes, I know that. I think I know that. I don't know what I know. "So you got it from her later, after the police left?"

"No. She didn't have any. And that was peculiar. Not that she didn't have any, but while the cops were there she was acting nervous and naturally I thought she was worried that they'd find her stash."

"Couldn't she've been nervous because of the holdup?" Kip asks.

"Sure. And she was. But there was something else going on. She was twitchy. Kept looking toward the door to the basement."

"Did you ask her about it later, when she said she didn't have any coke?"

"No."

"Why not?"

He shrugs.

I know it was because he didn't care. All he wanted was to get out of there to try to score somewhere else. I glance at Kip. She knows this, too.

"What do you mean, *twitchy?*"

"Overwrought, anxious. I was so surprised when she said she didn't have any blow. Do you think she was lying to me?"

God forbid that anyone should be lying to anyone else these days!

"I mean," he goes on, "maybe she was afraid the cops would come back or something. She hustled me out of there as soon as they left. Practically locked the door on my shirt."

"Locked the door?"

"She always locked the door after eight."

That's right! I remember what Meg told me about deciding who to let in and who not.

"If I don't know them I go on instinct, Laur. Good old-fashioned instinct. That's why I've never been held up. Everybody else on the block has, but not your favorite paranoid."

"Hell, who'd open the door to anyone you didn't know after you've just been held up?" I say.

"That's true," Kip agrees.

"Come to think of it, what was she still doing there?"

William says, "Funny she didn't call you about what happened."

"If she had called," I say, "what would I have done?"

"Gone there," Kip answers.

"Exactly."

"I can't remember anything ever happening to Meg that she didn't call you about."

"Me either. So what's the conclusion? Meg knew if she let me know about the holdup I'd come over, no matter how much she protested, and she didn't want that because she was expecting someone."

"Who?" William asks.

"Her killer," I say.

Chapter
Sixteen

"COME ON," I say, heading for the door.

"Where?" asks Kip.

William still lies in the chair, looking more and more like a beached whale. I return to him and pull at one of his hands.

"You're coming too."

"I can't go anywhere. My life is over."

"No, William," I say, somewhat cruelly. "Meg's life is over."

Our eyes meet and I see that he's chagrined. But I don't want to minimize his pain. "I know you're going through a lot. And it's terrible that Rick left like that, but there's something we have to do. Sitting here isn't going to change anything."

"What do we have to do?"

"We have to go to Meg's store."

"Why?"

"So we can find out what it was that Meg was afraid the cops would discover."

"How are we going to get in?" Kip asks.

"You must be kidding," I say.

I stop at our apartment to get two flashlights and the extra set of lock picks I have hidden in a pig-shaped cookie jar that Meg had given me. The better picks are in my office but these will do.

We hit the street at ten-thirty and a drone, like a plague of locusts, assails us. It's not the hum of bugs, but simply the din of Greenwich Village on an unusually warm fall evening. We wait at Seventh Avenue for the light to change.

Kip says, "How're you going to do this with millions of people around?"

"You and William are going to shield me."

"One can shield you, Lauren, but once you have the door open, then what?"

"Let's play it by ear."

"Why do I let myself get into these things?" Kip says. "I can see it now: 'THERAPIST BREAKS INTO STORE OF MURDER VICTIM.'"

"Well, then you'll be part of the sleaze you love so much."

William says, "Maybe you can get on the Ron Reagan show."

"Geraldo or no one," Kip says.

We cross Seventh and continue on Perry to Greenwich Avenue. The street is teeming with people. Perhaps I was impetuous in my zeal to find truth!

"One doesn't think this is going to be possible," William says.

When we near Meg's store I see that the yellow crime-scene tape is down. This is good. I also take in the vases of flowers and tributes to Meg that are miraculously still in place. In fact, have been added to. I find it interesting that no one has stolen or desecrated these things. It gives me renewed faith in humankind. New Yorkkind.

As we come adjacent to the store my emotions surface and I have to control myself or I'll weep.

"I can't believe all this stuff," Kip says.

I forgot that she hasn't been here since the murder.

"It must signify something," I say.

"What do you mean?"

"She couldn't have been . . . I mean . . . she must've been partly who I thought she was." I hear my cogent plea for corroboration.

Kip touches my shoulder. "Of course she was, Lauren."

I smile wanly, her witness to my desire ineffectual. "I guess it is too early to try this."

"Let's have a drink," William suggests.

We go to a bar called Dew Drop Inn on the corner of Greenwich and Charles. This appears to be what I call a drunk's bar. A hangout. Inside, it's dark and thick with smoke. Blaring music forces everyone to shout, which gives the impression of people having a good time. Yet, when I look at them closely, instead of fun, I see desperation. I'm not sure I want to stay, then someone taps my shoulder.

When I turn I recognize the face, but can't quite place who it is. He realizes this and says, "Jed Langevin. I have the boot shop, two up from Meg's."

"Oh, sure. Sorry." I'd met him once or twice in her store.

He waves a hand as if to say it doesn't matter. I introduce him to Kip and William. Langevin looks as though he's had a few; his brown eyes gleam with the hubris of a dedicated drinker. "Join me. I got a table." This is issued as a command rather than an invitation.

"Thanks," I say, "but it's a little too smoky in here for us."

As if I've reminded him of something he's forgotten to do, he takes out a cigarette and lights it, but blows the smoke away from us. "Any news on Meg?"

"Nothing," I shout.

"Son-of-a-bitching bastard," he growls. "They robbed me four times in the last year. I told her, I told Meg not to open the door to strangers."

"What makes you think she did?" I yell.

"Huh?"

"Let's step outside a minute, okay?"

He nods, holds up a finger, grabs his drink from a table that's occupied by two women. "Right back."

Outside, Langevin drinks and smokes. "Now, what d'you want to know?"

"When you told her not to open the door to strangers, what did she say?"

"Say? Oh. She said, 'How ya going to make a living if you only open the door to people ya know.'"

"She had a point."

"Yeah, in a way. But ya can tell, know what I mean?"

"No."

He leans in close to our group. "Nigs," he says.

The word jolts me. I'm not used to being with people who speak this way. I catch Kip's and William's expressions and I know they feel the same.

Langevin launches into a speech. "They're the ones ruining this city, the nigs and spics. Scum. Lazy bums. Crackheads, all of 'em. And they got no respect for life. Life is cheap to them. Know what the mortality rate is for male jigs? It's . . ."

"Mr. Langevin," I say.

"Jed."

"None of us wants to hear this shit you're spouting so why don't you just go back into the bar, finish your drink, and put on your sheet."

"Sheet? Oh, I get it. You think I'm a racist, huh?"

"It crosses one's mind," William says.

"You liberals make me puke. Look at the Koreans and Pakis, you hear me say anything against them? No. 'Cause they work their butts off, don't expect something for nothing like the others. Who do you think knocked off your good friend? Huh? It was niggers who held up the store."

"And a white man who shot her later," I say. "Good night." I turn to leave. Langevin lunges and grabs my arm.

With my eyes I get across to Kip and William not to interfere. I take my .38 from my purse. "Keep your hand there," I encourage. "I'd like a change." This is my parody of Eastwood's "Make my day."

"Dyke," he says.

"Nevertheless, take your hand off me."

He does.

"Now go back inside before I lose my temper."

Langevin spits on the sidewalk. I imagine that this means something important but I don't know what, nor care. He glares at us and I see his teeth touch his bottom lip, forming an F word as he looks at William, gauges the height and weight between them, then wisely reconsiders.

When Langevin has gone inside, William says, "Thank

God. I thought for a minute I was going to have to defend my faggotry."

And he could've done it easily, as William works out every day and is in great shape. But he hates violence.

"Great guy," Kip says. "Can we go home now?"

"You can if you want to. I'm going to have some coffee and . . . some coffee and wait for the street to clear."

Both agree to come with me.

We've had three cappuccinos each, one lemon tart (William), one order of pecan pie (Kip), and one slice of blackout cake (me), which is about as dense a piece of chocolate as you can get. Kip was too tired to argue.

It's quarter to two in the morning and even with all the caffeine we're fighting to stay awake. We're in the Caffe Degli Artisti, which is one flight up from the street. Our table is next to the window.

"Looks pretty quiet out there," I say.

"It looks like Times Square to me," says Kip.

"Well, we can wait until the bars close in another two hours but I really think we could give it a try now."

"I'm willing," William announces, raising his hand as if he's in school.

Reluctantly, Kip agrees. We get the check and leave.

The thing about New York is that the streets are *never* completely empty, certainly not in the Village. This is part of the city's charm, as well as its threat. It depends on what you're after.

Except for cars shooting up Sixth Avenue, the ubiquitous hum has died down. The street is dotted with leftover people like remainders in a book sale.

As we attempt to cross Greenwich we're stopped by a young woman who's drunk or stoned. She's wearing shredded clothes that would make my mother think she'd been in a car crash, but I know these threads cost plenty.

"Please, kind sir," she says to William, "take me to your leader."

"I have none," he says.

"Are you forsaken? Is that what you are?"

He turns to me. "How does she know?"

I guide him around the young woman, whose hair is the color of a robin's egg; nice for eyes, disconcerting for hair.

"What is that child doing out at this hour?" Kip asks indignantly.

"Kip, she's not a child. She's in her twenties."

"Come on, Lauren, she can't be more than thirteen . . . fourteen at most."

I smile. "It's your perspective, darling. As we get older . . . they look younger."

"Oh," she says softly, saddened by the truth of my statement.

When we reach Meg's store the street is fairly empty. A homeless man sleeps in the entranceway of Cicero's and another man is peeing in Langevin's doorway. Usually it disgusts me that men seem to think they have the right to urinate anywhere because it's so easy for them, but tonight I'm delighted by this sight. We wait until he finishes and walks off in the opposite direction.

Kip and William stand so it appears that they're looking in the window of the store while they shield me from possible passersby.

I take out my picks, select one, and with my free hand I grab the knob. The door swings open.

"That's incredible," Kip says.

"No," I protest. "I didn't."

"Didn't what?"

"Pick it. It's not locked." I'm momentarily disappointed that I can't show off my adeptness with the picks to Kip. She's only heard about it and it's not the same thing. But this shallowness is quickly put to rest as I contemplate the ramifications of the unlocked door.

1. The cops forgot to lock it.
2. Someone else has broken in.
3. Someone else has broken in and is still inside.

I tell them these possibilities.

"Let's go home," Kip says.

"I think number one is out," I say.

"What about three?" William asks.

I shrug. "I'm going in."

"Lauren," Kip pleads.

"It's my job. Do I tell you how to run your sessions?" What can she say?

"Will you come with me?" I ask William.

He says he will.

"You stay out here, Kip, and warn us if anybody comes."

"Are you crazy? You think I'm going to stand on Greenwich Avenue at this hour in the morning by myself?"

"Fine."

Cautiously, I push the door open and we ease ourselves inside. When I shut it behind us some light leaks in from the street but we quickly step into the dark.

And it is dark! We listen. The only noise comes from the street and the thumping of my heart. I try to recall the layout.

"Now what?" Kip whispers.

"We go to the storeroom. Isn't that where you said she kept looking, William?"

"Yes. It seemed so."

"Take my hand, Kip, and William, take hers." Slowly, as I remember the ins and outs of the store, I make our way far enough in so that it's safe to switch on the flashlights. We breathe easier. The dark never ceases to frighten no matter how old you get, especially in circumstances like these.

But the flashlights create shadows, and monsters form, which makes our hesitant walk to the back seem as though we're in the middle of a Stephen King novel. All of us give gasps of fear as we encounter these apparitions, one after the other, and I know I feel like a fool so I assume they do too.

When we reach the door to the storeroom I'm not surprised to see it ajar. We stop. Listen. If someone's down there, there's no way for us to know. We could walk into a trap. I reach for a bowl, probably worth hundreds, but it doesn't matter, my priority is our safety. Good-bye bowl. I toss it through the doorway, down to the basement storeroom.

When it hits the floor it smashes, makes a noise that, to me, sounds like an A-bomb. I wait for a gunshot, something in retaliation. Nothing comes. I'm sure now we're alone.

"It's okay," I tell them. "Close the door behind you, William."

We huddle on the landing as I search the wall with my flashlight and finally locate a light switch. This can't be seen from the street so I feel relatively safe. Gingerly, we go down the steps. There are boxes and crates everywhere but it's not hard to know what to do because we see at once that two medium-sized cartons are open and empty. I know from experience that Meg wouldn't leave these boxes this way. She'd close them, pile them in a corner, or more likely cut them up and put them in the garbage.

Whoever has been here has removed what was in the boxes and taken it away. I hope to read what it says was in them, but all there is are things like: THIS SIDE UP and OPEN HERE. There's nothing to show where the boxes came from, and that in itself seems suspicious because all the others are marked with return addresses.

"What the hell was in these?" I ask.

Kip says: "Coke?"

"No," William says, "I really don't think so."

We speculate on one ridiculous thing after another until Kip interrupts with a healthy scream.

"What?"

She points toward the back of the room.

When I look where she's indicating I see it, too.

Feet.

Wearing black loafers.

In a position that reveals the person attached is lying on his back.

I'm almost sure he's not asleep.

Chapter
Seventeen

═══════════════════════════

I HATE TO ADMIT IT, but these late nights are too much for me. I feel like a noodle. I don't want to think what I *look* like.

And Kip?

Looks as if she's had a perfect eight hours! I can't believe that the two-year difference in our ages can be responsible for this contrast. Or is it in the eye of the beholder?

"How do I look to you?" I ask her.

"Tired."

"Why the hell don't *you* look tired?"

"Good genes," she says crisply.

"Give me a break."

"How else can you explain it?"

I ignore her. It's eight in the morning and we got home at five. *Three lousy hours of sleep!* How could anyone look like she does? She's dressed for the day in a smart pair of blue slacks and a light pink shirt, both neatly ironed. I'm in my rumpled robe.

"Actually," she says, "if I didn't have an eight-thirty I'd meet Kate Stimpson for a game of handball."

I glare.

"Just kidding," she says. "The truth is, I feel like you look."

"Thank you."

"Think about it this way: I don't have your skin. You're going to age much better than I."

Somehow this doesn't appease me. Though Kip is behaving

normally, I know she's still in shock from having discovered a body. A first for her.

"I can't believe this," she says, reading her paper.

I sing, "I feel a rant coming on. Please, oh, please, don't let it be sleaze."

"We now have a magazine coming out called *Crime Beat*. This is appalling."

"Why? The mystery genre is very popular right now."

"It's *not* about fiction." She reads again. "The monthly newsmagazine of crime. The first issue will feature the sole survivor of Jeffrey Dahmer. I can't believe this. Also included in this issue: 'She starred in America's bloodiest home video.'"

"Who?"

"Does it matter? Honestly, Lauren."

The phone rings. It's Cecchi.

"We've I.D.'d him," he says. "Wallace Faye, a.k.a. Wally, a.k.a. Fingers Faye. Got a sheet three pages long."

"What kind of stuff?"

"Small time. Scams mostly. Last known association: Alan Pesh, a.k.a. Alice."

"Alice?"

"As in Wonderland. Likes little girls. Pesh is a grifter. Been back on the streets for almost two years. Going there now."

"Can . . ."

"Yeah, you can come. Meet me at the place in ten."

I jump up.

"What?"

"Meeting Cecchi."

"Lauren? You do remember the funeral's this afternoon?"

I give her a withering look.

"Sorry. Will you come home first?"

"Not sure."

I kiss her lightly and run upstairs to get dressed.

Cecchi's at the counter of the Waverly Place coffee shop. When he sees me he gets up, pays, and we're out the door and into his car, which is double-parked on Sixth.

"The punk lives over by the docks on Twelfth between Twenty-fifth and -sixth."

"Lucky him."

"Yeah, nice digs."

"You know what Pesh is into right now?" I ask.

"No. But it's gotta be something. Man's never idle, so to speak."

"What's this thing with little girls?" I ask with distaste.

"Just what you think."

"How little?"

"Young teens."

"You mean, like thirteen?"

"Yeah."

"How old is Pesh?"

"Fifty-eight, maybe sixty."

I feel furious. I despise child abusers. I don't care what their backgrounds are, what made them who they are, I have no patience with or sympathy for them. Yes, I judge them, and I always will.

"What could Fingers Faye have been doing in Meg's basement?" I ask.

"I thought you might tell me."

We haven't had time to discuss it before now.

"I don't know."

"What made you look down there?"

I explain about William's noticing Meg's nervousness and her glancing at the cellar door.

"Why didn't you tell me this? You have to stop breaking in places, Lauren."

"You're angry."

"How long do you think I can keep you out of trouble?"

"I know. I'm sorry. I'll try not to do it anymore."

"What d'you mean, try?"

"I can't promise."

"Jesus," he says to himself. "And what were the empty boxes? You think it was coke?"

"William doesn't."

"Maybe William didn't know she was a dealer."

"It's possible," I say, because I feel almost anything is, at this point.

"I know this is hard for you."

"It's harder having her dead. I want to find her killer no matter what was going on."

"They could be connected, but not necessarily."

"Right."

"I think the holdup earlier in the evening is coincidental."

"Me, too."

"So after that experience, why didn't she go home?"

"Because she was waiting for someone," I say easily.

"Right."

"And you think the someone was Wally Faye or Al Pesh?"

"Could be," he says.

"If it was one of them, why didn't he get what he was after and go?"

"Spooked. Maybe he hadn't planned to kill Meg, but something happened, or didn't happen, that made him do it. Then he was afraid he'd get caught and there wasn't time to go down to the basement and unpack those boxes."

"The thing is," I say, "how could one person expect to carry what was in the boxes?"

"What d'you mean?"

"Wouldn't more than one person come to collect?"

"Depends on what it was."

"I don't care what it was, I don't think one person could carry off whatever took up two boxes."

"You have a point," Cecchi says, grudgingly.

He hates it and he loves it when I think of something he hasn't.

"And," he says, "we know it was just one person because Kornbluth was a witness to this jerk-off running out of the store and down the avenue."

"Right."

"She could be wrong."

"Sure."

"But not likely."

"Right. What about Meg's boyfriend?"

Cecchi says, "So far nothing. We can't place her with anybody and there's nothing in her apartment leads us to a particular man."

I almost tell him I know but catch myself.

"I think you're right, guy must be married. Wherever they met it wasn't in public."

"What about the guys Ruby mentioned?"

"Our favorite waitress? Well, she couldn't give me much but from what she said it didn't seem likely any of them was a romantic interest. But, hey, now that I think about it, one of them could've been Fingers."

"I just can't understand what Meg was doing with people like that," I say, more to myself than to him.

"In the end, nobody knows anybody," Cecchi says cynically as he parks.

The area is bleak, though there's the occasional oasis of a trendy restaurant or club. Most of the buildings are run-down, unkempt like drunken whores.

We get out of the car. "This is the one," Cecchi says, consulting a piece of paper.

The brick building is six stories, the facade is crumbling, and several windows on the first floor are broken and covered with plywood. The door is attached by one hinge, the entry strewn with garbage, the metal mailboxes sprung, nothing inside them.

"He's on the fourth," Cecchi tells me.

I know instinctively, because I'm a detective, that there's not going to be an elevator. Sometimes I amaze myself with the incredible deductions I make.

The hallway's even more disgusting than the entry and I cover my mouth and nose. It's hard to believe but I'm sure that I see piles of human feces, mounds of vomit, and, of course, more garbage.

We make our way up the littered stairs. Pesh can't be doing too well if this is where he has to live. On four we walk to the end of the dark hall and Cecchi pounds on a door, his other hand resting on the butt of his gun. I reach in my bag and do the same.

"Open up, Pesh. Police."

This is always a tense moment. I hate it more than anything. Cops do, too. You never know, if there *is* a person inside, what he might do. The door could be sprayed suddenly with an automatic weapon — the kind that hunters of small game insist they need. We stand to the side of the door. It's worse if we have to break it down, go in on our own. The perp might be waiting, gun in hand. I'm relieved when I hear a shuffling sound.

"Whoisit?" asks a voice that sounds like a dry razor on a heavy beard.

"Police. Open up, Pesh. I have a warrant." This is true.

"Whaddayawan?"

"Talk."

"Fuck this," he says, but he begins the unlocking process. When the door is finally eased open, all I see sticking out for the warrant is a hand the size of a shorn lamb.

Cecchi gives it to him. The hand is withdrawn and a year later the last chain is removed and Pesh opens the door for us.

I follow Cecchi into the putrid-smelling apartment. It's almost as bad as the halls but has a fishy aroma. Spoiled fish.

Al, a.k.a. Alice Pesh, is enormous; so mammoth he blocks the view of the room behind him. He wears an old-fashioned ribbed T-shirt and a pair of once white, now yellow, boxer shorts. His arms are hairy and as big around as my waist. Under the hair are indecipherable tattoos. The legs are hairier still, as if he's wearing black tights beneath the shorts. The size of these legs is bigger than Cecchi's body and they end in gigantic feet with long, curling brown toenails.

And oh, the face. The head is pumpkin-sized, fringed with wisps of colorless hair. His features are almost lost in the surfeit of flesh. Two blue eyes, like thumbtacks, peer out over a nose that's obviously been broken several times and is dwarfed by cheeks the size of melons. Jowls swing when he moves, as though they're separate people. But it's Pesh's mouth that's the most revolting. The lips are unnaturally glossy, gargantuan, and resemble two inner tubes.

Pesh is frightening and I'm glad I'm not alone. Of course,

I'd be too old for him so that's not a concern. When I imagine this monster in the same neighborhood as a child, bile burns my throat.

"Whaddayawan?"

Cecchi walks toward him and Pesh backs up until we're all three in what passes for a living room. It has a broken armchair and a dirty daybed, gray sheets in a tangle. The expected empty Chinese food cartons festoon the room along with crushed beer cans, and mashed cigar butts. I soon realize that the fishy odor is wafting off Pesh. I gag.

"What do you know about Wally Faye?" Cecchi asks.

"Who?"

"Don't bother, Pesh, we know you know him."

"Faye," he says as though he's capable of thinking. "Oh, yeah, ya mean Fingers?"

"Yeah, Fingers."

"Ain't seen 'im, two, tree mons. Fingers in trouble, somepin'?" he says, as if he's asking about an altar boy.

"Fingers is dead."

"Dead?"

"What's Faye been up to, Pesh?"

"How should I know?"

"You were seen with him earlier this week," Cecchi lies. The thumbtack eyes go slitty. "Sez who?"

"A good source."

"Liar punk said it, then. I ain't seen Faye for two, tree mons."

"Then who has?"

Pesh thinks. This resembles a child trying to go to the bathroom. "Who has what?"

"Who's seen him?"

"How should I know?" he answers, insulted.

"C'mon, Alice, you know everything that goes down."

Now he's flattered. I can tell because the pink inner-tube lips turn up and spittle forms in the corners of his mouth.

"True," he says. "Maybe I heard somepin'."

Cecchi reaches in his pocket, takes out a twenty, hands it to Pesh, who swallows it with his hand.

"Who's dat?" he asks about me.

"Laurano," Cecchi says.

Pesh accepts this as a full explanation, nods, the whole face wobbling. "Ya know Malcolm?"

"Lieface Malcolm?"

Malcolm got his moniker because he's a pathological liar. Whatever anyone says happened to them, it's already happened to him, but worse.

"He been hangin' with Fingers."

Lieface and Fingers, I think. Nice duo.

"What do you know about the murder of Megan Harbaugh?"

"Who?"

"Store on Greenwich Avenue. Somebody shot the owner."

"Don't know nothin'."

"Never hear her name?"

"Sounds familiar. Can't place it. Ask Lieface."

"Know where I can find him?"

"Might."

"Listen, Pesh," Cecchi says menacingly, "so far I haven't used the warrant. You want me to start searching?"

I detect definite fear in Pesh's expression.

"Last I hoid, Lieface was in Tompkins Square Park."

"The park's closed," Cecchi says.

"Oh, yeah, I forgot. Guess Lieface couldn't be dere, huh?"

"Where is he?"

"As God is my witness, dat's what I know about where Lieface Malcolm is. Somebody from the park might know."

"Like who?"

"Dere wuz tree a' dem hung. Lieface, Fingers, an' Eddie Margolis."

Margolis is mostly into dealing stolen goods. A fence.

"Where's he?"

"Got me."

"Well, you're just an innocent pup, aren't you, Pesh?"

"Hey, Cecchi, I been good. Ya t'ink I live here I got any t'ing goin'?"

My very thought.

"Give me an address for Margolis and I'll leave without looking around," Cecchi bargains.

"Les see. Oh, yeah. Margolis lives on Avenue B. I t'ink maybe it's one ninety-one. Yeah, it's comin' back to me. Second floor, one ninety-one Avenue B, Alphabet City, U.S. of A." He grins, rictuslike. "You goin' now?"

"I'm comin' back if this address is shit. You understand?"

Pesh nods. "It's all I got. Ain't seen any a' dem in a long time."

"And you don't know what they were up to, right?"

"Right."

"You're full of shit, Pesh."

"Ya said ya'd leave, I tole ya where Margolis lives."

"I lied," Cecchi says.

Pesh actually looks hurt.

"I want to know what they were into. And don't bullshit me."

"As God is . . ."

"Save it, Pesh. God's never going to be your witness."

"Hey, I don't know. Honest."

Cecchi motions to leave. On the way down the stairs he says, "Notice he didn't ask how Faye died?"

"I noticed."

We spend the rest of the morning looking for Margolis but can't find him. The image of Pesh, and the possibility that Meg could know such a person, bewilder me.

"How could Meg get involved with people like this?" I ask Cecchi directly.

"Only one reason I can think of," he says. "Money."

I know I should tell him about her cash outlays but I don't. I want to hear his take on this first. "Money was never important to her," I say.

"Yeah? How would you know?"

It's like a slap across my face but it's true. How would *I* know? I continue to protest. "Meg ran a legitimate business."

"And she had something going on the side. You have to face it, Lauren."

Yeah, I do.

Chapter
Eighteen

ANOTHER FUNERAL. But this one is Meg's, my oldest friend. And in this one I'm a pallbearer, a first for me. Kip sits on one side of me and William on the other.

We are assembled at Grace Church on Broadway and Tenth. It's a beautiful old church and often Meg, Kip, and I came here for Christmas and Easter services. Meg and Kip needed the ritual. I went to be with them.

The place is packed. My parents and Meg's huddle together, as though if they stay close enough this won't be true. Meg's sister Rosie; her husband, Karl; their two grown children, Charles and Fritz; and Lorraine, Meg's other sister, share the pew.

Sasha, looking predictably seedy, has shown up with Tamari.

Blythe sits with her father, Nick. Ray Davies, my employer, is behind them. Cecchi stands in the back with his partner, Meyers.

I recognize Arlene Kornbluth, the boutique owner whom I'd spoken to the morning after the murder. She's with a blond woman I assume is her lover, Jane. In another pew are the racist Jed Langevin, Jim Darling from the leather store, and a woman I guess is his wife, Sally.

At the end of the pew are two male faces I recognize but can't name. I suspect they're store owners too. An African-American man sits by himself in front of them. I recognize him as the owner of an exclusive pottery shop.

Jenny and Jill are with Susan and Stan. Behind them is Jason Lightbourne, with an attractive woman and two small children. He nods at me, I nod back, smile, and turn around. I recall that when I asked him if he'd dated Blythe he'd said a simple no. So what? So most married men would answer no and add that they were married. He didn't. Is that a crime? Other people I don't recognize surround the Lightbournes; I assume they're other neighbors of Blythe's.

Looking to my right I see Harry, the doorman, other friends of Meg's, her three employees, and people I don't know. I can't help wondering if Topic A is here.

I speculate on how well any of these people knew Meg, or like me, if they only knew the side she chose to reveal. And were they disparate sides from the one I saw?

If asked, would my friends describe me as though I were different people? Would there be a common denominator, like a black thread running through a woven white mat?

I've always thought of myself as an open book, but Kip laughs when I say this. She says I'm guarded and well defended. So it's possible that Cecchi has a dissimilar picture of me from Susan, and Susan views me unlike William. This isn't hard to believe or accept because it's not the same thing as what I've discovered about Meg. I have no BIG secret from any of my friends, unless I have a secret from myself, and I don't think that counts.

How many people here know that Meg was involved in something dishonest? Criminal?

The minister speaks about Meg, says what a wonderful person she was. And she was! What do I expect him to say?

I stare at the coffin at the front and wonder if Meg wears the black-and-white shoes. I'm obsessed with this question and picture myself running up, opening the lid, and checking it out. But the lid is nailed shut by now, and what would I do if I discovered that the shoes were missing?

Jesus! Meg's in there. Dead. It hits me as if for the first time. How many more first times will I admit that she's dead? Kip takes my hand and I realize I must've made some sort of noise. She squeezes and I do the same. Various people go to the altar and speak of Meg. I cannot. I'd never get through it.

Rosie rises, walks to the front. She looks like Meg, as though they're distant cousins, with a faint family resemblance. She wears a polyester blue suit, a white blouse with a jabot. Her hair is the color of sweetheart roses and I wonder how she got it to be that way. And why?

"I'm Meg's sister," she starts. "I've known her all her life. Longer than anyone here, except our parents. But longevity doesn't necessarily mean better."

Yes, I think, that's right.

"The Meg I knew is probably different from the Meg you knew."

I can't believe Rosie is saying this.

"The Meg I knew could be an awful brat."

People laugh.

"But that was when she was little. That was when she wanted whatever I had, whatever I was allowed to do. Come to think of it, this lasted right until I went off to college two years before she did. Nevertheless, we were always close friends."

I know this to be untrue. Does Rosie really believe this? Meg used to tell me what a bitch Rosie was, how she twisted her arm, or lied to their mother about who started things. And later, in high school, they hated each other, as they competed for boys (Meg was the better-looking of the two) and their parents destructively compared their smarts, Rosie winning with better grades.

"My sister was a wonderful woman," she continues. "She was my confidant, my adviser, my role model. Yes, I was the older, but Meg was the wiser."

I recall Meg's telling me that Rosie told her to "butt out of my life" when Meg tried to suggest something about one of Rosie's kids. And as for confiding, according to Meg, neither told the other anything about their lives because they were so totally different. Role model? As in what?

Suddenly I wonder if Rosie killed Meg. I'm sure she has an alibi that Cecchi hasn't bothered to mention. I wish I knew if this woman actually believes what she's saying, or if it's a conscious act, perhaps for her parents, other family members, the crowd, because she deems it the right thing to do?

And then there's another possibility: Meg lied to me about their relationship. Of course I know the truth about them growing up because I was there. Still, my vision might've been skewed, shaped by Meg's emphasis on the horror of it all.

I feel there's nothing I can count on.

Rosie concludes and returns to her seat.

More people lionize my friend and I stop listening. It's too confusing. When the ceremony ends, my pallbearer job is required again. We don't actually lift the coffin. It rides on a gurney to the front of the church, where we do carry it down the stairs, then return it to the gurney and wheel it to the hearse. Here the funeral personnel take over.

Meg is to be buried in a plot in New Jersey the Harbaughs have owned for years. Kip, William, and I ride with my parents. There's no way around this.

My father drives. He's a handsome man in his sixties, with black hair turning gray, but his widow's peak untouched by signs of age. His nose, like mine, has a Roman cast. He has thin lips and deep dimples.

My mother, about the same age as he, looks amazingly healthy for an active alcoholic. She takes good cosmetic care of herself. I've decided this is to protect her right to drink. Her hair is dyed brown, and her makeup hides the tiny broken veins, the skin of a drunk. But her hazel eyes conceal nothing and advertise her despair, futility, and fear.

I feel trapped. I *am* trapped. My mother's perfume permeates the car and I'm instantly nauseated and thrown into the past. I could be anywhere from four to twelve, coming from the shore, my grandparents' house, going to visit friends. How I hated riding in the car with them. We always had to stop because I *always* got sick and had to vomit on the side of the road, humiliated. It wasn't until I was older that I realized my mother's perfume, often mixed with fumes of alcohol, was the culprit.

Suddenly I remember going to the Jersey shore with Meg, singing "Ninety-nine Bottles of Beer on the Wall" the whole way. Funny how when Meg was with me I didn't get sick. Distraction or something else? A feeling of unity, I think. To be alone with my parents felt lonely because they were never really there. Meg was my solace, my parent. I start crying.

Kip and William, on either side, take a hand and hold it.

"You have to pull yourself together," my mother says, swiveling her head to look at me over her seat.

"Why?" I ask.

She tsks, as though I'm a hopeless imbecile. "You tell her, Kip."

"I can't," Kip says, "because I don't know why either."

My mother looks at William, who shrugs. She turns front, saying: "You kids." This is meant to imply that we're all out of control.

My father tries a different tack. He relates one of his cases that he thinks will divert and amuse us. It does neither. For the rest of the ride my mother takes over, and rambles on about people we don't know or care about.

Two decades later we arrive at the cemetery. After parking, we walk a short distance to the Harbaugh family plot. Sasha and Tamari, Blythe, the senior Harbaughs, Rosie and family, and Lorraine are waiting for us with the minister and Lorenzo. There are some older faces I don't know and I assume they're friends of Meg's parents. Neither ex-husband has come, nor any of Meg's colleagues and friends. They know we're going to give the party in a few weeks and will do their mourning or celebrating then.

It's the depth of the hole that gets me. Next to it, the coffin rests on a contraption that will lower it into the ground. Into the hole. I feel I might go insane, start screaming, laughing, something inappropriate, and I grab Kip's hand. William puts an arm around me.

The minister begins. I go into a trancelike state and hear nothing. The next thing I know it's over and I'm being led away by friend and lover. I look back and see the coffin disappearing. A big mistake. In my head I say, *Okay, every-body, the joke's over now!*

In my heart I know the truth.

Having had to go to the Harbaughs' for the after-funeral do, we don't get home until well after eight. My mother was quite herself, consuming numerous Manhattans, and when we were leaving, Hildy Harbaugh was comforting her.

All I want is to go to bed, hide for a while. In the entryway William stands staring at us. He makes no attempt to climb the stairs to his place.

Kip invites him in.

He accepts.

I can't remember ever not wanting William around but I feel that way now. Still, I understand that he doesn't want to be alone.

There are three messages on the answering machine. They are all from Cecchi. In the first he says that Lieface Malcolm has been found, strangled, in an abandoned building. The second tells about the untimely death of Eddie Margolis. Same M.O. Both appear to have been dead for several days, probably predating Fingers Faye's death. And the third relates that Al Pesh has an alibi, a good one, for the approximate time of the two most recent murders.

Kip says, "I think you should get off this case."

I nod.

"Lauren, don't give me that. I mean it. People are dying."

"Let's not talk about it now, okay?"

William says, "Can I sleep here tonight?"

The couch converts to a bed, as he knows.

"I can't face going up there to an empty apartment."

"Are you afraid you might do some coke?" Kip asks.

Childlike, he nods.

"Maybe you should consider a rehab," she says.

"I don't think I need that," he says adamantly.

"What do you plan to do, then?" I ask.

"Do?"

"Yes, William," I say testily, "*do*. About your habit."

"I wish you wouldn't call it that, Lauren."

"Okay," I say. "What are you going to do about your addiction? Your compulsion, craving, obsession? You like that better?"

"I think I'll go home," he says.

"Oh, for Christ's sake," I yell. "You just admitted you were afraid to be alone because you might snort. You think that's normal?"

"You're just mad at your mother," he says.

This is probably true. "My feelings about my mother don't negate my feelings about you. I love you, William. I don't want to lose you. Don't you get it?"

He says nothing.

"Are you planning to live with us forever so that you won't do coke?"

"Of course not," he says, indignant.

"Then what? What is it you're planning to do about this thing?"

"I'm not planning anything. I don't need to. You're making such a big deal about this. I can control it," he says.

"Then why are you afraid to go upstairs?" Kip asks.

Not waiting for some excuse, I say, "Don't you want Rick back?"

"That's a stupid question."

"Is it? I don't think so, because if you don't do something about this coke thing, Rick isn't going to come back."

Alarmed, he asks, "He told you that?"

"It was clear," I say.

"Then *he* has a problem."

I laugh. "And you don't."

Kip says, "If you promise to get help, William, you can stay."

I look at her, mystified. Does she actually think any promise he'd make now would mean anything? What the hell, she's only a therapist. What do they know? Me? I'm the child of an alcoholic. I know about promises.

I no longer want to go to bed. I want to talk to some sane

people with my modem and computer. "You two do what you want, I'm going to check out my E-mail."

"I thought you were my friend," he says predictably.

"I am."

"William, promise you'll think about a rehab."

As I enter the study I hear William promise and Kip believe. The room is dark and I leave it that way when I flip the switch on my surge protector. Everything whirs into tech life as I remove the vinyl covers from my computer and printer.

I have a new Sony monitor, and it bleeps and burps and brings up the Norton Commander in living color. My Cardinal modem, little yellow lights twinkling, rests on the surface of my EPS 386SX-20 CPU. On top of it is my Logitech scanner, and to the right of my 101-key EPS keyboard is a shiny white Microsoft mouse that sits on its gray pad. Oh, yes, we've grown.

I put the cursor on the Telix directory by moving my mouse, depress a button or two, and in milliseconds I'm in the Telix program and dialing AARDVARK, my favorite Bulletin Board. With this modem I hear the whole thing: dial tone, the singsong notes of the phone number, the ringing and . . . the busy signal.

I move down the directory to Invention Factory. This BBS has live chat and if I'm lucky maybe Phantom Two, or Lovable, or Gefilte Mish will be on the board ready to talk about Madonna or Bart Simpson. Hey, I never said this was an intellectual pursuit.

While I wait to connect I think about the case. I have to find Meg's killer. And now that those creeps are dead, and Pesh is in the clear, the only suspect I have is Topic A, and since I don't know who he is I don't know much. But what I do know is that there's a killer out there . . . maybe Topic A . . . maybe someone else.

Chapter
Nineteen

WE SIT IN THE LIVING ROOM waiting for Tom and Sam.
We're going with them to meet Dr. Woo. I have an emotional
hangover from the funeral. Depression sits on my chest like a
sumo wrestler. We're reading magazines. I turn the pages but
barely see the print.

Kip says, "I can't believe this!"

SLEAZE RANT COMING!!!

"Kimberly Bergalis," she says.

I'm blank.

"The woman who got AIDS from her dentist."

"Right."

"They're going to bring her before a congressional com-
mittee, wheel her in in her hospital bed, and have her testify
that she's, and I quote, 'an innocent victim of AIDS.' Meaning, of course, that the homosexuals and drug users are *not*
innocent."

"Helms?"

"Who else?"

"Why're they doing this?"

"It's the goddamn testing thing again. But wait, that's not
all. This display, this obvious exploitation of a dying woman
. . . are you ready . . . will be televised. Can you hardly wait?
Jesus. I mean, I feel sorry for Kimberly Bergalis, but using a
dying person like this is so disgusting." She flings the magazine across the room. "Do you know what Bob Sklar told
me?"

Her dentist. "Nope."

"The dental students at NYU *must* work on AIDS patients but, should they contract AIDS, they won't graduate. Can you believe it?"

"They're not going to get it that way."

"Honey, I know that and you know that, but some right-winger at NYU doesn't. Someone spurred on by Jesse Helms, who may as well be a mouthpiece for Bush. I hate that man. He's nothing but a panderer."

"Which one?"

"All of them. But I'm talking about Bush. The man will say and do anything he thinks will get him reelected."

I'm in awe of how she's managed to get to the Bush harangue. But horrified too, as once the Bush invective starts we are lost.

"War on drugs," she snarls. "Ha! The education president," she sneers. "Do you know . . ."

The bell rings. I cannot believe I'm actually saved by it!

Tom and Sam come in. They beam. Tom's glow is less bright than Sam's. Though it's only ten in the morning he looks tired.

"All ready?" Sam asks.

We say we are and leave the house with them. It's a crisp day, the way it should be. Tom insists we walk to Thirty-first but Sam says it's too long a walk for him, not Tom. I admire the way Sam handles this.

"Let me treat us to a cab," Kip says.

They protest. We insist. They give in.

Not only is the ride bumpy, it takes four weeks to get there.

Thirty-first between Seventh and Eighth is a busy block. We're in the garment district and men push racks of clothing through the streets. Dr. Woo is in your basic boring building. Second floor. Elevator.

When we enter the waiting room there's another man there. It's clear he has AIDS. Tom urges us to take the remaining two seats, and we do because it seems so important to him.

This is unlike any waiting room I've ever been in. There's

nothing plush about the place. The chairs are wooden and, in a glass-enclosed cabinet, there are rows of jars and bottles. The walls are bare and painted puce, though faded. There's also a woman who is mixing what I assume are herbs in a bag at a wooden table. She appears to be Chinese but I don't think she's Dr. Woo. She has the aura of an assistant. The dress she wears is Western and is what is known as a housedress. Black slippers like ballet shoes are on her feet and she slides back and forth between cabinet and table.

The door to an inner office opens and a young woman, gaunt and ghostlike, comes into the waiting room, a Chinese woman behind her. This must be Dr. Woo.

The assistant ties up the bag of herbs she's been mixing, gives it to the woman. The man rises. Both shake the doctor's hand and she bows her head several times.

"You know what to do, yes?" the doctor says.

"Yes. We do."

"Thank you," the man says. I see that he carries a bag also. They leave together.

Dr. Woo is a plump woman in her forties. She's about my height with black hair, no gray. She wears a blue gabardine suit: a boxy jacket with a skirt to the knees and a mauve blouse. She smiles.

"Mr. Adams?" she says, looking at the two men.

Tom identifies himself and she shakes his hand, and asks him to accompany her into her office. He tells her that he wants us all to come.

I had no idea we'd be going in with him and it frightens me. I don't know why.

"Of course," she says. "Come along." She's experienced this before.

It's a small room. The walls are a cream color in here and are adorned by photographs of Dr. Woo with others. Against the far wall is a conventional leather examining table and opposite a small couch, where the three of us crowd together.

"You take off shirt," she instructs Tom. "Leave on pants."

He follows her orders and my heart nearly breaks when I

see the devastation of his once marvelous upper body. The ribs show clearly, like thin tree branches.

She tells him to lie down on the examining table, and when he's settled she steps out of her shoes, climbs up, and stands on his chest. Remarkably, he doesn't make a sound, as I would've expected with a 125-, 130-pound woman standing on him.

"You fine?"

"Yes."

Now she walks his chest the way another doctor would use his hands. And it doesn't seem to bother Tom at all. We look at each other, astonished. When she's finished mapping out his body, she steps back down, puts on her shoes, and sits next to him. With her hands she feels every inch of his face and head. Her eyes are closed. After this she looks inside his mouth, at his tongue, and into his eyes. She uses no instruments.

"Put shirt on," she says.

While he does this, she turns to us but speaks to Sam.

"No more ice cream. He eat lot of ice cream, right?"

"Yes, he does," Sam says, surprised.

"No dairy any kind. And no sugar."

Tom groans.

She whirls on him, shakes her forefinger. "You want to get better you listen to me. I know you like these things but not good for you. I'm giving you diet plan. Also, herbs. You drink herbs four times a day, like tea. You won't like this. Taste is bitter but good for you."

Tom nods.

She turns back to us. To Kip she says, "You his sister?"

"Yes." She's pleased Dr. Woo has identified her.

"You big sister, you help, too."

"I will."

"You sister-in-law?" she asks me.

"Yes."

"Good. All help."

"We live in San Francisco," Sam says.

"Move here with family, then."

"Well, I . . ."

"Best thing. You move." And that is an order. To Tom she says, "You come here next week?"

"I have to go back to San Francisco."

Dr. Woo thinks. "I give you name of associate and I write out herbs. He will give them to you until you move here."

"Thank you."

In the outer room the doctor speaks to her assistant in Chinese. To us, "I write out herbs. I also give you diet." She goes back into her office.

The assistant does her dance between cabinet and table, measuring and mixing. By the time she finishes Dr. Woo is back with the written formula, which she gives to Tom. She shakes his hand. "Who pay?"

"We do," Tom and Sam say in unison.

She hands Tom another slip of paper; he passes it to Sam, who writes out a check.

"Nice family," she says.

We agree.

Outside Tom says, "Can I have one last normal meal before I'm condemned to the horror of macroneurotic?"

"Why not?" Sam says.

"Italian, Indian, Greek, French, Chinese . . ."

"Not Chinese."

We laugh.

"Indian."

"Know just the place," I say and hail a cab.

In my office, I drink from my Styrofoam cup and eat a brownie (I eschewed dessert at lunch because Indian ones don't interest me) as I look out the window at the scene on Sheridan Square. I can see quite a distance from here on Waverly Place. My view takes in the square, also Seventh Avenue South and the streets running perpendicular to it.

Things are as usual: cars blow their horns; several men race down the avenue on roller blades; people buy their papers at the newsstand, rush down the subway stairs, hail cabs. Nothing new. A typical afternoon in Greenwich Village.

Except that Meg has left me.

Left me to deal with the world, never mind her murder. Left me to find her killer and to learn things I don't want to know about her.

But when *exactly* did she leave? Was it the moment she was killed or was it way before that when she involved herself in things she couldn't or wouldn't tell me? Or had she left me time and time again through the years? Does everyone always leave everyone?

Rick's left William, even if it's temporary.

Unless there's a miracle, Tom will leave Sam.

And William, in his way, has left me.

Has Kip left me?

Will she?

I look at my watch and note that she's between patients. At the desk I punch in her number, let it ring once, then punch it in again.

"Hi," Kip says. "What's up?"

"Promise me you'll never leave me," I command.

"What's wrong, honey?"

"Just promise me."

"Okay. I promise."

"I don't believe you," I say.

She sighs. "How can I make you believe me, Lauren?"

"What if you get sick and die first?"

"I guess I'll be leaving you," she says.

"You see? How can I believe you?"

Patiently Kip says, "How about this: I promise not to leave you unless it's due to death."

"I hate that."

"It's the best I can do."

I consider this and realize what she says is true. It's impossible for her to promise not to die first. "If you die first," I say, "I'll kill you. 'Bye."

The phone rings.

"Lauren? Honey?"

"What?" I've now gotten myself into a state where I believe she's going to leave me momentarily.

"You sound furious," she says. "I'm not leaving you, I promise. And I have no intention of dying anytime soon."

"Neither did Meg."

"I know, honey."

We don't mention Tom but I know we're both thinking of him. I feel so selfish now. Poor Kip. How could I call her with my insecurity when she's spent the morning watching her brother scramble for life?

"I'm sorry, Kip."

"It's okay. Want to guess what the topic is on one of the talk shows today?"

"What?"

"Plastic surgery that went wrong! Can you imagine them parading these deformed people across a stage? This is beyond sleaze."

"Which show?"

"Does it matter? I don't know if I can go on living in this country, Lauren."

"See, you're getting ready to leave."

"Stop it. Finish your coffee and brownie and get to work."

"How do you know I'm eating a brownie?"

"I have my ways." I can hear her smiling.

"This is appalling."

"I wish I could talk more but my next patient's here. Try to remember that I'm not going anywhere and I'll see you later."

They were a wasted set of phone calls. I don't feel any better, any more reassured, although I have to admit if she does leave me, it probably will be through death. I don't believe she'll dump me for someone else.

I can't imagine my life without Kip. Who would soothe me, listen to my stories more than once, make love to me the way she does? And who else would know through the telephone exactly what I was eating? No one. She'd better stick around.

Meg had three employees: Mary Jane Vineburgh, Julie Fisher, and Lorry Stone. None had been present at the time of the murder, all had alibis. Still, it occurs to me that one or all of them might know what Meg was up to, what was in the two cartons. I've invited them to meet me at the Caffe Degli Artisti. If any of them knows anything I think it'll be harder to lie in front of the others.

As I climb the stairs I promise myself to have nothing more than coffee. There's only one other customer in the place, a skinny man with white clumps of hair like an ungroomed Persian cat. Idly, I wonder why he prefers sitting in the entrance level rather than up near the window.

I go up the three steps and take a window table for four. Before I'm settled the women come in. It's obvious they've met first so that they could come together. They spot me at once. We all order cappuccinos.

As a trio they look like the three weird sisters. One would never find them together in a social setting.

Mary Jane, in her late fifties, is the oldest. She has a cap of gray hair, wire-rimmed glasses that sit on a beaked nose, and wears a plaid cape over a shirt and slacks.

Lorry Stone is the youngest, still in her twenties. She has big blue eyes, brown hair twisted into one braid, and skin the texture and color of a rose petal.

"Gawd," Mary Jane says, "I wish I could have one of those desserts."

"Why can't you?" asks Julie Fisher. She's about thirty-five, gorgeous, and has the kind of body you only see in movies. Her long dark hair is matched by her eyes, like paint chips.

Mary Jane answers, "Be-cause if I even sniff a dessert it goes right to the thighs. And I'm on a diet anyway."

"You're always on a diet," Lorry says.

"So? What do you know, a kid? You want to take off weight" — she snaps her fingers — "it's off. Me, I have to work and work at it. Wait. You'll see when you get to be my age."

Julie says, "Does anyone ever wonder where all the fat goes that people lose? I mean, does it go into the air or what?"

"I hate to interrupt," I say, "but I'm sort of on a tight schedule."

"Oh, yeah, sure," says Mary Jane. "You want to talk about our Meg, huh? I still can't believe it. Gawd."

"You know, don't you, that the police have interviewed all of us and we're in the clear?" Lorry asks.

"Yes, I know. What did you think of Meg's boyfriend?" I ask suddenly.

They look at each other blankly.

"Didn't know she had one," Julie says.

The others agree.

So she'd kept him hidden from everyone. He *must've* been married, or maybe very, very young. Someone she wasn't proud of, knew she'd be judged for, and not by me alone.

I go right on to the next point. "I'd like some information about the store."

"The store? What about it? Is it going to open again? We got to find jobs, you know."

"I don't know if it'll open. I doubt it."

"I think I'm going to write a screenplay," Lorry says, as if she's talking about mowing the lawn or doing a wash.

"I'd like to talk about the storeroom. The deliveries in particular. How did that work?"

"Deliveries?" Mary Jane says. "What about deliveries? You think I got time to check deliveries? Deliveries aren't anything a person would look at anyway. Deliveries go on all day long."

I want her to stop saying *deliveries*.

The other two look at each other.

"C'mon," says Julie, "you guys know what she's talking about."

My detective's heart ripples.

Mary Jane gives Julie a look that shouts betrayal. It's going around, I guess.

"What, Julie? What do you all know?"

"Something was going on. We don't know what, but there were these boxes we weren't allowed to open. One day they'd be there, the next they'd be gone. Meg was very specific about us not opening them."

"I can't believe this," Mary Jane says. "We agreed."

"Well, it was a stupid agreement. Maybe this is important. Maybe this has to do with her murder."

"Yes," I say. "Julie's right."

Lorry says, "The boxes came once a week. Usually Monday afternoon."

"Turncoats," Mary Jane says. "Who could a person trust?"

I know how she feels. "And then they were gone Tuesday?"

"Yeah."

"What reason did Meg give you for not opening them?"

"You serious? She didn't have to give a reason," Julie says. "She was the boss."

"Do you have any idea what was in those boxes?"

Again they look at one another.

"Try about seven hundred," Lorry says. "Ideas."

"Gawd, this is awful."

"Could've been almost anything. But, whatever it was, it wasn't good."

"Do you think it was drugs?"

"I do," Julie says.

I look at the other two.

Mary Jane shakes her head, refusing to speculate.

Lorry shrugs. "Hey, why not? It's gonna be drugs in my screenplay."

Outraged, Mary Jane says, "You're gonna write about Meg?"

"I'm not going to use her name, for fuck's sake."

"Language," Mary Jane says.

"Fuck language. We're not in the store anymore."

"Besides the boxes, was there anything else unusual going on?"

They all say no.

Julie says, "Meg was a great boss. Fair. Pleasant."

"Yeah, except you know when," Mary Jane says, then covers her mouth, chagrined.

"When?"

"When the brat came in," says Lorry.

"The brat?"

"Blythe," they say together.

Blythe.

"Meg was always in a lousy mood after Blythe was there."

"She come to the store much?"

"Well, until about two weeks ago she came in every Wednesday."

"Always on Wednesday?"

"Yeah."

The day after the boxes disappeared.

"What happened two weeks ago?" I ask.

"There was a fight," Julie says.

"Where?"

"Right there. In front of the store." She points as if I don't know where Meg's store is. "It was weird because like all the store owners were on the street, like a convention or something."

"What do you mean?"

"You don't know what a convention is?" Mary Jane asks.

She may drive me to mousse cake. "I know what a convention is," I say patiently. "I want to know what Julie means by that analogy. How many were there?"

"Maybe six, seven."

"Who were they?"

"The usual," Lorry says.

"What's that mean?"

Julie answers, "The regular members of the Merchants Association."

Why hadn't I ever heard Meg talk about this group? "How long ago was this association formed?"

"Two years, maybe."

"Who belonged?"

I write down the list of names and note that Arlene Kornbluth's not among them. "You said there was a fight. What did you mean?"

"Pushing, shoving."

"How long did it go on?"

"I didn't time it," Lorry says.

"Your impression."

"Mmmm. Five minutes, tops. Then they left, except Blythe."

"Then what happened?"

"She and Meg screamed at each other," Julie says. "Couldn't hear what they said but I could tell they were screaming because I could see through the door that their mouths were big and they were sort a' hunched over. I felt embarrassed watching so I looked away. Next thing, Meg comes back in the store and when I look out I see a car pull up and Blythe gets in, drives off. That's it."

That is a lot.

I need to talk to the store owners.

And Blythe.

Why is it that everything seems to come back to Blythe?

Chapter
Twenty

I DECIDE TO START my interviews of the shop owners with Jim Darling of the leather store. He's on the opposite side of Greenwich Avenue from Meg's but I walk down her side to stop in front of her place. The crime-scene tape is up again, the door padlocked. And on the sidewalk, there are additions to the memorials. It's my best guess that they're none of them for Wallace "Fingers" Faye.

I wonder how long these remembrances are going to be placed here. These tributes to Megan have to mean something. Whatever she was doing, whatever she was into, it was only one part of her.

I glance at the signatures on the new cards: Tom and Linda; Paul and Elzbieta; Bill and Valden; Pearl and Joe; Alana, Norman, and Josh; Lita and Ellen; Marsha and Cookie; and Winx. I recognize some of the names. After a while, I cross the street and enter Jim's shop.

It's small, no more than twenty by fifteen, but the space is used efficiently. The leather goods are handmade, although not by Jim. He features black motorcycle jackets decorated with metal studs. There are pants, bags, and more conventional jackets, too. Nothing is specifically for women to wear but I know some do.

Jim is in the store alone, behind the counter. When he sees me he looks as though he can't place me but then, smiling, he does. "Lauren," he says confidently.

"Hi, Jim."

"How're ya doing?"

"Okay. You?"

"Not great. Can't get Sally to stop crying."

"Why try?"

He looks at me as if I've just asked him who's buried in Grant's Tomb. "Well, it's over now."

How can people think that because the deceased is buried, grief should end?

"No, it really isn't, Jim. If nothing else we haven't caught the killer. So that part's not over."

"True." Carefully, he smooths his hand over his awful black toupee.

I point to the motorcycle jackets. "Who buys those?"

"Mostly GOBIs." Pronounced *Go*-bees.

"What are GOBIs?"

"Gay outlaw biker impersonators."

"What's that?"

"You know the Hell's Angels and gangs like that? Well, these gay guys impersonate them. Most of them don't even have bikes. They dress up and go to certain bars. Aside from the jackets the look they're after is pretty seedy and dirty. Turns people on."

"To look at them or to dress that way?"

"Both, I guess."

Sometimes I don't understand gay men at all. I try to think of a comparable lesbian twist and come up empty.

"What's this about somebody else having their ticket punched in Meg's store?" Jim asks this like a tough guy.

"What do you want to know about it?"

"Well, hell, what's going on?"

"A man was found murdered in the basement."

"No kidding?" He raises his delicate eyebrows.

"A small-time thief."

"Grifter?" he asks, inordinately pleased he knows this word. I don't tell him that since the movie everybody knows it.

"Maybe."

"How'd they do him?"

I notice that he uses a plural, but this could mean nothing.

"Shot him."

"So maybe it was the same shooter, then." I don't bother telling him that ballistics has said the bullets have come from two different guns.

And I'm tired of this pitiful presentation of movie dialogue. "You know Meg long?" I ask, suddenly switching subjects to throw him off guard.

"Five years, about. Since I started the store."

"Were you in on the deal?"

He blinks once, which could mean anything. "Deal?"

"The scam."

"Scam?" he asks, as if he's never heard the word before.

"Look, Jim, if you know anything it'd be smart to tell me."

"I don't know anything," he says quickly, takes out a rag and some Windex, and begins cleaning the countertop as though the thing is filthy.

"Maybe Sally knows?"

"Sally?" He stops wiping. "Why would Sally know?"

"I gather she was a buddy of Meg's." How come, I wonder, if these people were such good friends, I never heard anything about them? How can I ask myself this? I continue to deny the evidence.

"Well, yeah, they were like pretty close, I guess."

"Closer than you and Meg?"

"Different." He won't look at me now. Then it dawns on me. Maybe he's Topic A, Meg's secret lover.

"You having an affair with Meg?"

"Je-sus," he says, beads of sweat dotting his forehead like tiny blisters. "It was a long time ago. Sally never knew."

And neither did I, I think. "When exactly was it?"

"About two and a half years ago. It only lasted a few months."

"How many?"

"Nine."

"That's long. Pillow talk?"

"I don't get you."

"Surely, Meg told you what was going on in her life when you were sleeping with her."

"You know," he says, crossing his arms over his scrawny chest. "Funny thing about Meg was I couldn't ever get her to talk about herself. She asked plenty of questions but she wouldn't answer any."

"And how was she with Sally?"

"Same. Kept it zipped up, so to speak. But she was always real interested in the other guy."

But I was different. She told me . . . nothing.

"You belong to the Merchants Association?"

"Right."

"What were you fighting about a few weeks ago?"

"Fighting about?"

"In front of Meg's store."

"I don't know what you mean."

He's lying but he's not going to tell me anything.

"Ever see any odd types going into her store?"

"Lauren, that's *all* we see around here."

"I mean toughs, gangster types."

He looks up at the ceiling as if he'll find the answer there, then back at me. "No, I don't think so. Naturally, I didn't see every person who went into her store."

"Naturally." I hand him my card. "You think of anything, anything at all, even if it seems unimportant, call me, okay?"

"If it's unimportant how will I know I should call you?"

"Just anything to do with Meg you haven't told me."

"Sure."

Arlene Kornbluth's, Cicero's Boutique, is my next stop. She's sitting behind her counter on a tall stool. When she sees me through the glass her face reflects recognition and she buzzes me in.

Cicero's is your typical Village boutique. The clothes are less dramatic, less bizarre than those in SoHo stores. Still, they're designed for the young and for people who regularly wear size 1. On a hanger, facing front, there's a black dress shaped as if someone is already inside. It's the size of my underpants. Maybe a little bigger but it seems impossible that any adult could fit into this garment.

"Do people actually buy dresses that size?"

Arlene looks to where I'm pointing, then back to me as if I've asked her if UFOs land in the store.

"Why would I carry it if no one bought it?"

She has a point. The store's decorated with posters of Italy showing the ruins. Dressing rooms are fashioned out of fake rock, their corners Roman pillars.

"Why Cicero's?" I ask.

"You mean why'd I pick the name? The truth is I had a cat called Cicero so I named it after him. He's dead now. It also gave me inspiration for decor."

We talk about Wallace "Fingers" Faye's murder. Arlene tells me she didn't know him or any of the other creeps: Pesh, Malcolm, Margolis. Then I get to why I've come.

"Arlene, about two weeks ago there was some kind of disagreement on the street in front of Meg's that involved a bunch of the store owners. You know anything about that?"

"I wasn't here that day."

"But you know about it?"

"Only that it happened. Nobody would tell me what went on. Matter of fact, we all used to be pretty close on this block until maybe two years ago, then, I don't know what happened, it was like suddenly I was poison."

"Meaning?"

Arlene twists some fingers through her springy curls. "I just wasn't one of the group anymore. Sometimes I'd walk into the Egg's Nest, the luncheonette on the corner, and two or three of them'd be in there, and when they saw me they'd shut up real fast, like they had a secret. I guess maybe they did, huh?"

"Was Meg one of those people?"

"Sometimes. She was totally different with me when we were alone, that's why I cared for her. But when she was with those others, I don't know." She shakes her head.

"Did you ever ask her why she was that way when she was with the others?"

"No, because they'd formed an association. A merchants' association and they didn't invite me to join."

"Who was this group composed of?"

"Let's see. Jim and Sally Darling of the leather store; Jed Langevin, boots; Peter Wood and Paul Steele, pet shop; and . . ."

"Peter and Paul?" I say skeptically.

"Yeah, and Wood and Steele too. Truth is stranger than fiction. Anyway, the other one is Winston Daignault, better known as Winx, pottery. That was the whole group, I think."

These are the same names I got earlier.

"Yeah, I'm pretty sure no one else was involved."

"Involved? That sounds like you don't believe it was really a merchants' association."

"I had my doubts. I mean, why wouldn't they ask me to join if that's what they really were? They're all nice people . . . except Langevin. Racist," she hisses.

"I've had the pleasure," I say.

My sarcasm isn't lost on Arlene. "Isn't he the worst? See, that was part of what confused me. I mean, that Meg would be mixed up in something that included Langevin. Even a merchants' association."

"Especially when it didn't include you?"

"Well, yes."

"You were hurt by Meg, weren't you?" And, I think, were the only one who saw the shooter.

She looks down, mechanically moves a wedding band up and down her finger, shrugs. "I guess."

"You take drugs?"

Arlene's head snaps up like a rubber ball against a paddle. "No. Never."

"I'm not interested in turning you in or anything, please believe me."

"That's not it. I don't take drugs, is all."

"Okay. How about the others you named?"

"Let me think. Peter and Paul might. Pot, maybe. Langevin's a drinker. The Darlings? Don't think so. Winx? Could be."

"And Meg?"

Arlene's gaze darts around the room like a trapped animal, ricocheting from one place to another. It feels like she'll never look at me again.

"I know Meg did coke now and then," I say.

Now she looks at me. "Yeah, she did. But it wasn't a problem, know what I mean? Hey, you think they were into drugs, that group?"

"Maybe."

"Like how? Dealing?"

"Don't know."

"I find that hard to believe," Arlene says. "Dealing coke? It doesn't feel right."

"It doesn't to me either. But I base this only on Meg. I can't believe she'd do something so disgusting." I realize how specious this thinking is after all I've learned about my old friend. Still, dealing drugs is a whole other category and even as I think this I have to wonder what in hell else it could be. There is still the mystery of the empty boxes, the murder of Fingers in Meg's store.

"You must've wondered what they were into, that bunch."

"Jane and I speculated on it all the time."

"And what did you come up with?"

"Oh, shit," Arlene says, and raises her arms as if I'm pointing a gun at her, drops them back in her lap like heavy things she lacks control over. A giant gesture of futility. "Drugs."

"It kept coming back to that?"

"Yeah. What else could it be, you know what I mean? Let's face it, Lauren, when people get secretive these days it's usually about drugs, isn't it?"

I don't say anything.

"I mean, they weren't running an illegal baby-selling thing or making counterfeit money or running guns to Saddam, were they?"

"These are the things you and Jane thought of?"

"They crossed our minds but they didn't fly."

"I can understand why they wouldn't. On the other hand, counterfeit money isn't too off the wall."

"Yeah, but how would these people come across anything like that?"

"Same way they came across whatever it really was: someone approached them, or one of them, and then that person approached the others."

"You mean, maybe they were asked to pass counterfeit money, as in giving change?"

It's hard for me to believe too and I say that to Arlene. "Even if they'd all agree to it I don't think it would be such a great outlet for counterfeiters. If you were going to give counterfeit change, how much do you think that'd amount to in a day?"

"Negligible. Most people use credit cards."

"Exactly." I wish I could tell Arlene about the boxes in Meg's cellar, but I can't because I haven't ruled this woman out, suspectwise. She was hurt by Meg and she was kept out of a group that called itself the Merchants Association. And since she's a merchant she could easily translate that into an exclusive club. Arlene had a motive and an opportunity. Did she have the means?

"You have a permit for your gun?" I ask.

"Gun?"

"Don't all you store owners keep a gun under the counter?"

"No. Not me, anyway."

I'm sure Cecchi has looked into this and Arlene is telling the truth. So no means. And her motive is flimsy, I have to admit. Opportunity is the only thing that's strong. She claims to have heard a shot, seen a white man running away from Meg's shop, then discovered the body. But it didn't have to have happened that way. She could as easily have shot Meg, called for help, and then made up her story. Why don't I believe this? Not because Arlene Kornbluth doesn't have a perfect MOM, or doesn't look like a killer, whatever that means, but because I'm convinced Meg's murder is connected to whatever that group of store owners was involved in.

I have to talk to Peter and Paul and this Winx person. I

know the police have questioned them all but it doesn't matter. When they interrogated them they didn't know about the boxes in Meg's basement, and Fingers Faye was still alive and kicking. Not to mention the other two dead guys.

"One more thing, Arlene. The day the big argument took place on the street, the day you weren't around, someone said Blythe was there, too. Any thoughts about that?"

"Well, you probably know that Meg and Blythe had a volatile relationship, to say the least. I'm not sure what she'd be doing with that bunch, though."

A volatile relationship. Yes, I knew that once. And now I know about Ray Davies. But for the last few years Meg had said she and Blythe were getting along fine. Big deal. Who cares what Meg had told me? I have to face facts: what Meg said to me and what Meg did could be completely opposite.

"Hadn't the relationship improved over the last few years?"

"Yeah, I guess. A little. Blythe was talking to Meg, anyway. There were a few years in there where there was no communication."

Ludicrously, I feel privileged because this is something I *did* know. I am pathetic. The slightest suggestion of loyalty, intimacy, feeds my need to deny what becomes more obvious each day. I thank Arlene, leave the store, and cross the street to the pet shop called Claw & Paw.

Having no pets, because of Kip's allergies, I've never been in this store, although I've passed it many times. It's not, thank God, the kind of store that carries pets. Except fish, turtles, and obviously snakes, one of which is wrapped around the neck of a man who sits behind the counter.

Snakes are not some of my favorite things. This snake is long and thin, the color of dried leaves. Its eyes are hooded and a hideous dark tongue flicks in and out for no particular reason I can determine.

The man, although seated, is clearly tall. He wears a red Harley-Davidson T-shirt, muscles bulge below the sleeves, and he has a well-developed chest beneath the shirt. I suspect he works out, as everyone in New York City does, except Kip, me, and the homeless. People have personal trainers now with names like Buck, Sly, Del. Even Susan has a trainer of her own, named Todd. It's obvious to me that no trainer can have more than a one-syllable name.

The snake man has short blond hair, a ripoff of the Fade. Why, when racism is so prevalent, do white people want to copy the styles of African-Americans? On the shaved part of his head the initial *P* stands out. This could be either owner.

"Peter?" I ask.

He eyes me as if I'm trying to find out his Social Security number, and *Who wants to know* is implicit.

I answer his unasked question. "I'm Lauren Laurano, private investigator."

"You're kidding," he says.

This is not the first time I've had this response, nor will it be the last, I'm sure. Still, it's annoying and boring to have to tell him that I'm not kidding.

"Got any I.D.?"

I reach in my bag, take out my wallet, show him my license.

He snorts derisively. "I've already told the cops everything I know, which is nothing, about Meg's murder and the guy, what'shisname."

"I'm not the police and I'm not working for them."

"Who you working for?"

"I can't tell you that."

He laughs, showing small uneven teeth. "This is just like TV."

I'm so glad he's enjoying himself. "Want to tell me your name?"

"Not particularly. But I will. I'm Paul Steele. What kind of pet do you have?"

"I don't have a pet."

"Gimme a break," he says. "Everybody's got a pet. Especially lesbians."

How does he know I'm a lesbian? "Well, I don't."

"Never did?"

"My lover's allergic."

"Ah. I knew there had to be a real reason."

"And when we got together, before she knew she was allergic, we swore we wouldn't get a pet."

"Why?"

"Because all lesbians have pets," I say, defeated.

He smiles with the look of someone who needs to be right. "What can I do you?"

I plunge right in. "I want to know about the deal."

I see his eyes flicker like an inferior computer monitor. "What deal?"

"The one you had with Meg and the others?"

"Whoa, dudette," he says, and stands up, the snake writhing round his neck.

"Don't call me dudette," I say.

"Oh, please, what're you, some kind of feminist?"

"Right."

"So you want to be called *dude?*"

"I just want some answers. About two weeks ago you, your partner, Meg, the Darlings, Langevin, Winx, and Blythe had some sort of argument on the street. What was it about?"

His wheels spin. "Don't remember." He and the snake come out from behind the counter.

As I suspected, he's extremely tall and he stands so close to me I'm forced to step backward. The snake is the real offender, although I don't like to be crowded by humans. He gets the picture and moves in on me again, the snake close enough to strike.

Steele smiles. "I forgot to introduce you. This is Bertha."

"Great."

Bertha narrows her eyes and flicks her tongue.

"Know how old she is?"

"I don't care," I say. "I think you do remember that day, Steele, and I want you to tell me what it was about."

As he's about to say something, the door opens and a handsome man comes in. He's shorter than Steele by a few inches, wears a T-shirt that says LIFE IS A BEACH and a pair of worn jeans.

"What's going on?" he asks, alarmed.

It doesn't take much to figure this is Peter Wood. He's as dark as Steele is fair, his hair identical to his partner's, *P* and all.

"*Nada*," Steele says. "Just introducing Bertha to this dick here."

Wood's mouth drops open — he misunderstands his partner's use of the word *dick*. "Paul," he says, reproachfully.

Steele laughs. It sounds like a plunger in a toilet. "Private eye."

Wood is frightened. Twitches break out across his face like acne. I seize the moment, ask him about that day in front of Meg's.

His gaze flits between me and Steele and back. Suddenly tears well up in his perfect blue eyes and his face folds in on itself like a magazine left in the rain.

"Peter," Steele says sternly.

Wood brings his hands up to his face, covers it, but the sound he makes lets me know he's crying.

"Shit," Steele says. "Stop being such a pussy."

"I canhepit" come the muffled words.

My detective's heart gives a joyous thump. At last, I think, a break.

Chapter
Twenty-one

PAUL GRABS PETER by the shoulders. "Will you pull yourself together, for God's sake."

"Why don't you let him talk?" I say.

"Why don't you fuck off?" comes Paul's answer. When he turns to look at me his eyes flash hatred like two hornets on a mission.

"What are you afraid of?"

"I think you better leave."

Peter continues to cry as Paul leads him to the chair behind the counter.

Paul says, "Are you so damn insensitive you can't see what's happening here? God, I hate dykes."

This last remark cuts me deeply, though it comes as no surprise. There are loads of gay men who hate lesbians, and vice versa. Still, it's always a shock, like one African-American calling another *nigger*.

Peter wipes his eyes, calms down. "I'm all right now, Paul."

Paul pats him roughly, then faces me. "You still here?"

"Still here," I say jauntily, as if I'm the last guest at a party.

"You're a real ball-breaker, aren't you?"

"Only if there are any balls around to break," I state.

"Huh?"

I ignore him, move to the side so I can see Peter better. "Why did you cry?"

He glances at Paul, presses his lips together.

Steele says, "Shut up, Peter."

"This is stupid. You're not going to get away with it so why not tell me?" To Peter I say, "I know about the fight you all had a few weeks ago in front of Meg's store."

He looks frightened but says nothing.

"I want you out of my store," Steele says.

"What are you afraid of?" I ask again.

"Nothing. I just don't like your face."

"You just don't like women," I say.

"Only if there are any women around not to like," he mimics, smiling.

"Where do you keep your gun?" I ask Peter.

He glances at a place behind the counter, quickly looks away.

"We don't have a gun," Steele says. "Are you going to leave, or not?"

"What if I told you I know about the scam, Peter?" I venture.

"Paul, please," he begs.

"Shut the fuck up, Peter. I told you before: scam, deal, shmeel . . . I don't know what you're talking about."

"We didn't kill Meg," Peter wails. "We loved her."

"I find that hard to believe," I say to Steele. "You loved Meg?"

"She was okay," he says grudgingly.

"Well, *I* loved her. She was like a mother to me," Peter says. "That's why I was crying. I can't get over her being dead."

I detect a look of relief in Steele's brown eyes. "Yeah, that's why he lost it. Petey was very attached to Meg."

"Why was Blythe at the meeting?"

"She wasn't," Peter says.

Paul wheels on him. "Shut up."

"Oh, what's the big deal, Paul? So we had a Merchants Association meeting, is that a crime now?"

"Yeah, that a crime?" Steele asks me, going on the offensive.

"Do you usually have your meetings on the street?"

"It wasn't on the street. We had it at Meg's."

"You were seen arguing on the street."

"Oh, well, that," Peter says. "That was after the meeting, when we were leaving."

"And what happened?"

"I don't know who told you what, but that was just an argument between Meg and Blythe. I mean, we were all still there but it had nothing to do with us."

"That's right," Steele adds.

This is bullshit. But I pretend to believe them. "What were they arguing about?"

Peter warms to the subject. "Well, they had problems. The usual mother-daughter stuff. Blythe accused Meg of trying to run her life and Meg denied it, that kind of thing."

"And you all got into it, is that what you're saying?" I ask spuriously.

"Yeah, that's what we're saying," Steele affirms.

It's pointless to go on with these two because I'm never going to get the truth.

Suddenly Peter says, "Do you think we're all in danger?"

Steele gives his partner a hard look.

"Why would you be in danger?"

"I don't know," he backs down. "It was just a thought."

"A stupid thought as usual," Steele says.

I want to say something about Steele's abusive behavior toward his lover but I don't. It would only muddy the waters at this juncture.

I say to Peter, "Unless you think someone's after the members of the Merchants Association, you're probably safe. By the way, why wasn't every store owner a member?"

Peter looks blank.

Steele says, "Everybody who wanted to be was."

"What about Arlene Kornbluth?"

"We asked her to join. She didn't want to."

I know this is a lie. "Thanks for your help," I say facetiously.

Steele wraps Bertha around his neck like a stole. "You're

extremely welcome," he says, echoing my tone. "Want to say bye-bye to Bertha?"

Bertha growls. Okay, so it's not a growl. But it seems like one. I leave my card on the counter and say the usual bit about if they should remember anything, et cetera, et cetera.

The weather has taken a turn and it looks like rain. I debate the merits of going home for an umbrella now, or interviewing Winx first, umbrella later. I check the time and decide umbrella now. Kip has a two-hour break and I think we should spend it together. Besides, I'm still harboring the shadowy feeling of being abandoned. I *know* Kip's not going anywhere but there's leaving and leaving. One thing I do know is never take anything for granted. Or as Kip and I say to each other: "Don't take me for granite!"

Kip's lying on the bed reading bound galleys of Jane Smiley's new novel. The generous Js often give them to us. We love the feeling of being the first on our block.

"What are you doing here?" she asks.

"I wanted to see you."

She pats the bed next to her. "See me? You forgot what I look like?"

"Don't make fun," I say and curl up next to her.

She puts down the galleys. "Sorry. C'mere."

I wriggle underneath the arm she offers, put my head on her breast, which she adjusts. "I know they're small but they still need pampering."

"Who says they're small?"

"I sez."

"What d'you know?"

"You mean . . . they're *not* small? I must've been insane all these years, deluded."

"I haven't wanted to tell you."

"Why not? A breast is a terrible thing to waste!"

We laugh.

"I didn't think I ever wasted it," I say lasciviously, and reach out and touch one.

"Mmmm."

"Is that a go?" I ask.

"Yeah," Kip says, voice husky. "I think it is."

Slowly we undress each other. Then, teasing, I caress her, and like a skier, trail my hand over the slopes and vales of her body. She does the same to me. We massage, tickle, stroke, our fingers dancing fools. At last our mouths meander and our tongues survey the sites, like architects of love.

We lie tangled and sweaty in each other's arms and Kip says, "Darling? What are you thinking about?"

How can you tell your lover, after a sensational sexual experience, that you're thinking about the chocolate peanut butter pie at the Egg's Nest? I'm always hungry afterward. Let's face it, I'm always hungry. But especially after making love. To lie or not to lie?

I fudge it, so to speak, and kiss her.

She says, "Mudcake or mousse?"

Sometimes I wonder which of us is the detective.

"I have a gorgeous salad downstairs. Sound good?"

"Mmmm. Yum."

"Thought you'd go for it. C'mon, let's eat and you can tell me where things are with the case."

Before rising we kiss again and almost don't get up. But the truth is, after twelve years, no matter how much we might feel aroused, we both know we're not going to do it twice. This is reality.

We break apart, dress, and go down to the kitchen for rabbit food.

The pottery in Winx's store is like no other I've ever seen. It's whimsical and engaging: teapots tipped as though they're drunk; fat butter dishes in wonderful colors; unorthodox cups curved crazily. And then there are the sculptures. They're the best. Eccentric, fanciful, funny.

This store is not strange to me. I've been drawn to its windows many times, lured inside by the merchandise, and have bought many things. But I don't know Winx Daignault personally and he can't possibly remember me among thousands of people who go in and out of his shop.

Winx is a medium-sized man the color of espresso, with dark eyes, a wide nose, sensuous lips. He wears a bright red short-sleeved shirt and crisp, ironed jeans, his silver belt buckle large and ornate.

"Good afternoon," he greets me with his Jamaican lilt. "How are you today and may I help you?"

I tell him who I am, show my I.D.

"Ah. Megan. Yes. We shall all miss her very much. She was a good neighbor, a good friend." His eyes glisten with a sheen of tears; he blinks them away. "She spoke of you often, Lauren. Do you mind if I call you Lauren? You must call me Winx."

I nod, surprised that this man's heard of me from Meg. "What did she say about me?" I ask, unable to control my curiosity.

"Oh, she cared for you very much, Lauren. I believe she said you were her best friend and that you had known each other almost all your lives."

But what did she say ABOUT me? I want to ask.

As if Winx senses this, he adds, "Megan said you were the most honorable person she knew ever." A look of panic skims his eyes, as if he's afraid he's said too much, then quickly he smiles.

The scenario I write, based on his statement and expression, is that Meg was doing something illegal with Winx and mentioned that if her best friend knew about it she'd be horrified because "she's the most honorable person I know."

"You mean, she was scared I'd find out what was going on?" I venture, trying to catch him off guard.

"Going on?"

"Were you a member of the Merchants Association?"

"Of course," he answers smoothly.

He's a cool one. Still, I feel the possibility I might learn something from him, so I lay out everything I know as honestly as I can.

"Megan was correct," he says. "You *are* honorable. I wish I could tell you something, Lauren, but I cannot."

"You mean, you won't."

"There are varieties of fealty," he says enigmatically.

"Meaning you have to be loyal to your friends."

He nods almost imperceptibly, eyes closed in a prolonged blink. The agreement is clear.

"Let me say this, Lauren. Meg's murder is a tragic and evil thing. I hope the perpetrator is found soon. I do not believe he is anyone we know."

"In other words, not a member of the Merchants Association."

"Precisely."

"Therefore, there's no reason to tell me or the cops what you people were doing?"

"Allow me to rephrase. The meetings of the Merchants Association have no bearing on the murder."

Stonewalling. "It's a very elite association, isn't it? I mean, why aren't the Korean grocers on the corner members? Why not the Pakistanis who run the newspaper store?"

"They did not wish to join."

I don't believe this and intend to check it out. "Winx, suppose you're wrong. Suppose one of the Merchants Association *did* kill Meg?"

The corners of his mouth twitch. This obviously hasn't occurred to him. "I thought it was a robber."

"I don't think so. Meg opened the door to this person *after* being held up earlier. If the person were a stranger, doesn't it seem unlikely that Meg would do this, even though she was usually fairly relaxed about whom she let in the store?" I note conflict in his eyes.

"This is a conundrum. Still, why would a friend kill her?"

"You tell me. What was the argument about the day you were all on the sidewalk, the day Blythe was there?"

He gives me the bull about Blythe and Megan, and I realize that Steele has gotten to him.

"Winx, I don't believe that and I'm going to make it my business to find out what that was really about."

"Do you think that wise?"

"What do you mean?"

He laughs uncomfortably, like a stutter. "I only mean, Lauren, that should you be correct, then you are putting yourself in danger."

"Danger is my business," I say, after waiting over a decade to use this line. Unfortunately, it's lost on Winx.

"A nice girl like you should not make it your business. What does the husband think of this profession you have chosen?"

"I have no husband."

"Yet you wear a wedding ring?"

"I'm married to another woman."

"I see. I meet many women in here like you and still I cannot understand."

"What don't you understand?"

For a moment he's perplexed, unsure how to express it. But then he asks the usual question. "What can you do?"

He means sexually. This is what gets men. They believe that without a penis nothing of any importance or satisfaction can take place.

"We can do a great deal," I tell him. But I'm unwilling to go further with this conversation as it's one I've had too often and I'm not interested in educating this man. "Winx, I want you to think carefully about the people in the Merchants Association, what it was you were involved in, and then if something should occur to you, I want you to get in touch with me." I put my card on the counter.

With long brown fingers, he picks it up and slips it in his red silk shirt pocket. "Let me say this, Lauren: Meg was speaking of resigning from the association."

My detective's heart stands up on its back legs. What he's saying is that Meg was trying to pull out of whatever it was they were doing. "And did she also say she might tell outsiders private things about the association?"

"She did not say that. But it occurs to me now that this might have been a thought of someone's."

"Who?"

"This I have no way of knowing."

That's it. That's all I'm going to get from Winx, but it's something. More than I've gotten so far. He's supplied a motive for one of them killing her. I thank him and go for the door. He stops me with a question.

"May I ask something personal, Lauren?"

I think I know what's coming but I tell him he may.

"What is a woman without a man?"

"Look at it this way: what is a muskrat without a telephone?"

When I glance back through the glass door he's standing in the same spot, looking bewildered. Good.

I go into the news and magazine store and check out what the owners know about a merchants' association. As I suspected, no one ever approached them. I don't bother with the grocery people because I know the answer.

It's time to talk turkey to Blythe.

Chapter
Twenty-two

I CAN'T BELIEVE that I forgot my umbrella. After all, that's what I went home for, wasn't it? Who asked you?

The rain catches me as I hit the corner of Greenwich and Sixth avenues. It's that shocking type of rain that starts as though it has been going on for hours and has built to this, often known as a downpour. Within seconds I'm completely soaked. And cold, as I wear very lightweight tan slacks and a cotton shirt.

I have several choices: I can go inside and wait; I can continue to the subway, as the quantity of my wetness doesn't matter . . . drenched is drenched; I can go home; I can buy an umbrella from the man on the corner with hopes that I'll dry off by the time I get uptown; I can perform an exercise in futility and wait for a cab. Home looms large. But the longer the investigation goes on, the less likely it is to be solved.

"How much?" I ask the umbrella seller. It always amazes me how they appear at the first raindrop. Where do they live when the sun shines?

"Ten dollar," he says.

"Ten?" I squawk.

"This one last," he explains.

"But ten is outrageous. I can get one for five anywhere."

He shrugs, as if to say it's my decision, he doesn't care if I get wet or not, or if I want something inferior; he'll sell these. Maybe he will, but ten dollars is ridiculous. On principle (not to mention cheapness), I refuse.

"Good-bye," he says cheerfully.

I don't answer. The light changes and I cross to the east side of Sixth. I notice a new sign in the window of Gray's Papaya: "Back by Popular Demand, 50-Cent Hot Dogs." I feel a thrill. The "gorgeous" salad has already faded but I don't have time.

Another umbrella dealer stands in front of Dalton's.

"Five bucks," he tells me before I ask.

That's more like it. I scrounge around in my purse, find a five. He holds out a plastic bag that contains six or seven to choose from. I pick a blue one.

As I open my new umbrella I walk down Sixth. This is your basic no-frills model: the plastic covering, a handle, a metal thing you push to open it, another metal thing it clicks into. Who needs anything more?

The enigma is this: I still get wet. Rain sloshes the front of me, so I tip the umbrella in the direction I think it's coming from. It works. But now the entire back of me gets saturated. I play with the angles and just as I get it right I'm at the subway station.

Halfway down the steps I close the umbrella, hold it out to the side so it doesn't touch my wet clothing. This makes no sense but it's part of umbrella etiquette.

Under the street it's hot, steamy. Wafts of vapor hover around each person like an aura. The platform is crowded, so I assume they've been waiting for a while and that the train will come any minute. But why don't I know better? *A* does not mean *B* in the wonderful world of subways.

I look around at the riders; not a smiling face among them. Even people together don't make each other happy. Everyone looks tortured.

The inevitable amateur musician plays a guitar and sings. His case lies open in front of him, and on the faded green interior, there are a few bills and a collection of coins. This entertainer sounds as though he's hog calling, which is not much worse than others of his profession, who resemble anything from cement mixers to wounded crows.

I try to decipher what he's singing but cannot. It's not that he vocalizes in a foreign language, because I can discern the occasional *the, he, she, I.*

The songster is young, looks well fed, and his clothes, though not stylish, are serviceable. I watch a woman drop some coins into his case. I can only assume that she has hopes that if he gets enough money he'll stop singing. He nods his appreciation to the woman and continues to strum and warble.

It gets on my nerves. I know he doesn't have a permit and consider mentioning this to him. But it'll serve only to create a scene and the train should come any second. *Should* is the operative word here.

He finishes his song. No one claps. There's a blissful moment of subway silence and then he starts again. I hear a train and feel relief that I don't have to stand through another number.

The train pulls in.

On the other side.

Two years later, the one I want arrives. Inside it's hotter and stickier than on the platform, though it's not packed. I get a seat.

It seems like heaven to be squashed between an enormous man and a teenage girl because I don't have to hear the guitarist anymore. I note my pathetic preference.

As soon as the train starts a dark-skinned man comes into my car hawking a newspaper. In the last few years the homeless have been employed to do this. The paper's called the *Subway Times.*

A white woman, of indeterminate age, carries a paper cup and asks for donations, while she tells the story of her life, and works her way toward the news seller.

"I haven't always been on the streets," she says. "Once I was an account executive for a top advertising company."

This is hard to believe but I suppose it's possible. I've noticed that this kind of identification (presidents of corporations; college professors; bankers) has become the norm in the last year, and suspect it's to make us, who have jobs, think it could happen to anyone. And I guess it could, though I can't see how it could happen to me. Am I a dupe in detective's clothing?

The two indigents meet in the center of the car, give each other filthy competitive looks, and move on. I know that some homeless in New York are not really homeless but most are legitimate. I cannot give to everyone; I do give to some. Sometimes it makes me feel like a Roman emperor, deciding who will live or die, and I don't like this sense of power, but can't come up with a different procedure. I carry small Baggies of change in my pockets. It's hardest for me to pass up women. I drop a Baggie in the cup of the ex–account executive, but don't buy a paper because I already have this issue.

When they've gone to other cars it's relatively quiet until the next stop, where another beggar boards. It's endless. In a country where your president would rather play war than face poverty there's little hope for these people.

The conductor speaks over the intercom. It might as well be in another language because the combination of equipment and enunciation makes it impossible to understand. I know the announcement is of the upcoming station and what train to take to go somewhere, but that's because I'm a New Yorker. I wonder what tourists make of this.

At the next stop the fat man next to me leaves, and two women and a child take his place.

It is the twenty-first century when I arrive at my destination. I step from the car and the usual smells of body odor and urine, combined today with wet dog, momentarily stagger me.

As I ascend the stairs I feel a hand on my bottom. I whirl around. Behind me is a well-dressed man, who looks at me as though he's annoyed by my halting the succession of climbers. I look directly in his eyes.

"What?" he says to me.

"Don't do that again."

"Do what?"

"Touch me."

"You kidding?" he says, as if I'm unworthy of his fondling. In back of him, others are yelling.

There's always the possibility that it was an accident, but even so I give the man another one of my best watch-it looks, turn away, and continue upward. A moment later he does it again. There can be no mistaking it this time because he takes hold of one cheek and squeezes. I spin around.

"Listen, creep," I say, "you want to be arrested?"

He blinks innocent gray eyes. "Lady, I don't know what you're talking about," he says facilely.

People come down the other staircase and look at us as the crowd behind the perp begins to sound like angry geese. It's too difficult to get out my I.D. so I color the truth.

"I'm a law officer. Once more and you've had it."

"Why don't you just keep going," he says, anger covering embarrassment, "and we'll all be a lot happier."

"Move it," someone shouts.

"Yeah, les go."

"I gonna miss my twain."

This time he doesn't do anything. At the top of the stairs, as he's about to go one way, and I another, he taps me on the shoulder.

"You have a nice ass," he says nonchalantly, and scurries away.

Why does this astonish me? Is it because people are getting more and more brazen, as though they have the right to do anything they feel like to anyone? There's nothing to do with my outrage, the man's gone, so I do what millions of women before me have done: I swallow it.

When I reach the street it's still pouring. I open my new umbrella and immediately it's turned inside out by a strong gust of wind. I'm so glad the ten-dollar vendor is not nearby to see this. I can't quite accept this fate so continue to get wetter while I try to make the damn thing work, but it's been rendered useless. I throw it in an orange sanitation basket, which already houses four other dead umbrellas, and slosh as quickly as possible toward Fifth Avenue.

The offices of Nichols & Thompson are on the fourteenth floor of a new building. In the elevator, as water collects on the beige carpet around my soaked sneakers, people treat me as if I'm contagious. My hair is plastered to my ears, cheeks, neck, and my clothes cling obscenely.

When I exit I imagine I hear a huge sigh of relief as though the passengers have escaped something nasty. I make a squashy sound and trail water like Gretel in the forest as I follow the sign that points the way to Blythe's company.

Two huge glass doors with glass handles trumpet the entrance to Nichols & Thompson. I try to open one but it doesn't move. Inside, a woman behind a white desk is talking on the phone and not looking my way.

The door handles are backed by brass plates and on one there's a button.

I push.

The woman looks up.

And does nothing.

She stares at me and I realize it's my soaked condition that causes her to be apprehensive. She says something into the receiver, returns it to its cradle.

The woman, who's in her late fifties, early sixties, pats her dyed brown hair at the sides. She comes from behind the desk. Her flowered dress covers a lumpy body, as if she's stuffed with eggplants.

At the glass door, frightened, she says: "What do you want?"

I can't hear her words but I can read her lips.

I mouth my reply. "I'm here to see Blythe Benning." And I know what she'll say next.

"Have you an appointment?"

I'm right. "Yes," I lie.

"What's your name?"

I tell her.

She pauses, trying to recall if the name's in her book. Although I look horrible, I suppose she decides I don't appear dangerous, so she opens the door.

Her nostrils flare and I wonder if I smell. I follow her to the desk, where she checks her book, looks up at me without raising her head. "You lied."

"Yes," I say. "But Blythe will see me." I glance at her nameplate: Deanna Rosner. "Ms. Rosner, just buzz her, please."

"How could you've lied to me?" she asks, sincerely shocked.

"Could you please buzz her?"

She sits with a thump as if someone's pushed her. "What's happening here?" she asks rhetorically. "Once it was a world where a person could trust; where a person wasn't afraid all the time; where a person could take her tired, her poor, and believe; where a person . . ."

"Ms. Rosner?"

". . . could watch the antelopes play. Where a person could be deep in the heart of Texas. Where . . ."

"Deanna?"

"Yes?"

"Lovely name," I say.

"Named after Deanna Durbin, but you wouldn't remember her. You see, this is what I mean."

"I do remember her."

"Really?"

"I've seen her in old movies." She sang and was a simp.

"My mother loved her," she says, voice cracking. "In fact, I think my mother loved her more than she loved me." Her face curls from happy reverie to snarling reality. "I mean, what the hell did she think, just because she named me Deanna I'd be able to sing? Crazy bitch."

I don't know what to say to this and fear Deanna Rosner is about to go into a rant so I remind her again of Blythe.

She squints at me. "You Eyetalian?"

I nod. Wait.

"You should be ashamed," she says.

This one I'm not prepared for and I try not to lose my grip. "Of what?"

"All the people you kill, the drugs, the whole nine yards."

"Ms. Rosner, I'm not a member of the Mafia, nor is anyone in my family. Nor are most Italians."

"Yeah? What about Al Pacino?"

"Pacino's an actor."

"And De Niro? You going to tell me he's an actor, too?"
The woman's mad. "No," I say slowly, "De Niro's Mafia."

"That's what I mean."

"Right. Could you please buzz Ms. Benning now?"

She does. "She'll see you in a minute," she says, sounding surprised.

I thank her and walk across the room to stare at an ugly painting so that Rosner won't engage me in any more conversation. I don't sit on the gray upholstered banquette because of my soggy condition.

"Ms. Laurano?"

I turn to see a young woman in a black leather skirt the size of a quilt patch, a white silk blouse, and very high heels of the sort we all thought would never come back.

"I'm Ms. Benning's secretary, Ellen Holland. Would you follow me, please?"

Ellen Holland is trying hard to pretend that I look like a dry person but she doesn't quite succeed; there are little twitches in her cheeks like blips on a heart monitor.

As we pass Deanna Rosner's desk she says, sotto voce: "And Marlon Brando. What about him, huh?"

"Not Italian," I say over my shoulder.

Ms. Holland appears not to hear us and I follow her through a door and down a corridor, left, right, left again, and then she stops.

"Ms. Benning's in here." She knocks once and opens the door. "Ms. Laurano," she announces.

I go in. It's a nice office but small. The furniture is functional. There's no window. It's clear to me that Blythe doesn't have a high-paying job, and again I wonder how she manages to live the way she does.

"You look lovely," Blythe says.

"Thanks. It's all the rage."

"I would've thought it was all the rain." She smiles falsely. "Not bad."

"Why didn't you let me know you were coming?"

"So you could've baked a cake?"

"Huh?"

"Nothing." Deanna Rosner would've gotten it.

"I'd ask you to sit but I don't have a surfboard."

"But you do have a chair." I sit.

"Hey!"

"It's only water. It'll dry."

Blythe is wearing an expensive gray-striped power suit, yellow silk blouse. "Can I ask why you didn't use an umbrella?"

"No. Can I ask where you get your money?"

She takes a cigarette from a silver box, taps it on the desk, sticks it in her mouth, and lights it with a silver Dunhill. "What's that supposed to mean?"

"What part of the sentence didn't you understand?"

She blows smoke streams from her nostrils. "I work for a living in case you haven't noticed."

"And you make about what, twenty-five, thirty thousand?"

She doesn't answer but her cheeks redden like wine stains on a white tablecloth.

"Somehow that doesn't add up. I mean, your apartment, your clothes, jewelry, and . . ."

"So I manage my money well. Is that a criminal offense?" Innocent as William Kennedy Smith.

Then to get her off balance I throw one in from left field: "How could you have had an affair with Ray Davies?"

Her eyes flash fury. "Why don't you just get out of here, Lauren?"

"He was married to your mother."

"And half her age," she spits out.

"Not quite."

The look in her eyes changes from anger to anguish. "I thought he loved me," she says simply.

I feel a momentary pang of compassion as I imagine the child flattered by the older man's attention; perhaps needing love, love her mother didn't provide. I'd always thought Meg was great with her kids, but maybe that was another fantasy of mine; maybe I chose to see Meg through a prism of my making: the perfect mother.

"I'm sure it wasn't your fault, Blythe."

"There was no fault involved. I wanted him and made it clear. God knows my mother didn't love *him.* Sometimes I wonder if she loved anyone."

"She loved you and Sasha," I say ingenuously.

Blythe smiles crookedly and I recall that expression on the five-year-old; realize now that it was far too sophisticated for a child and not cute.

"Don't you think Meg loved you?"

"No. Well, that's not fair. I suppose she loved us as much as she could love anyone."

What does this mean? I'd always thought Meg *loved* me.

As if reading my mind, Blythe says, "You, too. She loved you as much as she knew how. I understand her limitations now, but as a kid, well, you don't grasp those subtleties. You're just a big blob of need and either it's filled or it isn't."

"And you're saying that Meg didn't fill your needs?"

"Yeah, Lauren, that's what I'm saying."

I feel cold suddenly, frightened. I'm afraid to ask my next question but I force myself. "She, she didn't abuse you, did she?"

"No."

Guilt pervades me for having asked. "So what did she do, then?"

"She didn't *do* anything, that's the point. She wasn't there even when she was there, if you know what I mean."

I do. Pictures of Meg and the kids flutter behind my eyes like a shuffling deck of cards. I see her feeding, bathing, dressing, playing with them. So why don't I see her kissing and hugging them? This is crazy. Of course she was affectionate with them. Wasn't she?

"She was always more interested in us when people were around. But when it was the three of us she was cold, Lauren. That's the only way I know how to put it."

"She had to make a living to support you. She was working her tail off during those years."

"I know," Blythe says simply. To her Meg's work was no excuse for what she perceived as lack of interest.

"Wasn't there anything you loved about her?" I ask dismally.

Blythe gives a mirthless laugh. "You don't understand. I loved *everything* about her. So did Sasha. We just couldn't get her attention."

"So you got it by sleeping with her husband."

"Yes."

"And Sasha got her attention by becoming an addict."

"Yes."

"Negative attention."

"Better than nothing," Blythe says sadly, stubs out her cigarette.

"Meg was having an affair at the time of her death."

"How very unusual for her."

"Who was he?"

"You probably won't believe this, but I don't know. She kept him . . . hidden."

"Hidden?"

"Well, at least from me. Maybe she was afraid history might repeat itself." She laughs. "No, that doesn't make sense. I've met others. Unless this was a young one like Ray was."

"You had a party and Meg came with a date."

"No, she didn't. I distinctly remember her coming alone."

"Then she met someone there, someone she liked, spent a lot of time with at the party?"

"Could be. I wasn't watching her every minute, Lauren."

I abruptly switch my line of questioning. "Who was the man who brought you home the night Meg was murdered?"

"Who said it was a man?" She gives me a look as though she's bested me.

"So who was it?"

"I can't think of one reason on earth why I should tell you.

You know where I was when Mother was murdered so why should it matter who I was with later?"

"If it doesn't matter, why won't you tell me?"

"I can't see getting an innocent person involved."

"I'm not going to involve . . . her."

"Good. Can we drop it now?"

I don't know why, but I don't believe she's protecting a woman friend. I'm almost positive she was with a man. So why is she lying? Even if she wants to protect a man, why? Has Blythe continued the pattern of dating married men?

"Is he married?" I ask.

"Who?"

"The man you were with that night."

She laughs. "You're relentless and ridiculous. I was with a woman friend and if I had to prove it in a court of law, I could. But I don't. So get off this or get out."

She's right, she doesn't have to answer. I don't want to leave before I ask the most important question, so I relinquish the subject of the mysterious person and throw her what I hope will be the proverbial curve. "Why was Meg giving you money?"

"Because I wanted it."

My detective's heart does a figure eight. "That's it? You wanted it so she gave it to you?"

"She'd sort of changed. I guess she realized she'd been an absentee parent, after all."

"Where was she getting the money to give you?"

Blythe shrugs.

"Didn't you know her business was in trouble?"

"Not my affair," she says, inculpable.

"But you knew?"

"I suspected. So what?"

"Well, where the hell did you think she was getting the money she gave you?"

"Lauren, I didn't care where she got it as long as she gave it to me."

"Did it ever occur to you that she might be doing something illegal?"

"Yes."

"And that didn't matter to you?"

"No."

I'd like to smack her. Instead, as calmly as possible, I ask her about the fight on the street weeks before.

"She was having one of her dumb Merchants Association meetings and I needed some cash. I saw a fab jacket I wanted," she says defiantly. "After the others were gone, Mother said she wasn't giving me any more money. So we argued."

"Did she say why?"

"Not really. She just said she couldn't continue giving it to me. She didn't have it."

"And then what?"

"And then I slapped her across the face and left. It was the last time I saw her."

Chapter
Twenty-three

I'M ON THE STREET AGAIN but at least it's stopped raining. And what have I learned from my trouble? Not much. I've confirmed that it's almost certain Meg was into something illegal, probably so she could bribe love from her children. Did she also give Sasha money, knowing he'd use it for drugs? This is extremely hard to believe, yet things are becoming easier to accept as I learn more ... more than I want to know, as a friend, not as a detective. Perhaps Sasha knows where Meg was getting the money.

The thought of going to his apartment isn't appealing; nevertheless it seems in order. No longer as wet as I was, I still look like undried laundry. Back to the subway.

This time I'm lucky and catch a train straightaway. It's stuffed with passengers in various stages of drying. Idly, I wonder if the motorman is drunk or on crack. Since the crash in August that killed three, I board trains with more trepidation than in the past.

A man, wearing weary pants that almost cover his scuffed shoes, a big dirty jacket over a filthy T-shirt, enters from the car in front of this one. He sports a ragged beard and shakes himself like a dog trying to rid himself of fleas. I immediately smell him: urine and booze, a common combination.

My luck holds as he stops directly in front of me, grabs the overhead bar with one hand, and looks down, red-rimmed eyes crazed, particles of food like tiny tree ornaments hanging from his beard.

"So are they hiring in this dump, or what?" he shouts at me.

Hiring? I don't answer.

"Hey, they fucking hiring, or not?" He bends down and his breath hits me like a fume from hell.

The question is always the same: do I answer so that he will go away, or not answer with the same hope? And if I do answer, will it accomplish my goal or encourage? But I don't like the inherent violence I see in those too-bright blue eyes, the forced intimacy of this situation.

"Yes," I say. "They're hiring. Get off at the next station."

But he's not fooled by my obvious ploy and bends even closer, holding the bar with the tips of his fingers, unsteady on his feet. I fear he'll fall on me.

"You think I'm some sort of asshole, or what?"

Answering *or what* in this situation doesn't seem the smart thing to do. I continue to bluff. "I heard they were hiring at the next stop," I say.

"Gorbachev told you, or who?"

I nod.

"Yeah?"

The train slows and pulls into Eighty-sixth Street. He peers past me through the window.

"Thanks for the tip," he says, and surprises me by getting off.

As the doors close I feel my body sag and realize how stiffly I've been holding myself.

When I reach my destination I feel better. Until I step out onto the street at 104th. Though the area feels somewhat less threatening in the daytime, there's still the undercurrent of disorder, chaos, and congenital crime, due mainly to poverty. Most faces here are dark-skinned and I stand out like a plastic cup among china. I purposely don't meet the eyes of passersby, but still keep aware, my hand in my purse on the butt of my gun.

Sasha's stoop is empty this time. Inside, breathing through my mouth, I climb the ten flights and, panting, make my way to his door.

Throughout the building, noise reverberates like sound bites gone amok. I put my ear to the door but it's hard to hear the inside life of Sasha's place. I knock feverishly as though my insistence will force him to appear.

But it doesn't. It's hard for me to accept that I've come all this way for nothing and I can't make myself leave. Across from Sasha's, the apartment door opens and a dark woman, wearing a brightly colored dress and matching head scarf, looks over her shoulder at me as she locks and double locks. When she's finished she faces me.

"What you want?" She's suspicious, angry.

"I want to see the man who lives here, Sasha Benning."

"What for?"

It seems an impertinent question but perhaps these tenants all protect each other.

"I'm a friend."

"His mamma jus' die. That boy take it hard."

"I know," I say.

"He out of it," she says.

"On coke?"

She looks at me skeptically, then a cynical smile twists her lips. "It make a difference what he on?"

I see the wisdom in her question. "No."

She nods for punctuation.

Then I hear the undoing of locks behind me and turn to see Sasha's door opened about two inches, a chain still in place. It's because of the purple flash that I discern it's Tamari.

"What d'ya want?" she asks in a husky voice.

"I want to see Sasha. It's Lauren Laurano. We met."

She shuts the door before I think to put my foot in the open space. I assume the best: she's asking him.

The woman from the other apartment says, "You a dago?"

Why is it all right for her to call me this ethnic slur? It isn't. "I'm Italian," I say.

"You don't seem like a wop. No wop I never knew."

Fury parades in my chest. "How would you like it if I called you a nigger?"

"Don't you?" she asks without artifice.

"No."

We are staring at each other warily when his door is opened again. This time the chain is off and Sasha stands there.

"Sash," I say.

"Come in." He nods to the woman in the hall as she moves past me.

Inside the place is still a shambles, as is Sasha. He seems thinner than at the funeral and the blond hair is separated into oily coils that touch his shoulders. He wears cutoff jeans and an old navy sweatshirt. His feet are bare and dirty.

Tamari sits in the corner on the floor. She wears a soiled sleeveless plaid robe. Lean arms hang at her sides like old soup bones. Her face is expressionless.

"You want to sit?" he asks.

I don't but I do. I pick a wooden chair, something that's less likely to be inhabited.

"Want something to drink?" he asks, like an amnesia victim who vaguely recalls the amenities.

"All I want is to talk, Sash."

He shrugs, sits on the floor looking up at me. Tamari scoots over and joins him. I feel like I'm their guru. *How* stoned are they? Will Sasha understand my questions?

I give it a try. "Did your mother ever give you money?"

He and Tamari look at each other.

"Not really," he answers.

I sigh. What could *not really* possibly mean? "She did or she didn't," I say, and try to keep the impatience out of my voice.

"We were hungry and she didn't exactly give us money. But she took us to a restaurant now and then?"

Tamari says, "Meggy fed us."

I'd forgotten she talked like this. I have to try to not let it get on my nerves. "She never gave you cash, then?"

"No."

"Did you know she gave money to Blythe?"

"She did?"

"Bitchy Blythe," Tamari says.

"Yes. She gave her a lot."

"Who says?"

"Blythe says."

Sasha lights a cigarette.

"Why d'you believe *her?*" asks Tamari.

"For one thing I've seen evidence of it."

"Well . . . ," Sasha says enigmatically.

We look at him.

"She did say she'd give me some 'financial help,' she called it, if I'd go into a rehab, give up coke and stuff."

Tamari says, "How come Sashie never told me?"

He doesn't answer, sucks on his cigarette, blows smoke at the floor.

"She didn't say where she was going to get this 'financial help,' did she, Sash?"

"No." He looks up at me. "She did a funny thing, though."

"What's that?"

"Every so often she'd give me a big jar of tokens."

I immediately recall the half-full jar in Meg's closet.

"How often?" I ask.

"I dunno. Maybe every three or four months. Started a couple years ago."

"Tamari never saw them," she complains.

"Sold 'em," he says. "Guess she didn't realize I could do that. I mean, you know, sell 'em, buy drugs with the money."

But of course Megan *did* know that. How could I have been so stupid? I jump up, thank Sasha, and make a dash for the door.

"Tokens," I say to Cecchi.

"Tokens?"

"I found a jar of tokens in Meg's closet."

"Yeah, I know," he says. "I saw them there."

"So why didn't you mention it?"

"What? Your friend hoarded tokens?"

"She never took the subway."

"That I didn't know."

We sit in Washington Square Park, drink coffee out of paper cups.

"You think it was tokens in the empty cartons?" I ask him.

"I didn't, but I do now," he says.

"So how does Meg fit in?" I want to know. I don't want to know.

"I'm not sure exactly. My guess is, she was a holder. She had deliveries all the time, nobody would notice extra boxes coming in."

"And her employees said she didn't let them open those boxes."

He shoots me a look and I realize I've given away my interrogation of them. "I have a job," I say defensively.

He shrugs. "They told me that, too."

"What's a *holder?*" It seems self-explanatory but I want to make sure.

"Like a fence. But she probably didn't do anything except store the stuff."

I still don't want to believe it. I know *why* she would've done it: to get money for Blythe and Sasha, desperately trying to make up for the past. But what I don't know is *how*. "How would she get involved in something like this? Meg ran a legitimate business. How would those people know to approach her?"

"I don't know exactly but I can guess. She needs money, she tells somebody, that somebody tells another somebody, and it trickles down, gets to some types, they pitch it to her, she bites. Shit happens and Meg was in it. Face it, Lauren."

I refuse.

I can't.

I won't.

I must.

I do.

Ah, hell.

I tell him about Blythe.

"So we got a motive. Meg was backing out. For whatever reason, she didn't want to do it anymore," Cecchi says.

"Because she was basically decent."

"Yeah," he says unconvincingly.

"She was," I insist. And she was. One thing doesn't cancel out another.

"Okay, okay."

"She was," I say again.

"Okay." He touches my hand. "You want to find out who killed her, or not?"

"You know I do."

"Then you have to be ruthless, like always. Forget your personal attachment, forget what you think you knew. What we have to find out is who else was involved in this token racket. Who else, besides Blythe, would be hurt if Meg pulled out?"

"Want to know what I think? I think that whole Merchants Association is involved."

"I think you're right," he says.

There's always a weak link. In this scheme it's one of the pet store owners, Peter Wood. Cecchi has had to go somewhere on another case and I've told him I think I can handle Wood by myself. But before I do I call William from my office.

"Oh, Lauren," he says phlegmatically. "How are you?"

"I'm fine. You?"

"All right, I guess."

"Have you made plans yet?"

"Plans?"

I sigh. This isn't going to be easy. Then, it never is. "To get some help, William."

Silence.

"William?"

"I know you mean well, Lauren, but I can do this myself."

"Why should you?"

"Do it myself? Because that's who I am."

"Have you heard from Rick?" I ask.

"Yes. He's ensconced at the Chateau Marmont."

"What did he say?"

"About what?"

This is infuriating. "William, don't you want Rick to come back?"

"Of course."

"Well, unless you *do* something about your habit I don't think he will."

"You don't understand. I've already done it. I'm not going to take the stuff anymore."

"Just say no, huh?"

He laughs. "Right."

I think I know better but maybe not. I try to take a different tone. "Good."

"Taking coke's simply not a viable option anymore."

He's saying all the right things but does he mean it? I wish him luck and tell him I'll see him soon. Then I walk over to Greenwich Avenue, pass Claw & Paw, determine that both men are inside, and lurk in a doorway across the street, a little down from them. No one notices me. As people pass by they're all too intent on where they're going, what they're thinking.

In ten minutes I count six citizens with multiple earrings, four with pierced noses, and one with a stud through his bottom lip. I wince at the thought of it. I know that some people have their nipples pierced. And other places, too. Eeeeuuw. I had my ears done when I was about twenty but piercing any other part of my body is anathema to me.

I'm in luck. Peter Wood comes out of his store and heads toward Sixth Avenue. I follow on my side of the street. He goes into the Peacock Cafe. I wait. When I think he's had time to settle himself, I cross over and go in.

The Peacock is one of the oldest coffeehouses in the Village. The service is slow, the chairs uncomfortable, the coffee mezzo mezzo, the decor amusing (a rococo statue in the back), and the music is usually opera. I think what keeps it going is that it feels authentic.

At this time of day most tables are empty. Peter sits in the back, near the counter where the gleaming, elaborate espresso machine resides. His eyes are closed and I assume he's listening to the music, a soprano singing something I can't identify because I hate opera. Kip loves it and goes to the Met with our friend Vonnie once a month.

I pull out a wire-backed chair and the sound makes Peter's lids snap open. His mouth forms an O but he doesn't say anything.

"Hello, Peter, mind if I join you?"

As I'm already seated there's not much he can say. He nervously looks at the door, then back at me.

"I know about the tokens," I say bluntly.

"Oh, please," he implores, drops his head to his hands, elbows on the table.

"You might as well tell me your part in it."

"Paul'll kill me."

I wonder if he means this literally.

"I won't tell Paul."

Peter looks at me, eyes like small starry specks. "You don't understand."

"Then help me to."

"I had nothing to do with it." He pushes up the sleeves of his blue sweatshirt as though he's readying himself for an unpleasant task.

"To do with what?"

"I thought you said you knew?"

"Not all of it. I need your help to fill in the missing pieces."

"Just what is it you know?" he asks.

This is the tricky part; neither of us wishes to reveal how much information he/she has. But I have to give something if I'm going to get something.

"I know that the so-called Merchants Association is bogus and that you were all involved in a token scam."

"I wasn't," he claims, panicky. "I told Paul we shouldn't be part of it but business has been so lousy. I didn't want to have anything to do with it. Paul insisted."

"How did it work?"

"Well, we . . . they, just held the tokens in the storerooms until the guys picked them up."

"The guys?"

"I don't know who they are. I told you, I didn't want anything to do with it."

"So then what? These guys would pay the holders?"

"Yeah. A weekly fee."

"How much?"

"Paul didn't tell me because I didn't want to know. But we were eating out three times a week again and we got a Mitsubishi thirty-five-inch TV. God, you should see it, it's unbelievable."

Typical. He didn't want to be involved but was delighted to share in the spoils. "What was the fight at Meg's about?"

"He's going to kill me."

"Do you really mean that, Peter?"

"Huh? No. Of course not. It's an expression. Now don't go twisting my words, okay?"

"So what was the fight about?"

"Meg wanted out. But more important, she wanted everybody else out too."

So Winx knew this.

"You mean she was threatening to blow the whistle on the others?"

"Yeah, I guess. Yes."

Why? I wonder. What had happened to make Meg change her mind about doing this illegal thing? And why was she threatening the rest of the group?

"Did anyone else want out?"

"No. Listen, I know how this sounds, but none of those people would've killed Meg."

"The night she was murdered, where was Paul?"

"He was with . . . he was . . . he said he was at the movies. I was having dinner with my mother. But Paul wouldn't have killed her. He couldn't kill anybody. You have to believe me."

I nod and he takes it for belief, as I intended, though I'm not sold. For now, Peter is the only one I don't suspect.

"Did Meg say *why* she wanted out?"

"I didn't listen. The less I heard about the whole thing the better I liked it."

"As much as you liked the Mitsubishi TV?" I can't help myself.

His cheeks flush like tropical flowers.

I push back my chair, ready to leave.

"Wait," he says, puts a hand on my wrist. "I think drugs were involved. I honestly don't know how."

I recall William's telling me that Meg took coke but that she wasn't a dealer. "Do you mean the store owners were involved in drugs?"

"Oh, no. Well, everybody uses, but I meant with the token guys."

"Everybody uses?"

"Sure. Don't you?"

"No."

Peter seems surprised, as if I've told him I've never had sex.

"Well, I don't do a lot of drugs," he says quickly.

"It's okay, Peter. I don't care. It's your business." This is, of course, a lie. But I don't want to seem totally judgmental. The new me.

I get up. Though no one has appeared to take an order, I don't want to drink coffee with him.

"You won't tell Paul we talked, will you?"

"You have my word."

He looks skeptical.

"My word means a lot."

He still doesn't seem convinced. Why should he be? In a world where a man like Clarence Thomas can be nominated to the Supreme Court, why should anyone's *word* mean anything?

Chapter
Twenty-four

ON THE WAY TO MY OFFICE I see William dart furtively into an apartment building. His movements are so stealthful that I'm immediately suspicious. It's true that I don't know all his friends, but I've never known him to have an acquaintance in this building.

Assuming my M.O. of the day, I find a doorway and lurk again. Fifteen minutes later William appears, but now he doesn't skulk. He seems quite confident, head held high, and walks toward Perry without glancing in any direction.

I follow him.

He goes to our building.

I wait, lurk once more to give him a chance to get into his apartment. When I do reach the front door, and before I open it, I can hear the blasting music. It's the score from *Follies*. He hasn't started it at the beginning and Lee Remick sings "Would I Leave You?" I feel sad. Remick *has* left us and never got her due, as far as I'm concerned. But then Julia Roberts makes more money per picture than Meryl Streep. Go know.

As I take the first step upstairs my apartment door swings open and Kip sticks out her head, with eyes that look the size of CDs.

"What the hell is going on?" she asks.

"It's William."

"I know that. What's he doing? He knows better than to play music that loud when I have clients."

"I was just going up to tell him."

"Christ," she says, and slams the door.

I don't take this personally. This is one key to a long relationship.

I pound on William's door.

*"Would I play on the grass with a boy half your age, bet your
ass,"* Remick sings.

I pound again.

"But I've done that already."

The door opens. William stands there mouthing the words
to the song. Remick's voice coming out of William's mouth
looks ridiculous.

"Turn it down," I say, and push past him into the apartment.

He reaches the CD player first, lowers the volume, and
continues to lip-sync the song accompanied by hand ges-
tures. It's nominally better than William actually singing (he
loves to sing and can't carry a tune), but not much.

"William, would you please stop?"

He heaves a sigh, drops his arms to his sides. "What's
wrong?"

"Oh, please." I sit on the couch. "Turn it off, okay?"

He does. "You're no fun."

It's clear to me that he actually believes I can't tell he's
high. True, I never realized it before and this might give him a
false confidence, but now that I know, I know. I lean my
elbow on the arm, my chin on my folded hand, and stare at
him.

"What are you looking at? Do you want something to eat?
Drink? What do you want, Lauren? Want to dance?"

I almost don't know how to begin. So I use one of my usual
oblique, wily ways: "You're stoned out of your head."

"Moi?"

"I thought you were going to 'just say no.' "

"I don't know what you mean," he says, turns away from
me, and fusses with a knickknack on a bookshelf.

"You had no idea the music was so loud, did you? Kip even
came out to . . ."

"Oh, Kip, shmip. You think I care? And who invited you in here, you self-righteous little prig?"

I'm stunned but remind myself he's high. Still, it stings.

"William, you need help," I press on.

"And you need to get the fuck out of my apartment." He grabs my arm, pulls me off the couch, drags me across the carpet, opens up, pushes me into the hall, and slams the door.

When I hit the wall with both palms it hurts. I turn, unable to move. Nothing like this has ever happened to me with a friend. Especially *this* friend. William has always been the most gentle of men. But it wasn't really William doing that ... it was some horror he'd become by using. Still, he shoved it up his nose and he is responsible. Tears threaten, but I hold them back.

I'm finally able to go downstairs and into our apartment through the nonpatient entrance. In the kitchen, tears run freely down my cheeks as I get myself a diet cherry Coke, pop the top, and sit at the table. But when I lift the can to my lips, I find I can't drink because I'm crying. These are two things you can't do at the same time.

Humiliation tears are one of the worst types. But that's not my only emotion. As I cross my arms on the table and lay my head down on them, I realize I'm crying from frustration as well. And who knows what else?

"Darling?"

I look up to find Kip bending over me, a hand on my shoulder, the unmistakable expression of concern and love on her face.

"Lauren, what is it?"

Her question, her obvious caring, make me sob. I push back my chair, fling my arms around her waist, press my face against her, as she holds me and strokes my hair.

The wonderful thing about Kip is that she doesn't say anything, doesn't reassure me with words like *everything will be all right*. She simply lets me cry until I'm through.

Then she hands me a tissue and sits down, moves her chair

close to mine, waits. I wipe my eyes, blow my nose. I tell her what occurred with William.

"I can't believe it," she says, astonished.

"What're we going to do?"

"There's nothing we *can* do. Except give him a wide berth until he's ready to get help. He knows how we feel."

"Calling Rick would be controlling, huh?"

"Very."

"What about this intervention stuff?"

"Hmmm. I suppose we could do that when Rick comes home if William hasn't gotten his act together."

"What if Rick isn't coming home?"

Kip thinks. "Let's see what happens. I have another client in five minutes."

"Listen, Kip, I need your help. I know what Meg was doing and I'll tell you about it later, but if the person will cooperate, do you think you could hypnotize the eyewitness and get her to remember in more detail whom she saw running away from Meg's store that night?"

"I can try."

"What time?"

"I have my last appointment at seven . . . so after eight?"

"Good."

"You okay now?"

"Yeah. Thanks."

We both rise, put our arms around each other.

"I feel like people are leaving me right and left," I say.

"I know. But I'm not."

We kiss, the buzzer sounds, and Kip is gone. I sit again. I have to put William out of my mind for now and concentrate on the case.

I'm sure that one of the store owners killed Meg because she was about to expose the scam. But which one? Peter is out. So there's Paul Steele, Jed Langevin, Jim and Sally Darling, and Winx Daignault. Arlene said she saw a *man*, a *white* man, but you never know. Still, if I believe Arlene, I have to rule out Sally and Winx. That leaves three suspects. The one thing that confuses me is the murder of Fingers Faye. Why would any of them kill him?

But if I can get Arlene Kornbluth to agree to be hypnotized, I think I can crack this thing.

I have managed to persuade Arlene to be hypnotized as long as she can bring her lover, Jane, with her. So the four of us sit in Kip's office.

Jane is in her early forties, with short blond hair and steel-rimmed glasses, and has a pleasant face. She wears jeans, an orange T-shirt, and white Nike Airs with a pink stripe.

She and I sit on the couch and Arlene and Kip face each other.

"Try to relax," Kip begins.

Arlene nods. She's very nervous; her fingers drum on her brown-slacked thighs.

"Think of a place in which you're comfortable. A place you find peaceful, relaxing. You don't have to tell me where it is, but let me know when you've thought of one."

Silence.

Tension tentacles come off Jane like electric rays in a cartoon.

Arlene says, "Okay, I have one."

"Good. There is a long marble staircase, which leads down to your place. Do you see it?"

"Yes."

"A banister runs alongside."

"Oak," Arlene says.

"Yes." Kip smiles. "Put your hand on the banister so you won't fall."

"The steps are steep," says Arlene, apprehensively.

"Grip the banister, you'll be all right. Got it?"

"Yes."

"Good. Now go down the steps."

"I don't know . . ."

"Trust me, Arlene. You'll be fine. Do you trust me?"

"I think so."

"Good. Take the first step."

Silence.

Arlene's eyes are closed and her fingers have stopped their tattoo.

"Go on," Kip encourages. "Take that first step."

Arlene takes a big breath, lets it out. "Okay. I took it."

"Great. Now, carefully, go down the rest. When you get to the bottom, tell me."

We wait sixteen or seventeen days.

"I'm at the bottom."

"Wonderful. Look around. See the door?"

"Oh, yes. It's also oak."

"Yes," Kip says, because the door, like everything else, can be whatever the subject wants it to be. "Open it."

"All right."

"When you do, go inside and find somewhere to sit. Tell me when you're settled."

I glance at Jane, who still looks stricken. I tap her shoulder, silently indicate there's no reason to worry. She presses her lips together and pretends to believe me.

Arlene tells Kip she's found a comfortable place to sit.

"Let your mind drift. Look at your surroundings. Notice colors, shapes, smells."

Hundreds of years of solitude pass by as Arlene does this.

Kip continues, "You feel lighter and lighter, almost as if you could float. Do you feel that, Arlene?"

"Yes." A small, sweet smile appears.

I wonder where Arlene is and wish I could be there, too.

"Raise your right arm," Kip instructs.

Arlene does.

"Now lower it."

She does.

"Good. Do you feel a sense of well-being?"

"Yes."

"I'm glad. That's lovely. Is it all right if Lauren asks you some questions?"

"Yes."

"Thank you, Arlene. I want you to answer them honestly.

You're going to recall details you've forgotten." Kip looks at me and nods.

I clear my throat. I admit it, I'm nervous. Kip and I have done this only once before on a case of mine, and it was some years back. As I know from that experience, and from what Kip's told me, the unexpected is liable to happen.

"It's a warm September night," I say. "There's been an attempted holdup at Megan Harbaugh's shop. But that's over. It's after nine now. Where are you, Arlene?"

"I'm in my store," she says flatly, eyes open.

"What're you doing?"

"I'm moving stock around."

"How do you feel?"

"Terrible."

"You're upset because of what happened at Meg's?"

"Yes."

"Why haven't you gone home?"

"I'm waiting for Jane. She's coming from a psychology class to pick me up. She doesn't know yet. I could leave her a note but I don't want to walk home alone."

"That's understandable. What time is Jane expected?"

"About quarter to ten." She gasps, and reflexively brings her hands to her chest.

"What is it?"

"A loud noise. Maybe a backfire, but I don't think so. I run to the door, open it, look down the avenue. I see a man come out of Meg's and run toward Charles."

"Stop the man like you would on a VCR. Pause him. Got him?"

"Yes."

"Are you sure it's a man?"

"Oh, yes."

"Why?"

"The build."

"What does he look like?"

"He's fairly tall. Maybe six feet. He has brown hair, combed back."

"What do you mean, combed back?"

"I . . . I'm not sure."

"He's running away from you, is that right?"

"Yes."

"Then how can you tell how he wears his hair?"

"I . . . I can't."

Arlene appears anxious and Kip signals that I should go on to something else.

"Do you get a feeling of his age?"

"I can't see his face, you know."

"How do you know he's white?"

"I don't know. I don't know."

"Don't worry about it, go on."

"He moves well. Still, I don't get the feeling of a very young man. Forty . . . forty-two. Oh wait. He looks over his shoulder." She smiles. "He's white. And his hair is combed straight back, no part."

"What's he wearing?"

"Sweats. They're black. And running shoes. Also black."

"Is the gun in his hand?"

"Gun?"

"You heard a gunshot, remember?"

"Yes."

"So, do you see the gun?"

She squeezes her eyebrows together in concentration, says softly, sadly, "I don't see a gun."

"That's all right. Don't worry about it. Can you describe him any further?"

"That's all," she says as though she's disappointed a parent. "No, wait. There's something else." She grins: good child.

"What is it, Arlene?"

"Flashing," she says.

We all look at each other, bewildered. *Flashing?*

"It flies out when he runs. Whips around from the front, I think. Something around his neck."

I feel excited by this revelation but I'm not sure why.

"It's hanging down his back," she continues. "Something around his neck. A cross, maybe?"

"You can't see what it is?"

"A medal?"

But it's a question and I know she hasn't really seen it.

"No. No. Oh, God."

"What?"

"He's getting away. He's turned the corner. Gone."

I look at Kip, who nods. There's nothing more to be gained. Arlene's done a spectacular job. But the description doesn't sound like Steele, Darling, or Langevin, and definitely not Winx. Yet the portrait means *something* to me. I have vague echoes of having seen this perp.

When Arlene and Jane are gone, Kip and I discuss the results of the session.

"The description doesn't fit anyone?" she asks.

"It doesn't match any of the store owners, but it's familiar."

"Well, she didn't depict anyone unusual."

"That's true." Still, something nags. "Here's the thing: if Meg was about to blow the whistle, whoever dealt with the store owners probably knew about it and had some mechanic take her out."

"I hate it when you talk like that."

"Like what?"

" 'Mechanic take her out.' "

"That's what hit men are called."

"You do it so you don't have to feel anything."

I ignore this because it's true. "But for the bosses to know, one of the store owners had to have said something. The description doesn't fit Faye, Malcolm, Margolis, or Pesh. The point is, it's next to impossible for me to track down a mech — . . . hit man."

"How about the person who hired him? Could that be a store owner?"

"It's possible but not probable. I think this is mob stuff, Kip." I feel dispirited, defeated.

She puts an arm around me. "Maybe you have to leave this to the cops, honey."

"Yeah. I think you're right." Even as I say this I know I can't.

Kip says, "You know I'm right, but you're going on with it, aren't you?"

How does she always know? "It must be boring to be with someone so predictable."

She smiles. "Not yet. Lauren, I know what this means to you, but it scares me, mob involvement."

"On the one hand I think it's mob-related, but on the other, I don't know, I can't imagine them being associated with a token scam. How much money could there really be in it for them?"

"Maybe it translated into something else."

"Meaning?"

"Tokens to drugs?"

"Yes, I've thought of that. And that's probably right. But in a small-time way." This makes me think of William and an incredible sadness overwhelms me.

"What is it?"

I tell her.

"He'll come around, Lauren. He's not going down the tubes."

"How can you be so sure?"

"Because he wants to live. Basically he's not self-destructive."

"He's an addict, Kip."

"I know."

I shake my head as if to rid myself of William thoughts. "I need to concentrate on this other problem now. Tokens and drugs. And the hit man. Where was the gun? Why didn't Arlene see the gun?"

"Maybe it was in his waistband."

"Or maybe he left it behind, in Meg's store. And then later went back for it and ran into Fingers Faye."

"But didn't the police comb every inch of that store the night of the murder?" Kip asks.

"Yeah, that's right."

"Besides, wouldn't a professional take the gun with him?"

"Yes. And a professional wouldn't have a problem running

into Fingers. This is screwy. I can't believe he had the gun in his waistband. If he was running, it more than likely would've dropped out. And here's another problem I have with this scenario: I can't picture a pro in sweat clothes."

"I have some trouble with that myself."

"I've changed my mind. I don't think it *was* a pro. I think that the shooter left the gun in the store somewhere and the cops couldn't find it. Which means he knew a secret place, which means he knew the store, which confirms he knew Meg — what I said from the beginning, because she wouldn't have opened the door to a stranger — and that Meg's killer went back for the gun, which he retrieved. Then he met up with Fingers, who was there looking for the tokens, killed Faye, and took the tokens himself."

"But the tokens would've been too heavy for him to take alone."

"Right."

The arms of depression open like Shiva. NO. "Okay, if he couldn't carry the stuff alone then others are involved."

"And we're back to the big token cartel?" Kip asks skeptically.

"You mean the store owners?"

"Yes."

We look at each other.

"Well, why not?" I ask pitifully.

"But what about Arlene's description?"

"Shit. Forget the store owners. As I said, her description isn't totally alien to me. It seems familiar but I can't place him."

"What about a disguise, a wig?"

"Then Meg wouldn't have opened the door. Oh, I don't know, there's nothing distinguishing about the description...."

But there is!

"What?"

"Boy, have I been stupid." My detective's heart slaps itself.

"Tell me," she demands.

And I do.

Chapter
Twenty-five

═══════════════════

AS I PREPARE TO LEAVE the house I bump into William, who walks down the stairs, suitcase in hand.

"Lauren, I was just coming to see you."

I feel wary, as if I'm with a stranger who might hurt me.

"I wanted to apologize."

I nod in a grudging acceptance. "Where're you going?"

"Rick called last night. I'm going to California."

"I see." I want to ask what he's going to do about his drug problem but I zip my lip. "So you're leaving."

"You don't have to say it like that."

"Like what?"

"Well, it sounds so personal, like we're breaking up or something."

Funny, but I feel we already have. The hurt place inside needs to heal. "I presume you've told Cecchi."

"Told Cecchi? Why would I tell him?"

"Didn't he tell you not to leave town?"

"Oh, no. I forgot about that." He looks at his watch. "I have to catch a plane. I'll call him from the airport."

"He may not like that."

"I can't help it. I have to go." He leans down to give me a kiss but I turn away. "Oh, great. What if my plane crashes? How'll you feel then?"

"William, you can't do what you did to me and expect an apology to wipe it away, as though it never happened."

"I was stoned," he says.

"I know. That doesn't excuse you."

"You want to know something, Lauren? You've gotten really rigid lately. I have to go." He opens the outer door.

"One thing. Where did Meg keep her coke stash?"

"You mean in the store?"

"Yes."

"She had a secret spot."

I momentarily overcome my hurt feelings. "Where?"

"It's behind the counter on the wall, in the jewelry case. Inside there's a button under a ring box . . . you have to know it's there to see it when you move the box. Anyway, if you push it, it opens a place in the wall."

"Who knew about it?"

"I don't know. Anybody who did coke with her, I guess. I really have to go, Lauren."

"Good-bye," I say coldly.

He hears the tone.

"Oh, lighten up." And he's gone.

I can't remember William's ever leaving without my knowing when he was coming back. This is a very different kind of leaving. I don't know when I'll see him again; what condition he'll be in; or how I'll feel about him. Right now I ache. I exit the building in time to see him get into a cab, drive away. I put him out of my mind and walk toward my office.

I call Cecchi. I'm lucky, he's in.

"I think I know where the Harbaugh murder weapon is."

"Where?"

"Can you meet me at Meg's store now?"

"Give me ten."

"Right."

I take my time as I walk down Greenwich. So much has changed, is changing. Angelina's Restaurant, a fixture as long as I've been in New York, is gone. Jean's Patio, which turned into Arthur's, is now an unappealing Italian restaurant. The old record shop, which was once the Idle Bookstore, is gone. Stores are empty, too. Nothing's as it was. What will go into Meg's place?

As I approach I can see that the sidewalk in front still has pots of flowers and other tributes to my old friend. They're pushed back against the building, but new ones have been added. It's amazing that there hasn't been any vandalism or defilement of these offerings. For some reason even the street hoods respect this outpouring of grief.

The weather is growing warm and humid again; the smell that rises from the sidewalk is a cross between rancid oil and old feet.

I spot Cecchi coming toward me. We wave.

When he arrives he takes out a bunch of keys and opens Meg's door. Inside the air is stale. Everything is still in place: the jewelry, pottery, pieces of furniture, artifacts, as though Meg's on vacation, the store will reopen. I'm struck anew that she's gone forever.

"When is it going to be cleared out?" I ask.

"When we no longer consider it a crime scene. Soon. If there hadn't been the second murder it would've been dismantled by now. So?" He raises two dark eyebrows.

What if the gun's not there? What if I've gotten him here on a hunch? Cecchi hates hunches. But I barrel on as if I know exactly what I'm doing. I go behind the counter to the glass case on the wall. It's locked. I look at him.

"What the hell," he says.

"Do you have keys to everything?"

"No."

"Know where they are?"

"Nope. I hope this doesn't mean the assholes never looked in that case."

The assholes are his detectives.

"I'll have to use my magic key," he says. Cecchi comes around the counter, removes his .38 from his shoulder holster. "Stand over there," he tells me, then takes it by the barrel and breaks the case with the butt. "Magic key."

We both know he shouldn't have done this but neither of us says anything. Cecchi picks out the jagged pieces of glass, opens the case, and looks at me expectantly.

Inside are several pieces of jewelry, but only one in a ring box. I pick it up and, at first, I see nothing on the shelf. When I look closer I distinguish a circle of a slightly different hue. I push the spot. Amazingly, a door slides open on the wall.

"I'll be damned," Cecchi says.

I reach inside and my detective's heart gyrates as I touch steel. "It's here," I tell him.

"Let me do it." We exchange places and Cecchi, white handkerchief in hand, removes the gun. "How do we know this wasn't Meg's gun?"

"We don't. But I don't think it is. I think her killer put it there the night he shot her. Then, when he came back to get it he ran into Fingers."

"And left the gun here?"

"I admit that's weird. But maybe there was a time element. After all, Fingers was shot with his own gun. Maybe the killer thought he'd come back yet another time, or that nobody would find the gun."

"And I suppose you know who the killer is? Who the gun belongs to?"

"Well, yes, I think I do."

"Would you care to share this information with me?" he says a shade sarcastically.

"No," I say. "I have a client I have to tell first."

"Do you realize I could run you in for obstructing justice?"

"I can't believe you're saying that. That's what the cop is always telling the P.I. in books."

"Lauren, *I* can't believe you won't tell me."

"If you run a check on the gun you'll find out whom it belongs to."

"Oh, thank you very much. I wish I'd thought of that. This is ridiculous." He wraps the gun in his handkerchief and drops it in his pocket. "C'mon, let's get out of here."

On the street he starts to walk away.

"Cecchi?"

"What?"

"You wouldn't have even found the gun if it weren't for me."

He glares. "That's supposed to mollify me?"

"Yes."

"Well, it doesn't."

He walks away, leaving me on the street staring at his back. Then he stops, turns, and says: "Don't go mucking around in this case, Laurano. Don't screw it up. I don't give a damn about your client. Keep out of this." I've never known him to be so mad at me.

I can't keep out of it any more than he can. We both have our jobs to do. And I can't wait for documentation on who owns the gun, because I have to get to him before he gets to me.

I call Ray Davies and tell him I'm very close. He wants to know who I think it is but I don't reveal this as I'm not 100 percent sure.

There's a part of me that hopes I'm wrong because the implication is so revolting. On the other hand, I want to wrap this thing up so I can get on with my life. As long as Meg's killer's out there I can't rest. And I don't feel safe.

What I *do* feel is very much alone. Meg, William, and now Cecchi have all left me in one way or another. I know this isn't about me, but I can't help my feelings.

I decide to start with Blythe. Perhaps it's sexist of me but she doesn't feel as threatening as he does. I stop at a phone booth, punch in her home number. She answers on one ring. I hang up.

Five minutes later I push her bell.

"Who is it?" Blythe's voice comes over the intercom, tinny and thin.

I tell her.

"I'm busy," she says.

"Blythe, open the door or I'm calling the cops."

There's a moment of silence and then she buzzes me in. Instantly, I can see that Blythe's preparing to leave. Although there aren't the customary half-packed suitcases in the living room, the bookshelves are empty and the room's devoid of its personality: only the large pieces of furniture remain.

Blythe is wearing tights and a blue button-down man's shirt. "What do you want, Lauren?"

"I want to talk to you about your mother."

"We've done that."

"And I want to talk to you about the token scam."

There's a quick sign of recognition in her eyes.

"Don't bother telling me you don't know what I'm talking about because I know you do," I lie.

"Okay. So big deal. I know about the token thing."

"How did it work?"

"I thought you knew."

"I know some things."

"Like what?"

"Like the Merchants Association holding stolen tokens. Getting a cut."

She gives me a half smile and I know I'm only partly right.

"Why don't you be a good girl and fill me in."

"Don't patronize me, Lauren. You've been doing that for years."

I'm shocked. "I haven't. That's not fair."

"Fair? Since when is anything in this goddamn world fair?"

"Since never," I concede. "But I've never patronized you, Blythe. You were Meg's kid and I loved you."

"Past tense?"

"You haven't been lovable lately."

Her eyes sparkle with nascent tears.

"Where're you going?"

"On vacation."

"Taking all your books with you?"

Her bottom lip trembles and I see Blythe the child, who's been reprimanded by Meg for something, more hurt than anything else.

"Okay. So I'm moving. So what?" There's very little heat behind her words.

"Where to?"

"What difference does it make?"

"Where to?"

"I'm going to Paris, okay?"

"*Moving* to Paris?"

"Yes. I've always wanted to live there."

"What about your job?"

"What about it? I quit."

"Going alone?" I know she's not.

She doesn't answer.

"Tell me how the token thing worked, Blythe."

"They weren't just holding. I mean, they were, but it was more involved. Jed Langevin runs it. You know all the token-booth robberies in the last year?"

I recall reading a figure of somewhere around sixty in the last six months alone. And there have been deaths, too. Murders of the token-booth clerks.

Blythe goes on. "Langevin has this gang of thieves he uses. Kids, really. They knocked off the booths and he paid them twenty-five cents a token. Then he sold them to the other merchants for fifty. And they sold them over the counter for seventy-five. Mom didn't. She was strictly a holder. Too many employees. She sold to a gang."

"Faye, Malcolm, and Margolis?"

"Yeah. I don't know why they were killed."

I think I do.

Blythe continues. "In July that clerk got murdered and Mom had a stab of conscience."

"So she wanted out?"

"That's when she started grumbling about it. But Langevin swore it wasn't one of his guys who did it. Who knows? Then, when she found out that the token money was going into drugs, that did it. I guess because of Sasha."

"What was Meg going to do?"

"She wanted everyone to stop. Langevin told her if she didn't want to hold anymore she didn't have to, but that wasn't enough for her. She said everybody had to get out of the scam and that she must've been crazy to have had anything to do with it in the first place. Murder and drugs were never part of the plan, as far as she was concerned."

I'm amazed at Meg's naïveté. "When the scheme was presented where did she think the tokens were going to come from?"

Blythe shrugs. "I don't think she thought about it."

It was an old, tired story. This intelligent woman saw only what she wanted to, so that she didn't have to justify the means to gain the end. Money for her daughter . . . money for her lover.

"And she did this for you," I say.

"Not completely. Let's not make her too much of a saint, okay? She spent some of the money."

She certainly did. "You had the fight when she refused to continue?"

"Yes."

"What about the others?"

"You mean, did they threaten her about turning them in? They all did."

"Didn't it occur to you that one of them might have killed her?"

"Of course."

"But you didn't think it was important to tell that to the police or me?"

"I was told . . ."

I nod. Of course. She was threatened herself.

"Is that all?"

"Is what all?"

"Is that everything you know?"

She takes a beat. "Yes. Sure. What else could there be?"

"You're leaving, just like that." I snap my fingers, a nice solid sound. "You don't care who killed your mother?"

"Don't try to lay a guilt trip on me, Lauren. My staying or not isn't going to help find the killer."

"In fact, it might."

She gives me a gelid look.

"You're a witness to the threats made by the others."

"You don't understand."

"Yeah, I think I do. One of them threatened you, too."

Blythe nods, almost imperceptibly.

"Going to Paris alone?" I ask.

"Why?"

"Curious."

"Oh, sure, right. Curious." She laughs and it sounds like an insult.

"Jason Lightbourne's going with you, isn't he?"

"How did . . . you make me sick, Lauren."

I don't bother telling her how sick she makes me. "His wife know?"

"Listen, I'm not the first woman in the world to go away with a married man."

"Nor is it the first time you've had an affair with a married man. But you might be the first woman to go away with the man who killed her mother."

A twisted expression, like a squall, comes over her face.

"Lightbourne killed Meg. But you knew that, didn't you?"

"No. And I don't believe you." She grabs the back of a chair as if to steady herself. "That's ridiculous. Why would Jason kill Mom?"

"How long have you been giving him money?"

Gingerly, Blythe makes her way around the chair and sits. "The money I gave Jason was a loan."

Sure it was. "When did you tell him Meg was blowing the whistle?"

"I never did. I mean, he didn't know anything about it, the token thing, Mother's wanting to end it. He'd met her but he didn't know her. And we weren't exactly *flaunting* our relationship."

If Lightbourne didn't know anything, why *would* he kill Meg? Then that last little piece slides into place, like laundry down a chute, and I know *exactly* why he killed her.

When I first realized who fit Arlene's description, I knew Lightbourne had to be the person in the cab Blythe wouldn't identify. And I recalled that I'd thought he must be a married man. But I didn't know then that the *two* married men were one and the same. I believe Blythe's innocence regarding Meg's murder and feel relief about that.

"I don't understand. Why would Jason kill my mother?"

"Let's ask him."

"Ask him?"

"Get him down here, Blythe. I'll be in the bedroom."

"You want me to entrap him?" she asks indignantly, as if we're talking about civil liberties.

"I don't think you get it. This boyfriend of yours killed your mother."

"So you say. I don't believe it."

"Then pick up the phone and ask him to come down."

"Why should I?"

"Are you afraid?"

"Why do you think this is true?"

I tell her about Arlene's description under hypnosis.

"And that's what you're basing this on?"

"That and something else. Call him."

Blythe remains still, as though she's paralyzed. I hand her the mobile phone. Finally, she pulls up the antenna and slowly punches in a number.

"Jason?" she says, almost whispering. "Could you come down for a minute? I know, but ... no, not on the phone. . Okay. Thanks." She hangs up. "He's coming right down."

I realize there's a chance that I'm wrong about Blythe's innocence and that I'm being set up. But I have to take the chance. "I'll go in here." I indicate the bedroom.

"What should I ask him?"

"If he killed your mother."

"I can't do that."

"Blythe, I have every confidence that you'll find a way. And if you're smart you won't let him know I'm here. This is a dangerous guy."

There's a sharp rap on the door. Blythe looks at it, back at me. I can see she's frightened. I give her an encouraging smile.

"Just a sec," she calls to him.

I go into the bedroom. The half-packed suitcases are here, yawning open on the bed. I take out my gun, press ear to wood, and listen. I hear Blythe unlock and open the door.

"What's up?" he asks, annoyed.

"We need to talk."

"What about? I'm packing."

"Jason, what do you know about my mother's death?"

"What are you talking about?"

There's the sound of shuffling feet. A match being struck.

"I'm talking about my mother's murder. Do you know anything about it?"

"Why the hell would I know anything about it? What's going on, Blythe? Who put you up to this?"

"No one. Jason, don't. That hurts."

I stiffen, put my free hand on the doorknob.

"Tell me what you know," he demands.

Silence. Then Blythe says, "Know? Is there something I *could* know?"

"Jesus, you're just like your goddamned mother."

"How do you know? You hardly knew her." Blythe sounds alarmed.

"I . . . I meant you sound like what you told me she was like."

"You're lying."

I was right. Lightbourne was Topic A, Meg's secret lover. That's why she opened the door to him.

"Look, Blythe, we have a plane to catch and . . ."

"How well, Jason? How well did you know her?"

It sounds like Blythe is beginning to put it together.

"Shut the fuck up."

Now it could get ugly.

The slap resounds like the crisp crack of a snapped bean. It's ugly.

Slowly, I turn the knob.

"Jason," she says, breathlessly.

"I didn't want to kill her but she didn't give me any option. And neither are you. Why the hell can't you girls just do what you're told?"

"You killed my mother?"

"I fucked her and I killed her. And I fucked you and now I'm going to kill . . ."

I fling open the door, take the combat position, hold my

gun in both hands, and point it at Lightbourne, who's pulled a knife from somewhere. "Drop it."

"What the fuck." He looks at me, then back at Blythe. "You fucking bitch," he says.

I tell him again to drop the knife and he does. He glares at me, that awful hair combed straight back, no part. And around his neck on a string are the keys Arlene thought might be a cross or medal.

"You couldn't keep your mouth shut about us, could you?" he says to Blythe.

She looks dazed. "You were Mom's lover?"

I wonder which upsets Blythe more, Jason's being Meg's lover or killer.

"She was a much better lay than you," he says cruelly.

"Blythe, call the police," I say, as I continue to level my gun at this pitiful excuse for a man.

She doesn't move. "I don't understand."

History has repeated itself and, in a way, settled a score. But Blythe can't believe it.

"You want to explain," he says to me, "or should I?"

I give him the go-ahead nod.

"It's simple. Meg and I were lovers. I knew about the token ring from the beginning. You think she did it for you? Think again. She did it for me. ME. And then the bitch was going to dump the whole thing. I went to see her that night to ask her one more time not to do it. She wouldn't listen."

"We were both giving you money?" Blythe asks, dumbfounded.

Lightbourne laughs smugly. "Not bad, huh?" He grins, then realizes the position he's in and his smile fades like a dying firefly.

"I thought if I got rid of her I could get in on things some other way. Maybe with that stupid bunch she sold to."

"Oh, God," Blythe says.

"But then you were poking around," he says to me. "I didn't know what I should do. I thought I'd lie low for a while, until things cooled down."

"And Fingers Faye?" I ask. "Why'd you kill *him*?"

"I went back for my gun, which I'd hidden the night I killed Meg, and the asshole was there. I tried to do business with him but he wasn't interested. So I took his gun away from him, marched him downstairs, and blew his brains out.

"An unopened shipment of tokens was still there. Guess that's what Faye wanted. There were two boxes, maybe eighty pounds, worth about ten thou. I got two shopping bags, put forty pounds in each. I'm in great shape." He flexes a muscle. "I made sure nobody saw me leave, came back here, stowed it in our basement storeroom, and went upstairs. Just one problem. I forgot my fucking gun."

"Pity," I say. "What about the other two, Margolis and Malcolm?"

"Before I whacked Faye he told me he did that. He was greedy, wanted the whole ball of wax. He threatened me, but like I said, he wasn't any match for me," Lightbourne says proudly.

"So the coast was clear. Nobody knew about you."

"Yeah, except I couldn't get back to get my gun and from what Blythe told me I figured you were getting closer." He laughs. "I had my plans for you . . . a nice karate chop before flight time."

"Jesus," Blythe says.

"I thought you might want to see me so that's why I came over," I say.

"Yeah, thanks."

"Blythe, make the call."

While she punches in 911, tears streak her cheeks and her face twists with pain as she grasps the full implication of what has happened. Her lover was her mother's lover; her lover murdered her mother. And Blythe's left with the knowledge that she'd been betrayed by both. With any luck, she's cognizant of the horrendous role she's played in this pathetic drama. Sure, maybe Meg wanted to give Lightbourne money, but I'm almost certain it was Blythe she'd intended to bribe love from first. Let her live with that for the rest of her life.

So it's over, or practically. My Megan is gone and it's true I didn't know her completely. But what I knew, what she gave me, is the important thing. Who was the real Meg? Different things to different people, nothing wrong with that. Like all of us she had many facets to her personality and it's true of William too. People are what they are and do the best they can. And my ideas of what they *should* do, or who they *should* be, can take a powder.

Except what I think *should* happen to Jason Lightbourne.

"You know what you did?" I ask him.

"What?"

"You murdered my oldest friend and I hate your guts. Want to know what I hope?"

He doesn't answer.

"I hope you stay in the great shape you're so proud of, and live to be at least ninety years old . . . in prison."

I know he couldn't care less, but it makes me feel better. Almost good.

Chapter
Twenty-six

═══════════════

KIP AND I GET READY for our twelfth-anniversary dinner party. She's already set the table, something she prefers to do early . . . like three. Now comes the seating discussion.

"How about Betsy next to you on the right, and Anne next to me on the right?" she asks, the neatly printed place cards in her hands.

"Do you think it's seemly for us each to have an ex-lover next to us on our anniversary?" At least my affair with Anne was short-lived.

"I don't know how we can avoid it. They're all ex-lovers."

"They are?" I'm appalled. "When did you find the time and how come you never told me?"

"I meant of someone's."

"We live in an incestuous world," I say.

"A small world."

"I wonder if heterosexuals invite their ex-lovers to their anniversary parties?"

"Who cares what they do. I think it's extremely modern of us."

"*Modern?* You sound like my mother."

"Please, Lauren. Not on our anniversary."

"We have a very sick guest list."

"What're you talking about?" asks Kip.

"Think about it. Not only have Betsy and Anne been with us, but they've also each been with Doris and Doris has been lovers with Joan, who has also been lovers with Phyllis, who has also been lovers with Anne and Anne has been lovers with Marion, who is now with Joan, who used to be with Betsy, who at one time went with Phyllis, who is now with Doris, who had a long affair with Anne, who is now with Betsy, who before that had a short affair with Marion, whom you went to bed with when you were drunk."

"You want to cancel?"

"I almost could. These are our best friends, Kip."

"I'd keep that quiet if I were you."

"Thank God for Jenny and Jill," I say. "We can use them to separate people. I told you we should've mixed groups."

"You know how I hate mixing people who don't know each other. Anyway, I didn't feel like having heteros to this. Call me crazy."

"What I'll call you is heterophobic."

"Hey," Kip says, "fair is fair."

"True. But it's still a sick, sick list."

"What difference does it make? We're having dinner together, not playing post office. Besides, it was all a long time ago and probably no one ever thinks about it." She gives me a long look. "Do you think about going to bed with Anne, for instance?"

"Occasionally."

"You do?"

"Rarely." I can tell my candid response has been a huge mistake.

"But you think about it. I mean, even once is disgusting."

"Oh, stop. What's disgusting about it?"

"You don't find it disgusting to think about you and Anne in bed together?" she asks.

"No. You want to go on with these cards or not?" I try to divert her.

"Never mind the cards for now. This is more important."

"There's nothing important about it."

"You know, it's incredible. Twelve years together. You think you know a person and then all of a sudden, by accident, something slips out and you realize you're with a stranger," Kip says.

"I'm not a stranger."

"Then tell me about Anne."

"Tell you *what* about Anne? I told you about her years ago."

"I want to hear about these *new* feelings."

"I don't have any new feelings. You're making something out of nothing, Kip."

"You said you think about going to bed with her."

"You asked if I ever think about going to bed with Anne and I said, occasionally, and that's the truth. On occasion it has crossed my mind that once upon a time Anne and I went to bed together. I don't long for the good old days, so to speak, nor do I wish to start it up again. It's just that once in a while I'll look at her and remember, and that's all there is to it."

"Anne's very attractive. Sometimes she's extremely attractive . . . sometimes she looks beautiful," Kip states.

"Sometimes."

"Is that when those thoughts cross your mind?"

"Oh, please. Either we finish the table or I take my shower. Which is it going to be?"

"You're afraid of this conversation, aren't you?"

"I'm bored with this conversation," I say.

"Bored with me on our twelfth anniversary. Well, it was bound to happen sooner or later, why not today? Is today that special, after all? What does it really mean when you get right down to it?"

"It means that we've stayed together through thick and thin, long ago passing the famous two-and-a-half-year mark; that we never fell into the famous Mommy-Baby trap; that you stopped writing your name on your belongings six years ago; that we still make love frequently; and that no one has managed to force us to split the dishes. That's what it means and that's a helluva lot."

She stares at me, lips tight. And then that smile lights her eyes, and she begins to laugh. It's infectious and moments later we are literally ROTFWL (in Bulletin Boardese that means rolling on the floor with laughter).

When we finally pull ourselves together, Kip says, "My God, we're lucky."

"Very."

We kiss. Lovely.

"Think of Rick and William. What will happen?" Kip asks.

"I guess we'll see when William gets out of the rehab."

"And Tom and Sam," she says softly.

"I know."

It's a sobering thought and for a few moments we lie quietly on the floor.

Then I say, "What about the place cards?"

She throws them in the air and they flutter down like lazy butterflies.

"Let the sluts find their own seats," she says. "I have better things to do."

She gazes into my eyes and I feel it as if she's never looked at me that way before.

"Me, too," I say. "*Much* better things."